BOUND TO A SAVAGE

P. WISE

P. WISE
Presents

P. WISE PUBLICATIONS

P.O Box 923

Brookhaven, PA 19015

Prettiwise.com

ISBN: 979-8-218-36844-9

DISCLAIMER

This book was written with intent to pull at your heart strings. Grab a bottle of wine and some tissue, but also have your significant other near by when my words arouse you.

CONTENTS

STAY CONNECTED!

Website: PrettiWise.com
 Instagram: @CEO.Pwise
 Facebook: Author P. Wise
 Facebook Business: Authoress P. Wise

Facebook Group: <u>Words of the Wise (P. Wise Book Group)</u>

P.O Box 923

Brookhaven, PA 19015

This book is dedicated to my two fed-baby angels:
Tony McDade & Tiffany "Remy" Jones.
Continue to sleep in peace.

PREFACE

Since a little girl, I've always had a ride or die instinct in me. I always put people's happiness before my own, thinking later on it would be recuperated. I lived a traumatic life, and all I ever wanted was to be loved and accepted. Searching for it landed me in a lot of compromising situations.

Who would've thought an honor student athlete who had a promising future would've ever landed a two year federal sentence? Never say never, because in this thing we call life, anything can happen in a blink of an eye. One bad decision could cost you more than you could bargain for.

I battled with severe depression, anxiety, PTSD, and borderline personality disorder. I've had to stand toe to toe with my demons while painting a picture that I was okay. I wouldn't wish anything I've went through on anyone, not even my worst enemy.

After fear of judgement took over my confidence, I felt no need to speak about my past. As time went on, and I got closer to Allah, I eventually felt compelled to tell my story. So here it is. Here's a glimpse of Kristen "Pretti Wise" Marin's life.

DICTIONARY

Philly phrases and their meaning:

Jawn: A person, place, or, thing
    Bul: This term is to refer to another male
    Young Bul: Is a young man
    Drawn: Somebody that is acting out of character.
    Ye Mean: Do you know what I mean?
    Bid: A fool or fooling around
    Type Time: What are your intentions?
    Ard: Alright/Ok
    Outta Pocket: Out of line

PROLOGUE

KEILANI "KEI" MILAN

*J*anuary 2017

"Ladies and gentlemen, American Airlines

welcomes you to Philadelphia. The local time is seven-thirty-five p.m. For your safety and the safety of those around you, please remain seated with your seat belt fastened and keep the aisles clear until we are parked at the gate," the pilot announced.

Looking out the window, it automatically annoyed me to be back in the cold weather. Being away on a business trip to Haiti was a little getaway I needed. The weather was hot, the food was great, and the culture was so humbling.

My friend and client I managed, who played for the Philadelphia 76ers, needed me to take a bunch of things to Haiti for him and his mother. A family member was getting married, and they were the ones hosting the wedding. It was a last-minute trip, but I made it happen for them while reaping the benefits of escaping my everyday reality.

The following day, I not only had class, but I also had work and a basketball event meeting to attend. My schedule was always booked up, but that's what I expected, being a full-time student with a full-time job and being a basketball personnel on top of things.

Gathering my belongings, I made my way off the plane and through immigration and customs. Once everything checked out, I retrieved my luggage from baggage claim and made my way outside. I knew my brother was waiting for me, so I made things quick. Besides, I wanted to just eat something, shower, and crawl in the bed.

The ride back home wasn't a long one since we only lived about ten minutes away from the airport in Chester. By the time I got in, I did just as I planned. I greeted my family, talked with them for a little, ate, then went and bathed. Before I knew it, I rested my head on my pillow and was knocked out almost immediately.

BOOM! BOOM! BOOM!

Loud bangs startled me out of my sleep. Reaching for my Rugger SR9C on the ground next to my bed, I cocked it back and took the safety off. I planted my feet on the ground and stood up. I ran into the hallway and positioned myself at the top of the stairs.

I heard tussling at the front door, then a man yelled, "Sit down and don't move!"

There were a ton of footsteps being heard downstairs, letting me know it was several people. When I took one step down, two men with rifles appeared at the bottom of the stairs. Looking a little closer, my heart dropped to the pit of my stomach when I realized who they were. Their vests and jackets read *FBI.*

This can't be real, I thought. *Fuck.*

I quickly tossed my gun to the floor, even though it was registered to me. Muthafuckers like them only needed one little reason to pull their triggers; I would've been laid out in a blink of an eye.

"Keilani Milan?" the familiar-looking agent asked.

"Yes," I answered reluctantly.

"Come down to me slowly with your hands where I can see them," he instructed.

With just a tank top on and underwear, I did what he told me to and slowly made my way to him. Once at the bottom and in the living room, I saw they had my mother and her boyfriend sitting on the couch.

"Who else is in the house?" an agent asked.

"My two sons," my mother spoke up.

"Okay and, Keilani, where's your gun and passport?"

"My gun is on the floor in the hall and passport is in my room," I answered lowly.

The same agent nodded his head to another, prompting him to go upstairs with his gun drawn. Moments later, my little brothers came walking down the stairs looking confused and scared. They were instructed to sit on the couch next to my mother.

"Okay, Ms. Milan, so we have a warrant for your arrest for federal charges, aggravated identity theft, bank fraud, and aiding and abetting that has been brought against you."

Wow, this shit is real, I said to myself.

Instantly, my mind wondered as I sat there motionless. My mother asked question after question in my defense. The agents sent her to my room to get my passport and some clothes for me to put on. Not long after, when she returned, the female agent escorted me to our downstairs bathroom.

The fact the agent was literally in the bathroom with me while I changed made me uncomfortable. She watched me like a hawk, as if I was already within a prison wall. With every clothing she handed over to me, my hands shook vigorously as my mind raced a thousand miles per second with all kinds of thoughts.

"It's going to be okay," the agent spoke.

I looked at her with a confused expression. Because who the fuck was she kidding? Instead of responding to her foolish comment, I just continued to get myself together.

"Remove all of your piercings. It will make the intake process smoother," she instructed.

Ain't shit about to be smooth with anything that's happening, lady, I thought to myself. I took out my belly and nose ring, resting them on the bathroom counter. Once I was fully dressed, she escorted me back out into the living room where everyone waited.

"So, what time will she see the judge?" my mom asked.

I sat at the computer desk while my mother continued to speak to the head agent. In the beginning, I was paying attention, but that quickly changed once I allowed the thoughts that plagued my mind to take over entirely.

Standing on my two feet with my hands being forced behind my back, I was brought back to reality. Cold iron cuffs were wrapped around my wrists and tightened. With every move I made, the handcuffs got tighter and dug into my skin. I was in pure agony within seconds, but they didn't care; I was removed from my home and away from my family.

Stepping out into the stinging winter air, it was still dark as hell when they led me out of the house and to the car. It was a few of my folks outside, which I assumed a phone call was made and they came running. Every step I took, shame and humiliation took over me as I felt tears finally falling.

"Yo, La, everything gon' be ard," I heard my best friend, Teef, yell.

I was too fucked up mentally to respond or even look his way. Others spoke words of encouragement and, at that point, I didn't understand why. I disappointed them and had everyone looking crazy; why did they even still care?

The agent helped me into the back of a Ford Taurus, then shut the door. The driver started to pull off but waited for what seemed like a hundred other vehicles to fall in line. It was two cars, including a Chester Police car, leading the way, while two more vehicles were behind.

Did I kill someone? I thought. Things looked too outrageous for a person like little ol' me.

My older brother came franticly, hopping out of his whip as they carried me away. I looked out the window and saw everyone watching on in a defeated state. My stomach turned into knots, while I felt anxious and empty at the same time.

Although I knew they were coming for me, I was praying they didn't. Prison wasn't for a girl like me. I was only twenty-two and had my whole life ahead of me, but the law and system didn't give no fucks about that; they came for whoever they wanted. It was up to me to decide if I wanted to deal with it or take the easy way out and kill myself before the judge banged their gavel.

CHAPTER ONE

KEILANI "KEI" MILAN

A year later...
    January 28th, 2018 (Graduation Day)

"I'm finna just leave all y'all. I can't be late to my graduation," I smacked my lips.

Dressed and ready to go, I was still waiting for my family to get their lives together and for my brother and his family to arrive. Graduation was scheduled for eleven a.m., and the time on my phone read nine-fifteen a.m. They instructed graduates to arrive by ten a.m. The ride to the Chase Center in Delaware was only going to be about thirty minutes, but I predicted traffic to be crazy due to the ceremony.

"Yo, chill out, baby," my boyfriend, Brix, pleaded.

I snapped my neck in his direction and shot him a death stare. Without having to say a word, he back-peddled with his hands in the air as if he was surrendering.

"Lani, we're coming, relax," my mother shouted from her room down the hall.

"Whatever. If y'all not walking out that door in the next ten minutes, I'm gone."

Irritated, I stomped my way back to my room and plopped down on my bed. For once, I just wanted everyone to be on one accord and allow me to not have any worries. My mind was already discombobulated that I had to self-surrender into Federal Prison two days later. I just needed that day to be full of bliss and lightheartedness.

Scrolling through my timeline on Instagram, I couldn't help but feel the uneasiness I was going to experience being away from the world and what it offered. Seeing people post cute pictures of themselves out and about doing things pinched a nerve, prompting me to lock my phone.

I grabbed my cap and gown off the hanger it was on, dropped my things in my small purse, and left out the room to go downstairs. To my surprise, my brother was just pulling up in front of the house and everyone else was making their way downstairs. Looking over in the corner of my eye, I saw my boyfriend looking at me with a smug expression. Being the brat I was, I didn't give any reaction to everyone being on time to leave. That's what they should've done anyway. Piling into four cars, we all pulled off, left out of Chester, and made our way to Delaware.

A half an hour later, we arrived at The Chase Center on the Waterfront, but finding a park was unbelievable. The rain started to pour down, making me upset because I knew my curls were going to drop after I spent a long time doing my hair. After circling around for ten minutes, I started to snap.

"Just drop me off in the front, please. Y'all deal with the parking," I huffed at Brix.

He looked at me but didn't say a word, which was in his best interest. Since I got sentenced earlier in the month, my attitude had shifted from being humble and optimistic to pessimistic and confrontational. It was hard to find the good in anything. I was easily triggered and didn't care what I said or did. When I looked in the mirror, I wasn't able to recognize myself; I was gone.

By the time I got inside, everyone was already in their line to walk into the ceremony. I quickly found where I needed to be and settled in. Looking around, the other graduates were all cheerful and smiling. It took all of me to dig deep and feel some kind of happiness about the date, especially for my mother's sake. I wasn't too excited about graduation, but the judge gave me some time to enjoy myself and walk the stage for my mother to see; it was all for her.

Before I knew it, the ceremony started and, in a blink of an eye, my name was being announced to cross the stage and get my degree.

"Bachelor of Science, Sports Management... Keilani Milan," the dean announced.

I looked into the crowd in search of my family before proceeding to get my degree, but it was so many people, I couldn't locate them.

As I walked towards the center of the stage, I felt the place become still. It was so quiet; I thought I was inside of the building alone. Looking back out into the crowd, I saw everyone staring at me with disgusted faces; there was not a smile in sight. Even the administrator, who was handing out the diplomas, wore a scowl on her face as I approached her.

That's when I knew for sure, I was a total disappointment. I looked at the seal on the hard folder that held my degree and the only thing I could think about was the waste of time I spent going to school and studying hard. Everything I had done prior was worth nothing.

"Congratulations hun, I love your cap," she praised.

I was snapped back into present time, and all the loud screams and claps invaded my ears. Smiling and waving, I made my way across the stage seeming to be the happiest girl alive, but instead, I felt like a worthless piece of shit.

After returning to my seat, the ceremony lasted about another ten minutes before we marched back out. My loved ones stood by the ropes as we exited on one side, while the Wilmington family I knew stood on the opposite. I went over to speak with my mentor, which was the chair of my program.

"Congratulations my dear. I'm so proud of you and how you pushed through despite the circumstances," Dr. Williams stated.

For a while, she was aware of my case and the verdict. Not once did she ever switch up the way she dealt with me or viewed me. If anything, the situation brought us closer.

"Thanks Doc. I appreciate everything you've done for me." I felt tears welling in my eyes.

If the case hadn't come about, I would've been pledging Delta and having countless opportunities because of her. She was well connected in the sports industry and was a respected Delta Soror.

"You're most welcome. Please remember, your situation now does not define you as a person. You still have a future ahead of you. Make sure to use that time wisely, Keilani. I'll be sending in things to keep you busy as well." She looked at me with saddened eyes. "Come here." She took me into her embrace and held onto me for a few moments.

We spoke our final goodbyes, for the time being that was, and I made my way to my family, who all wore bright smiles on their faces. It was endless hugs, kisses, and congratulations. Although I didn't know how to feel, having mixed emotions, being around the people I loved and who loved me just made that moment all better; I was a college graduate for the second time in my life.

After graduation, we all went back to the house to grab our things to head to New York. I had one more day of freedom and decided to do a grad and go away dinner party in my hometown. A few of my girls came along for the trip, along with my family. Others met us there for dinner and, afterwards, we turned up at an Airbnb Brix got for us for the night.

All I wanted to do was get drunk to where I passed out and have sex. Two things I knew for certain were going to be gone in my life for a while.

THE FOLLOWING MORNING, we woke up and checked out the Airbnb. Making a pit stop in Brooklyn, I saw a few people before hitting the NJ Turnpike to head back to Chester. Brix stayed back to handle some business while the girls and I went ahead, but he followed close behind. There were several things I had to do before I self-surrendered. Plus, I wanted to spend time with my mother and brothers.

After getting my room in order, amongst other things, one

of my girls, Kyra, came over to pamper me one last time. She washed and did my hair, and nails. We talked about how much we loved one another and how we would stay in contact. It was as if every conversation I had repeated itself. They became redundant. The emotions were the same.

I heard stories of when people went away no matter if it was to prison, or for work, or the military, when you were out of sight, you were out of mind. For the most part, I wanted to believe everyone about how much they would miss me and they'd write and make sure my books were filled with money. But I had this funny feeling that as time went on, I was going to see everyone's true colors.

Later at night, Brix got another Airbnb for a couple of us to just kick back and chill. Of course, my brothers, my mom, and some of their friends that I considered to be family, along with one of my closest cousins, came by to chill with me for my last night. We drank, ate food, and just talked about all kinds of memories. When the night was over and everyone left, it was only Brix and me.

I went to use the bathroom and, when I came back to sit on the couch beside Brix, he grabbed me onto his lap. Straddling him, I cupped his handsome face with my hands. Brix had a caramel complexion, like I did. He was the splitting image of NBA all-star, Derrick Rose.

"How you feeling?" he asked with a sincere tone.

Not answering right away, I started to think about how I truly was feeling. "I'm just here, for real," I answered lowly.

He picked my head up, using his index fingers to meet his eyes. "Talk to me. I need to know where your head at."

"It's all over Brix. I'm literally going to prison tomorrow. I don't know what the fuck it's like in there for real. I don't know who gon' stick beside me. I don't know what you finna be doing out here. I just don't know about anything," I expressed.

"Aye, I got you. Don't even start wild'n. I'ma be here, aight?"

"Yeah, until a big ass and a cute smile come around, then it's over for me."

"Lani, I ain't try—"

"Aht, aht, don't even fix your lips to speak no bullshit and lies. You're a man and you have needs and wants. It's no way I could expect you to not fuck on bitches for two years. While I would love that, it's unrealistic for a nigga like you and unfair at the same time. All I ask is that you let them hoes know you have a woman, no deep feelings, and strap up. I don't need news while I'm in there or even when I come home that you done knocked a bitch up. And I damn sure don't want no STD's. Understood?" I looked him dead in his eyes.

He knew I was speaking the truth because he looked at me intensely. It wasn't time to sell any fairytales or beat around the bush. I was being real with myself and I needed him to know what was really on my mind and in my heart.

"Understood. We good, babe."

He grabbed my face and brought it to his, making our lips touch. "I love you," he spoke.

"I love you, too."

I just prayed love was enough for him to keep his word.

Self-Surrender Day

I COULD BARELY SLEEP the night before. Anytime I closed my eyes, I jumped out of my sleep looking around to see if I was still free or within confined walls. Most times, instead of trying to go back to sleep, I would wake Brix up just to have sex. This happened at least four times throughout the night. My eyes were already open when the sun rose. I checked the time and saw it was seven a.m.

Going under the covers, I searched and found Brix's dick, placing it in my mouth. Seconds later, he stirred in his sleep, but it wasn't long before he was awoke and his manhood was standing straight up at attention.

"Oh shit," he groaned, grabbing a handful of my hair.

I felt the force of his hand pushing me lower into his midsection, making his dick hit the back of my throat. Brix loved when I made the slight gargle noise when I was deep throating him.

"Mmmhmm, take all this shit," he growled.

My eye watered like it usually did with his length and

girth. Brix was skilled in the bedroom when he wanted to be. There were times he'd give me lazy, quick sex, which always had me thinking he was outside fooling around. While other times, which was mostly when he was intoxicated, he'd dick me down long and proper.

Every time I woke him out of his sleep that night and morning, he fucked me so good. I guess it was because he knew it was going to be a while before I got penetrated that way again.

Finally, coming up for air, we locked eyes for a moment before he grabbed me on top of him. I slid down nice and slow, making sure to enjoy every inch of him.

"Fuckkk," I whispered, throwing my head back in complete bliss.

I rode him like sex was going out of fashion and he was the last bit of dick to go around. Even with the low self-esteem I had after gaining weight from stress eating, I showed out like I was the baddest bitch on planet earth.

We went at it for a while until we had no other choice but to stop because I had to stick to the schedule. Making it home one last time was imperative; then, it was a must I made it to the Marshals in Philadelphia. I was to be in their custody by one p.m.

By the time we arrived back at the house in Chester, where I shared with my mother and two younger brothers, everyone was sitting around waiting for me. Without any words being spoken, the place felt gloomy. Taking on everyone's energy with my own, I felt total anguish.

"What all you have to do?" my mother finally spoke up and asked, pulling me from the wild thoughts that were about to invade my mind.

"I just need to shower and gather everything I'm taking with me," I answered as I made my way to the stairs.

"Your pre-trial officer called and gave me your—" she stopped abruptly.

"My what?" I looked at her, then at everyone else who was in the living room.

"The number they'll use to identify you."

Oh, my inmate number, I thought.

I didn't utter a word. I simply made my way upstairs to my room. No one followed me, not even Brix. When inside, I stood in the middle of it, looking around at everything. My eyes zeroed in on my basketball that sat on the ground by my closet. I asked myself how life would've been if only had I stuck with just dating ball players. Would I have gotten caught up in scams?

My eyes peeled away from the ball and landed on my bed, then my dresser and closet. Everything I was used to was about to be inaccessible within a few hours. What I knew life to be was going to no longer be.

Knock! Knock!

My head whipped in the direction of my door. "Who is it?" I asked.

"It's me," my mom answered solemnly.

"Come in." I plopped down on my bed. She came in and sat right beside me.

For a moment, we just sat in silence, unable to speak or move a muscle. And in that moment, that was everything to me.

"I love you. And I want you to know that I'll be there every step of the way like I've been. Go in there knowing you have a team of people that care for you. There's a life after you complete your time. Don't lose sight of what matters," she expressed.

"Thanks, ma. I got you."

We hugged one another tightly before breaking our embrace. I looked her in her eyes and broke down completely. "I'm scared," I whispered, allowing tears to cascade down my cheeks.

Her eyes immediately started to water as she pulled me back into her embrace. With her touch, I became weak. I became her baby girl again, the one she would rock to sleep in her arms. If only I was able to go back in time to that very tender age and start all over again. I knew things would've ended up differently.

"You'll be fine, Lani. Just stay to yourself and don't get mixed up into bullshit," she advised. "It's easy to get sucked in."

My mother was a supervisor at a federal half-way house. She saw and heard so many things when it came to incarcerated individuals. We just never thought I would've been the one to go in to potentially experience the same as them.

Knock! Knock! Knock!

Before I could answer, my bedroom door swung open with my older brother, Tremaine, in the doorway.

"My fault, but look at the time," he stated with a worried look.

"Okay. Let me go hop in the shower. I'll be ready to leave soon." I grabbed my shower things and left out the room, leaving the two of them to converse.

Stripping out my clothes, I got in the shower and handled my hygiene. As the water fell down my body, my mind drifted off to thoughts of how things would be on the inside, something I caught myself thinking about from the moment I caught my case. It was as if I thought it into existence.

My thoughts went to the day I was sentenced.

"Ma, it's snowing so hard outside, you think I'll still have court?" I asked my moms, as we sat in the living room waiting for everyone to get ready.

"Those people don't care if it's a hurricane, it's still on. Plus, your lawyer would've already called and said something," she stated.

I toyed with my fingers as I felt myself becoming jittery. I was a mixture of nervous, afraid, and anxious about the day. It was when the judge had to decide my fate. And while I didn't want to hear it, I knew it had to be done so I could move on with my life. The case had been hanging over my head for two years. It was time to put it to rest.

"Mommy, Kayla, and your uncle is already near the courthouse," my mom informed me.

For my family to drive all the way from Brooklyn to Philadelphia for my sentencing showed me I had a solid support system. A lot of people told me they were coming, but I told myself I'd believe it when I saw it.

"Okay, let's go, y'all!" my mom yelled upstairs to the boys.

One by one, my two younger brothers came downstairs, along with my boyfriend, Brix. We all left out the house and quickly jumped in the vehicles. My older brother was already in his car waiting with his family. Once everyone was settled in, we took off three cars deep to Eastern District of Pennsylvania Federal Courthouse.

The ride took us a little longer than usual due to the weather, but nevertheless, we made it on time. Once parked in the garage, we took our time walking in the snow and made our way inside.

By the time we got through security and reached upstairs, mostly everyone who said they were going to be there were already there. I had family, friends, flings, and even coaches in attendance. I greeted everyone and stepped inside the courtroom with my heart in my stomach.

My lawyer was already seated in his designated place. I

kissed my mom, then my boyfriend, and made my way next to him.

"You ready?" he asked me.

"As ready as I can be." I shrugged.

A few minutes later, the court officer announced the judge. "All rise for the Honorable Judge Kennedy."

The man I'd been standing in front of for almost a year was about to either save my life or destroy it further than I already had done.

Not wasting any time, he jumped right into things. He read off the sentencing guidelines and explained where I lied within them. He then asked the courtroom if anyone wanted to speak. I had a few people stand and speak on my behalf, which warmed my heart.

When the time had finally come for him to read off my sentence, my heart started to skip beats.

"Will the defendant please stand," he requested.

My lawyer and I both stood up and awaited what was coming our way next.

"The defendant is hereby sentenced to be imprisoned for a total term of: one day as to count one to run consecutive, and two years as to counts two, three and four to run concurrently. Upon release from imprisonment, you will be on supervised release for a term of: two years as to count one to run consecutive, and one year as to counts two, three and four to run concurrently. The defendant is ordered to pay restitution in the amount

of $232,895.90. The court makes the following recommenda-
tions to the Bureau of Prisons: Defendant have access to mental
health treatment and programs and be designated to a facility
close to Philadelphia to continue to receive family support."

Everything else he stated became a blur. He stopped my
heart from beating when he told me I had to sit in prison for
two years and one day.

Knock! Knock!

The sound on the door snatched me from down a horrible memory lane.

"I'm coming!" I yelled.

ONCE I WAS FINISHED in the bathroom, I went back into my room and threw on a pair of old sweatpants, a t-shirt, and sweater. Grabbing the list of people's information I wrote, along with my small bible with my cousin and step dad's obituary inside, I got ready to leave. As I was leaving out of my room, I turned around one last time to look around.

Oddly, I walked into each room in the house, including the closets. I inhaled the different scents that made up my home, the place I shared with the people I loved with all my soul. I wanted to remember them; I needed to remember them.

"Babe, come on!" Brix called out to me as I was looking out the backdoor of the house.

"I'm coming!" I yelled back, closing and locking the door.

Everyone was already outside waiting for me when I got

out in front of the house. We were going four cars deep with about ten people just so everyone could spend my last moments of freedom with me.

Stepping off the porch and onto the steps, the cold winter air kissed my face, sending shivers down my spine. I looked up and down the street at the houses of my dear neighbors, wondering what they were doing in their supposed happy lives. Then, I looked down at my loved ones who were piling into the vehicles.

"Sis, you driving your car or nah?" one of my younger brothers asked.

It would've been the last spin inside of my Dodge Charger, but I decided not to.

"Nah, go ahead and drive it," I told him, then proceeded to Brix's Infiniti instead.

When I reached the passenger side door, before getting in the car, I turned around and looked at the house I called home. Staring intensely at it, a feeling came over me that it was going to be the last time I saw it.

Beep!

The car horn snapped me out of my brief trance, prompting me to get inside. Once secured, Brix put the car in drive, one hand on the wheel while the other held onto mine. I was leaving the small town of Chester, Pennsylvania and was heading to the big city of Philadelphia, where my memories were once sweet but were going to quickly turn bitter.

Lost in my mind for the entire ride, I didn't notice when

we arrived in the city. One by one, each car made its way inside the garage across the street from the federal building. Finally parked, everyone came out of the cars, except me.

My ass was stuck to the seat as if it was crazy glued to it. I was unable to move an inch, let alone speak. The only thing I could do was sit there and stare out the windshield at everyone staring back at me. Not one face read confusion, they all knew good and well what I was experiencing.

Most people would call me dumb and say they would've run off instead of turning themselves in. But for me, I wouldn't have been able to not be in contact with my family, nor did I want to live my life in fear of being captured. The best decision was to stand ten toes down and face things head on. It wasn't life in prison.

The passenger door opened, and Brix stood there with his hand out. Reluctantly, I placed my hand in his and exited out the car. We found our way upstairs and out of the garage.

Looking up, I saw the huge, tall gray building with small rectangular windows that you couldn't see inside of. It stood behind the federal building and courthouse. The very building I was going to make my place of residence for whatever amount of time they decided to keep me there before shipping me to another institution for whatever reason.

I caught myself staring at the gray slab until I was at the entrance of the federal building. When we walked inside, everyone stood to the side to let me through.

"I'm here to self-surrender," I stated as I approached the gentlemen behind the desk.

"What's your name?" one asked.

"Keilani Milan."

He quickly glanced over the screen and nodded his head.

"Do you have anything with you?" he asked.

I showed him my bible and paper filled with my contacts.

"Okay, I'll call up for your escort. You'll have a few minutes, so say your goodbyes," he informed me.

"Okay."

I turned around to face my family who all stood there with tears welling in their eyes, instantly making me more emotional than I already was.

Digging in my back pocket, I pulled out my phone and handed it over to my mother. I gave her the passcode and whatever else instructions I had for her. She called my grandparents, aunt, and uncle to speak with them quickly. By the time I was ending the call, two Marshals came walking towards us. When I looked over at the guy behind the desk, he gave me the sympathetic head nod, letting me know they were there for me.

Starting with the children, I hugged and kissed my nephews, who were babies and oblivious to where aunty was headed. I then moved my way around to my sisters-in-law, my cousin, and my three brothers. My siblings and I were close but never showed much affection towards one another, but that day, the moment each one hugged me, I felt their tears against my cheeks, and I felt the deep love within their arms.

I turned to Brix, who's eyes were bloodshot red, which broke me down even more. Brix was a whole street nigga who I never not once saw cry. To see him in a vulnerable state as he was in, it told me that he really loved and cared for me.

"I'll be fine, baby," I wiped his tears, as he grabbed me by the waist.

"I wish they could take me instead," he voiced, making tears flow down my cheeks at his sincerity.

"I love you." I kissed his lips.

"I love you, more, Lani. I got you, don't even worry."

Peeling myself away from his embrace was harder than I thought. But it was even harder to face my mother for the last time. She was my last stop and most devastating one.

I ran into her arms like I used to as a little girl and held onto her as tight as possible. The safe place I knew was going to be out of reach, physically that was. I knew I wasn't going to be able to get to her for every little thing and not exactly when I wanted to neither.

"Remember what I told you," she whispered.

I nodded in acknowledgement.

"I love you, mommy," I spoke in between loud sobs.

Even though we were in the lobby of the federal building with people moving about, it felt like the place stood still in that moment.

"I-I, I love you, Keilani," she cried loudly.

After a few moments, I felt hands separating us. When I looked, it was my brothers, but only because the Marshals had approached me.

"It's time to go, Ms. Milan," one announced.

I nodded, then slowly let go of my mother's trembling hands. Looking at everyone one last time, I blinked my tears away to clear my vision, but it was helpless, it was a river coming from my eyes.

My heart ached with every step I took away from them. I continued to look back every second to see if they'd moved, but they all stood there watching me walk away. One of my brothers had to hold my mother because she seemed so weak. It took all of me to not run back to her or even run straight out the door.

When we reached the corner, I looked at them one last time from a distance and waved goodbye.

"How many tattoos do you have?" the Marshall asked me.

The officer was a young Caucasian male who looked to be around thirty years old. He was undeniably handsome, with a sleeve of a tribal tattoo. His aura was laid back and not much of a dickhead like I'd seen others be.

"Thirteen," I simply answered.

"Where? I have to take pictures of them." He looked at me with a blank look.

At that moment, I was confused to why a male was processing me and asking me to reveal my tattoos. Some of them were in private places while others were visible. I wanted to contest and asked for a woman, but something told me it would've turned out bad; they'd look at me like I had no power or room to say anything.

Reluctantly, I lifted my shirt and sweats in order to show him all tattoos. Once he logged all of them into the computer, we moved on.

"What's your sexual orientation?" He raised his eyebrows curiously.

"Excuse me?" I looked at him dumbfounded.

"We have to ask." He shrugged.

"What for? What gender I allow to lick or penetrate me does not concern y'all."

Why the hell did I get myself in here? I asked myself.

The Marshals didn't care about my red, wet, puffy eyes. They continued to process me into the system.

Once finished, I was led to the same holding cell I was in when the feds first came and picked me up. I stayed there for a little while before they came to escort me across the street.

We got onto an elevator that took us downstairs into an underground garage that I remembered from when I first was taken into custody. My assumption was they were putting me into a car to drive over, but I was wrong.

They walked me to a huge cage-like gate and entered a long hallway that led into a tunnel; we walked and walked for a minute until we got to a steel door. An agent buzzed it and was allowed access. On the other side was a man and woman officer waiting for us. They exchanged paperwork and my belongings; then, I was handed off to them.

"Ms. Milan, are you suicidal at the moment?" the woman asked.

"No," I replied, short and simple.

We proceeded to intake, which was called R&D, receive and discharge. There were many holding cells, all filled with men hollering and acting wild. I tensed up immediately; I was not used to the environment. Plus, the attention I was receiving was not something I wanted.

"Yooo shawty!" one guy hollered.

"Aye Ma, you look good as fuck!" another man yelled.

They were shouting all sorts of things while banging on the glass windows. I just tried my best to block it out. Because I was ignoring them and not even looking their way, some started to curse me out. The CO that was processing me told me to not speak to them because it was against the rules.

Shit, I don't care to speak to these niggas. They in here like I am, hell they can do for me.

The officer made me step onto a machine that supposedly scanned my body and took my fingerprints and picture for my ID. I felt like I repeated all of those things a lot that day. I was seen by the nurse and then taken to change out of my clothes for some old used raggedy jailhouse clothes. I was even given used panties, sports bra and socks. Being naked in front of a woman was one thing, but having to squat, spread my cheeks and cough for her was a whole other story. It felt degrading and I couldn't do anything about it.

On my way to the holding cell, through the catcalls from the guys and the continuous banging, I noticed one particular guy. He stood out for some reason, and I didn't know why. He was talking to a CO by the door of one of the holding cells. They seemed to have been having a serious conversation too.

He turned and looked at me with his green eyes. They were pretty as fuck but piercing; I was mesmerized. He was tall, about six-two, and light skin with an athletic build.

The perfect criminal, I thought. It just amazed me how he captured my attention when I was in a shitty situation and had no business checking out a man. *Can't help what attracts.*

The CO tugged at my jumpsuit sleeve and snapped me out of my daze, finally placing me into a holding cell. Inside was one other female who wore a tan top and bottoms that resembled nursing scrubs. I wasn't sure why I had on a green jumpsuit like the guys and she had that on, but it wasn't a major concern at that moment. Few seconds in, she spoke.

"First time in?" she asked with a smirk.

She was a beautiful girl, light skin, long hair, and a body that looked like she bought it from Dr. Miami.

I was hesitant to answer, but I gave in. "Umm, yeah, why you ask?" I replied.

She laughed a little. "I can tell. Don't worry, it's gonna be ard." She smiled.

I nodded.

We spoke while waiting to be taken to the unit. She wasn't bad, but I wasn't trusting a soul. I didn't know her and I'd heard so many stories about jail and prison. But it also didn't hurt to kind of sort of know someone as well.

"Keep your circle small, don't speak about your business, especially your case if you're still fighting it. And stay lowkey, follow those rules and you'll be just fine," she lectured.

"Thanks, I'll remember that. Wait, I didn't even get your name," I pointed out.

"My bad, I'm Trouble." She grinned.

Trouble? I sized her up and down when she mentioned her name. I mean, it was self-explanatory, simple as could be. She was *trouble*. I made a mental note to keep my eyes on her because I literally didn't want or need any unnecessary drama while I was in that place.

"Cool, I'm Keilani." I returned the smile.

Not long after our official introduction, the CO came to escort us to the unit. She handed me a rolled-up blanket with a towel, a plastic cup with a small soap, a tiny toothbrush, toothpaste, and a tiny pencil without an eraser inside of it. I followed her out of R&D with Trouble behind me. *Here we go,* I took a deep breath.

Getting off the elevator, the CO gave me a sympathetic look and stopped me before we entered the heavy grayish, greenish door leading to the unit.

"Mind your business and keep your business to yourself," she coached.

I looked at her with a blank stare and gave her a head nod. I wasn't a rowdy hood bitch, but I damn sure wasn't pussy. I didn't need anybody's pity, especially walking into the lion's den. I had to keep my head on straight.

We were met with another CO at the entrance of the unit. When I walked in, it was a huge open area with tables in the middle and flat screen TVs hanging around. There was a top and bottom tier with so many cells.

The place was loud, and it was packed with all kinds of different walks of life. Once I was in the women's vision, they all started to yell and stare at me. They started to chant something that I couldn't quite make out what they were saying. I kept my head down, trying not to make any eye contact as we walked to the CO's booth.

"Here's Milan." The woman CO handed the male guard my ID slip.

Immediately, I was escorted to my cell, which was on the bottom floor of the two-tier unit, close to the officer's booth. It was a grayish, greenish color, many might actually have a name for it while others would just describe it like that. It had a funny smell when I entered but of course it would. There was a toilet and sink inside. *Just like on TV*, I thought to myself.

There was an older white woman sitting on the bottom bunk. She had a soft look about her. Before we introduced ourselves to one another, the guard told me to rest my things down and follow him to get a mattress. I followed him along the cells, passing by many women to the back of the unit where they kept the mattresses in a place called suicide watch. I quickly grabbed a mattress and hurried back to my cell, still making no eye contact with anyone in particular.

Once I got my mattress up on the top bunk, the woman finally spoke.

"Hi, I'm Lisa," she introduced herself with a soft smile.

"Hi, I'm Keilani," I responded.

By the time I finished introduce myself, there were women at my cell door. I didn't know what to think at first. I'd seen so many TV shows and movies and also heard so many stories. I started to question myself quickly. Do I have to fight this early on? I wouldn't say I was in a panic mode. I was more so trying to be prepared.

"Hellooo, I'm Lena," a black woman who looked to be in her early forties sang as she walked to me with items in her hand.

"Hello, I'm Keilani," I said back with a low voice.

"Here's a nightgown, a juice packet, a tuna pack and crackers." She handed over the things to me.

"Oh, ummm, I don't have any money right now on my accounts. My family should be doing that as we speak," I started to explain.

"Sweetie, that's fine, I don't want nothing for it; I'm just trying to help," she convinced me.

"Thank you, I appreciate that," I gave in and accepted the items.

I was skeptical because I knew there was a rule in prison. When someone gave you something, they always wanted something back in return. It may not be at that very moment, but the time would eventually come.

Two younger girls came in and introduced themselves and gave me a hair tie, toothpaste, and lotion. While visitors came and went, my bunky just looked on from her bottom bunk with a nosey stare; I didn't pay her any mind.

Once things got a bit settled, I stood on the chair that was in the cell and made my bed to the best of my ability, being it was on the top and I stood at only five-three. The mattress was thin; the sheet wasn't in good length and it wasn't a fitted one. There were two blankets when I unraveled the roll, so I used one as a pillow, since we weren't given any, and the other to cover my body from the cold air.

When I finally got my bed situated, I climbed up on the metal ladder, being careful, and got on my top bunk. Without another word to my cellmate or even eating or changing out of the jumpsuit, I curled up on my side with my knee to my chest and cried myself to sleep.

And my two-year federal bid began.

CHAPTER TWO

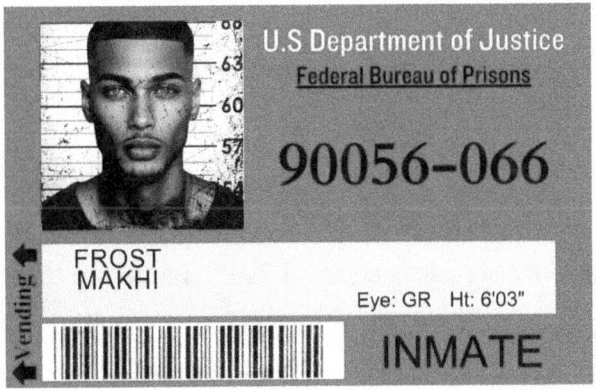

MAHKI "MANIC" FROST

*I*t was dark with just a dim little light preying through the rectangular window of the metal door. The place was still, cold, and had an unexplainable smell. For a minute, I laid on the bottom bunk in my cell, on top of my already properly made bed, lost in my thoughts.

The day marked the ninth month I'd been incarcerated in the Federal Detention Center Philadelphia. It wasn't my first run-in with the law, but this time around was very much different. After the first time getting hemmed up, I took extra precautions to not end up back inside these walls. But someway, somehow, I ended up taking the hit and landed right back in the very place I vowed not to go back to. They were trying to charge a nigga with a drug charge, amongst other shit.

Back in 2015, when I was introduced to the law on the federal level, I was under the guidance and protection of my ol' head, Reef. Reef ran the detention center in every aspect. He had control of the administration, guards and, of course, all inmates fell in line. What he did best on the outside, he did on the inside, ran the drug game. And I was his young'n under his wing.

Though my stay was short in 2015, I adhered to everything Reef taught me about the game inside the walls. Soaking up all the knowledge like a sponge and with my intellect, I returned to the streets a new profound boss within my family's organization.

After a few years of controlling the northeast distribution under my family, my reign took a fall, landing me right back behind the gloomy grey walls of FDC Philly. But when I returned, I returned to the inheritance of Reef's position and power.

My ol' head, as I once called him, passed away from health issues while he was still fighting his appeal for a retrial. Not only did I receive the title because of being Reef's protégé, but because of the weight my family and I held on the streets. There was no one in that vicinity matching my resume or ruthlessness.

As clicking sounds in the distance neared, I snapped out of my thoughts. I heard a big click indicating my cell door was now unlocked.

I sat up, rubbed the palm of my hands down my face. "Another fuckin' day," I whispered.

Touch opened the cell door moments later.

"Aye yo, Manic, I think you got court," he informed me while addressing me by my nickname.

Touch was my right hand, second in command. We were well acquainted before sharing the same federal address. I was Touch's connect on the streets and an associate, but luckily for us, we weren't on the same indictment. Touch never brought mess to my organization. He was a loyal, die-hard hustler who was a force to be reckoned with. If it was anyone worthy enough to be close to me, it was Tahir *Touch* Ahmed.

"Court?" I quizzed, creasing my forehead in confusion because I wasn't aware of any court date. Touch shrugged, looking just as lost as I was. He must've sensed my mood because as fast as he appeared, he disappeared.

I took a deep breath as I stood and slipped on my Crocs.

As soon as I was about to exit out of my cell, CO Wright approached my door.

"Yo Manic, put on your greens, gotta take you down to R&D, you have court," he informed me.

R&D was Receiving and Discharge. Every inmate proceeded through there when first entering a prison facility and when they're exiting one, even if it was to go to court. There, they searched you thoroughly and catalogued you into the system or removed you out of it.

"Brah, you sure I have court?" I asked him. "I don't know nothin' 'bout having court today. My lawyer ain't inform me of none of this."

"Shit, I wish I knew. I just got the call to come and get you." He shrugged.

Wright was one of my men, so I know he ain't on bullshit, but the prosecutor definitely seemed to had been on it. That shit caught me off guard, but I couldn't do nothing about it, so I got ready to go down to R&D with him.

Before I left the unit though, I went and made a quick phone call to my moms. It was seven in the morning, so I knew she was just waking up.

As always, on the first ring I heard her pickup, then the lady on the line continued, "To accept press five."

Beep!

"Good morning Ma," I spoke first.

"Good morning, wassup? Why this early call?" she quizzed.

"They taking me to court—"

Before I could finish what I was saying, she cut me off.

"What you mean court, why I didn't know about this?" she started getting hyped.

"It's news to me too, Ma. Call Hash and see what all this shit 'bout man," I told her.

"Okay, I'm gon' call him now. I'll be there though, see you in a lil' bit," she said before hanging up.

Hearing her voice always calmed me. She was my heart, my rider through any and everything. I had my whole family supporting me, but my mom was the go-to for everything. After we hung up, I went downstairs to R&D to get processed out to court.

EVERYONE NATURALLY HATED COURT, but going to court from prison was beyond the shittiest thing ever. It was a whole day process in holding for no reason. I wondered why they couldn't just take us over to court, and when we're done, bring us back and take us up to our units?

They wanted to have you sit in R&D from seven a.m. when your court time wasn't until ten or eleven in the morning or even after lunch. You'd sit in the Marshal's holding cells as well for a while, then when you're finished waiting there, they took you back to the detention center to wait in R&D until damn near dinner time around five p.m. You see why a nigga would be irritated all day?

What really had me hot and aggravated was, I went to court for literally two fuckin' minutes. It was just certain things the person shouldn't have to be present in court for if the lawyer was. It just be a whole hassle of getting to court for no reason. My lawyer somehow never received the new evidence that was found, so he had to make a motion to bring it to the judge's attention. Now, tell me why the fuck I needed to be there?

When I finally got back across the street to the detention center, it was damn near three p.m. Court was at eleven-fifteen a.m. The COs in R&D could tell I wasn't in the mood, so they hurried to get me back processed and limited interaction with me. They even went as far as to put me in a holding cell with Touch alone. He had court that same day, along with his sister, which was his co-defendant.

While sitting, caught up in my own thoughts, CO Wright waved me over to the door. He had a concerned look on his face, so I already knew some bullshit was up.

"Wassup?" I asked, walking up to him.

"You know anything about Bodhi getting high on yo shit?" he reluctantly asked.

Bodhi was one of my men that pushed weight in FDC for me. He was in another unit upstairs from where I was. We had no prior issues, so the question took me aback.

"If I knew that, do it look like he'd still be in possession of my shit?" I retorted.

"Well, now you know. I've heard it before, but I saw it with my own two eyes," he revealed.

I dropped my head and shook it in aggravation. "Okay, we have—"

My sentence was cut short once I saw this bad ass jawn. I'd seen some nice bitches roll up in the facility, but she was different on so many levels. I could tell she didn't belong. She had this innocent mien. I figured she was crying because her eyes were puffy, but it didn't take away from her beautifully shaped almond-brown eyes. Her caramel complexion still had its glow. Her black hair was nice and long down her back, with a silk press still in existence. She had on a jumpsuit, so I couldn't see exactly how her body was, but I definitely noticed a nice ass. She was very petite and thick, built nicely.

"Manic… Manic… Manic."

I heard Wright kept calling me. I snapped outta' my trance and returned to my initial conversation. "Can you get to Grace?" I asked Wright, referring to a lieutenant I had on my payroll.

"Yeah, I just left her office, as a matter of fact."

"Tell her I said to shake him down and get everything, but no shot; we don't need any heat." A shot was an incident report that followed with consequences.

"Ard, bet." He closed back the door and left out of R&D.

I sat back down, allowing my thoughts to consume me. I

never understood how muthafuckers could just get high from what they were selling. First, the shit was dangerous and addictive. Second, you wouldn't make no real money if you smoking everything up because you gotta pay for the shit. To each your own though because it wasn't in me to do.

Shaking Bodhi's stupidity out of my head, my thoughts drifted to the jawn I had seen moments before. She was no longer in my view, but she was on a nigga mind. *What the fuck was she in here for?* I wondered.

CHAPTER THREE

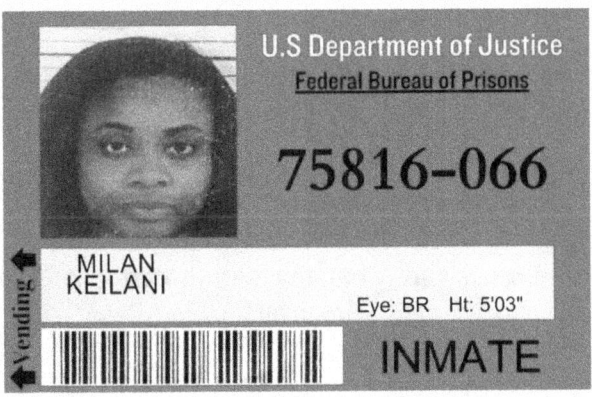

KEI

$\mathcal{T}$he next morning, I woke up shivering in a fetal position. My body ached, and it was extremely cold. Before I woke up fully, I was praying it was all a dream, but that was quickly dismissed once I heard the loud click of the cell door. I took a deep breath and let it out. I felt myself getting anxious and just wanted to shout and cry. I couldn't believe I was in prison, and what had me mostly on edge was the fact I hadn't spoken to my family since I went in. I felt completely alone.

My cellmate was already up and walking out of the door once it was unlocked. Through the small rectangle window on the door, I noticed movements in the common area. People were walking toward the entrance of the unit and returning to the tables with trays in their hands. I slowly climbed down the ladder and slipped on the thin-like Vans' shoe they gave me and proceeded out of the cell.

When I stepped foot toward everyone, all eyes were on me. I slowly approached the line like I saw others doing and received a breakfast tray, then went to sit at an empty table alone. It wasn't much on the tray but some dry, off-brand Raisin Bran cereal and a banana with a carton of milk. I was starving, so I ate everything, not paying the taste any attention.

"Hiii!" I heard a voice sing behind me.

I turned around to see a girl, who looked to be in her late twenties, approaching me. She sat down across from me with a smile on her face.

"How are you doing?" she asked.

"Hi, I'm doin' aight, thanks for asking."

When she was about to respond, four more girls came to

join us, all looking to be around the same age group as the first girl.

"You always tryna be the welcoming committee," one girl joked.

"Leave her alone Gia." Another one playfully nudged her.

"I'm sorry, these are my friends, Gia, Kali, Nami, and Noelle. I'm Zaara but everyone calls me Zee." All the girls waved when their name were mentioned. "What's your name?"

"Keilani."

"Cute name, where you from?" the girl Noelle asked.

"Brooklyn, but been in Chester and Philly for some years now," I replied.

"Hmmph, you caught your case in Philly?" the chick Gia asked with a raised eyebrow.

"Mind ya' business bitch, damn," Noelle told Gia, sucking her teeth.

"Damn, my fault, she can at least tell us what she in for," Gia spat.

I saw what type of timing this Gia chick was on, and I wasn't in the mood to deal with her, not then and not never. She was the type who wanted to get dragged across the floor and pounced on.

"Murder," I said with a straight face, then calmly stood up and took my tray back to the kitchen area and went into my cell. I saw no need to explain my case or situation to anyone, at least not until I felt comfortable or saw a reason to.

Not long after, the older woman Lena that gave me the things the night before came knocking on my cell door.

"Good morning hun, you good?" She walked in a bit more.

"Yeah, just aggravated. I need to speak with my family. I don't get a phone call or nothing?" I quizzed, scrunching up my face.

"Girl, are you even staying in? If so, you'll have to get your set-up from Ms. Walsh. She doesn't come in until eight or nine o'clock though, and once you get it from her, you won't be able to activate your voice for the phone until tomorrow. It's only Tuesdays and Thursdays to do that shit."

I literally wanted to just scream and tear shit up. If it wasn't one thing, it was another. All I wanted to do was to speak with my family. It should've been illegal to have someone in a place like that without being able to have an initial contact with their loved ones. It was pure bullshit.

"Are you serious?" I curled my lip.

"Girl, it's gon' be a lot of shit you don't like in here. I'm letting you know this now."

"Yeah, I already peeped that." My eyes went past her and out the window to where the girls sat.

Lena turned around to see what I was looking at when I said what I said.

"Oh, you're definitely not going to like a lot of people, but don't write them off so quickly. It's okay to get to know a few people, but don't speak too much about your personal business. These hoes are cutthroat," she advised.

I nodded. "Okay."

"You might wanna get out of this cell too."

"Why?" She had my full attention.

"Your cellmate is a chomo."

"A what?"

"A child molester."

"Dead ass?" My eyed bulged.

I knew I was going to come across different people with different and wild charges, but I didn't know it was going to be so early on that I was in close proximity to one.

"Yup, but don't worry. When Ms. Walsh come in today, we gon get you outta here."

"Please and thank you."

"Come with me, though," she stated.

"Where to?" I raised a brow.

"Girl, ain't many places for us to go. We're going to the computer room."

I followed behind her, leaving out my cell and to a room where there were five computers. Two were being occupied while two were free, right next to each other.

"What's your mom's number?" Lena asked, punching in a number into the computer and placing her thumb on a thumbprint machine.

Why the fuck would she ask me that, like I would just happily give it to her? I thought.

"Huh? For what?"

"So, I have this text app where I can message whoever and

it goes straight to their phones. I can shoot a text to your mom for you until you're able to get your stuff activated," she explained.

I looked at her skeptically but decided to give in. The way I was feeling without speaking to my family, I knew they were feeling the same way. So, I rattled out my mom's number, then told her what to message her. She showed me how she discreetly wrote it and, after I approved, she hit the send button.

She explained to me she wasn't supposed to do that, but if neither of us said anything, then no one would get in trouble. Apparently, the FBOP didn't want any third-party contact, especially not any inmates doing each other favors. But I was grateful for what she did. I felt a little more settled.

"Thank you so much."

"No problem, hun."

After we were finished, I returned to my cell, which I had to myself because my cellmate went to work. I had nothing to do, but let my thoughts consume me, which resulted in me crying off and on and falling back to sleep.

KNOCK! Knock!

With my heart beating, I jumped out of my slumber, looking bewildered. Any noise made me jump or had my heart racing. I was uneasy being around complete strangers, ones who I had no clue as to why they were inside those walls with me.

"Hey, Ms. Walsh is calling you," an unfamiliar person stood in my doorway and informed me.

I nodded while taking deep breaths. She closed back the door, leaving me to calm down alone. Once I settled, I got off my bunk, slipped the fake Vans on my feet, and washed my face quickly. When I walked out into the dayroom, I looked around to see if I saw Ms. Walsh, but there wasn't anyone in sight, so I went to the guard booth.

When I approached the booth, I stopped and waited for the CO to get off the phone.

"Wassup?" he asked when he hung up.

"Someone said Ms. Walsh was calling me, but I don't see her," I told him.

"She's in her office," he spoke as if I knew where that was.

"And where is that?"

"Right above this booth. Just walk up those steps and you'll see it," he directed.

"Okay, thanks."

"When did you come in?" he asked, just as I was walking off.

"Two days ago."

He sized me up and down as he leaned back in his chair. "Mmmhmm."

I raised a brow and shot him a sarcastic look before

walking off. He was giving off pervert vibes, which I knew for a fact many of the COs were on that type of timing.

Following his instructions, I took the steps up to the top tier and saw the office door. I knocked and was told to come in.

"Ms. Milan?" a short, older Hispanic woman asked.

"Yes. Ms. Walsh?" I wanted to confirm.

"Yes. Have a seat." She went and retrieved a folder from a file cabinet. "How's everything?"

"I'm not sure how to answer that, but I need to speak to my family," I cut straight to the chase.

"You will. I'll have your information to you by the end of the day, okay?"

I nodded and sat back in my seat. "Is it possible to move cells?" I came out and asked.

While I didn't confront Lisa about her charges, subconsciously, it made my skin crawl. Any adult who touched an innocent child needed to be locked away for life. It was a very touchy subject for me since I was a victim of molestation. That shit was a pure sickness.

"Who are you with?" She started looking at the computer.

"Lisa, I'm not sure of her last name."

"Mmmm. Okay. Go find an empty bed unless you want me to place you somewhere."

"Now?" I asked.

My eyes popped open because I didn't know she would've allowed me to move so easily and so fast.

"Yes. Go see where you want to move to and come back to tell me. Besides that, I will get your phone and Corrlinks set up today. I won't be assigning you to a job just yet. Also, grab one of those plastic bags in that box. That's your pads, tampons, and toilet paper," she quickly spoke.

"Thank you." I took one bag and dashed out of her office in search of Lena. If it was one person to help me find a new cell, it was her.

When I found her, we took a quick walk around the unit and saw who had empty beds. Narrowing it down, we pulled up to this chick that was known to be a loner. She was one of the people that had greeted me when I first got on the unit. Recollecting our introduction, she told me she was from the same city as me, so I thought it would've been an alright match. Besides, she was in for drugs, a charge I didn't care for.

We spoke briefly, and she agreed it was cool that I moved in. The moment she said yes, I was right back upstairs to Ms. Walsh's office.

"Okay, I changed it in the system. But you can't move until after four p.m. count," she directed.

"Thank you."

I left out her office feeling just a little better. Soon, I was going to be out of an uncomfortable space, even though, overall, I was uneasy. And I was about to be in contact with my family.

"Keilani!" I heard Lena yell as I was descending the steps.

She was standing by the computer room with the door open, waving me over.

"Wassup?" I quizzed, following her inside.

"Your mom wrote back." She stepped aside for me to see the message.

It read:

Baby girl, so good to know you're alright. We miss you so much already. I haven't been able to sleep and I won't until I hear your voice. I love you; we love you.

Reading those few sentences brought tears to my eyes. I turned into an emotional wreck within seconds. "Tell her, I love her more," I told Lena and left out the computer room.

I hurriedly made my way back to my cell before anyone else saw me in the state I was in. Climbing up on my bed, I let the tears soak my face and blanket until, eventually, I fell asleep.

I WOKE up to the sound of someone ruffling through something. My cellmate had returned from work. Remembering the revelation Lena told me earlier, I looked at the older white woman with much disgust.

"Oh, sorry. I didn't mean to wake you," she apologized.

"It's fine." I waved her off.

My throat was feeling dry as hell, so I got off my bunk to go out and get some water. I grabbed the cup they gave me from R&D and exited out the cell. The day room was filled with the ladies indulging in different activities. At a glance, there were some reading, watching TV, cooking, drawing, or just simply talking to each other.

When I got to the water, I saw it was only hot water. I observed the area to see if there was a water fountain, but there wasn't. Another girl walked past me and got some of the hot water, then proceeded to the ice machine and poured a bunch of ice inside. She took a sip and walked off. That's when I learned how they got their drinking water and followed suit.

"Recall, recall. All inmates return to your assigned cells for the four-p.m. count," blurred from the speakers around the unit, making me jump.

Everyone stopped what they were doing and gathered their things. Some started running around the unit to get ice from the ice machine and water, while others still procrastinated and were talking to their friends.

"What's going on?" I asked a girl who was walking slowly past me.

"It's count time. Just go to your cell," she said before stepping inside of hers.

I went into my cell and saw my cellmate sitting on her bed reading a book; she looked up at me then quickly returned her attention back to what she was reading.

"What time is dinner?" I asked, in hopes of getting an alright hot meal.

"Right after count," she said, not even taking her eyes off her book.

As I sat down on the chair, the CO came by the door and locked it, then walked away to lock everyone else's, I concluded from the clicks I kept hearing.

Within ten minutes, two COs, one after the other, walked past our door, looked inside, and walked off. They were conducting what I later found out was count. After what seemed like forever, the same CO who locked us in came and unlocked the door.

While some ladies fled from their cells, rushing to the tables to get a good spot in front of whichever TV they wanted to watch, others quickly formed a line at the computer room door and kitchen. Being as though nothing fazed me at that given time, I walked to stand in the line to get food, praying it was somewhat edible to eat.

When I received my tray, it was Philly cheesesteak with two hot dog buns, carrots, and a juice packet. Better than I thought. I went back into my cell, grabbed the cup they gave me the first day in, and went and made my drink. I sat down and ate my food, not having a care for anyone in there.

"Heyyy Keilani," sang Noelle, walking in my direction. "Or should I say Remy, you remind me so much of her, y'all talk and sound just alike."

"Hi," I shot her a shy smile.

I just found it funny when people would say us New

Yorkers all sounded the same and that we had a heavy accent, when it was them that had an accent.

"Hmmm, did that bullshit fill you?" she asked, scrunching up her face, referring to the tray.

"I mean, it's better than the cold sandwiches."

"Hold on," she said, putting up her finger and walking away.

She went over to the table where the other girls were and brought back a bowl of food in it.

"Here, it's good, trust me," she said as she handed me the bowl of food.

"What is it?" I raised my eyebrow.

"Mackerel and rice, with some sweet and hot sauce on it."

I looked at her blankly, as she motioned for me to try it. It didn't smell bad, and I was pretty sure it was more tasteful than the kitchen's food, so I went for it. When I took a spoonful, surprisingly, it was actually really good. I guess it showed on my face because Noelle laughed and said, "Told you so."

"Nah, this aight," I said in between chews. "Thank you."

"No problem, boo," she said and walked back to the table to join the girls.

I devoured the meal, not leaving a grain of rice in sight. I was beyond hungry. When I was getting ready to head into my cell, I heard my name being called, along with others on the intercom from the officer's booth. I walked over and stood in line until it was my turn to see what they wanted.

"Hi, you called for Milan?" I asked the CO when I reached the front of the line.

He shuffled through the stack of mails in front of him, pulled a paper out and handed it to me. I took it and walked away without asking any questions. When I opened it, it had my basic information on it and some codes. Instantly, I had a mind this was what I needed from Ms. Walsh. In perfect timing, Lena was walking past, so I quickly grabbed her attention.

"Hey Lena, what's this for?" I asked, showing her the piece of paper in my hand.

"Oh, that's for you to set up your phone and to get onto your email. You won't be able to do the phone setup until tomorrow, but I can show you how to get onto your email."

"Please, I'd appreciate it." I motioned my hands into praying hands.

We went and got in line for the computer. Once inside, she helped me set everything up and gave me the rundown on how to log in and how long I had to wait between sessions and such.

Lena was a heaven sent. I felt a good vibe from her. She was a cool ass ol' head. She was a good looker and had a calm body on her. The way she moved, she was hip and knew what was up in the world.

"You have medical in the morning," she informed me after we passed a paper that was on the wall.

"How you know?"

"This is the call-out sheet. Make sure and look for your name every single night. Around this time, they put it out. It tells us where we have to be and when the following day," she explained.

"Aight, thanks."

After we finished with the computer, Lena helped me move cells. Then, I took a shower and retired to my cell for the rest of the night. Lena gave me a book to read, so I did just that until sleep took over me.

CHAPTER FOUR

MANIC

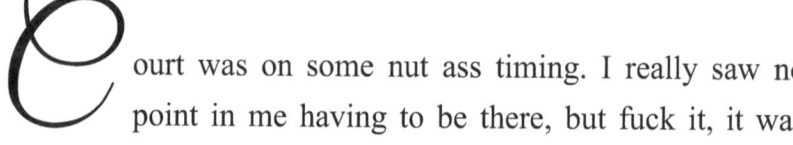

*C*ourt was on some nut ass timing. I really saw no point in me having to be there, but fuck it, it was over and done with. They said everything happened for a reason because if I didn't go to court, I wouldn't have seen shawty. She was a breath of fresh air. I hadn't seen someone have a glow like she did in a while, even in her darkest days.

Click! Click!

The sound of my cell being unlocked snatched me from my thoughts. As usual, I was already up and ready to start my day. I looked at the time on my G-shock, which happened to be worth a Rolex behind the walls, and it read six-thirty a.m. When I stepped out of my cell, I walked to the banister and looked over it. A few niggas were moving about, but for the most part, the place was silent.

There were two tiers in the unit. My cell was on the top tier in a position where I could look out my door and see everything that went on, including who entered and exited the unit; a spot I needed. Though I was untouchable for the most part, I always moved and operated militant.

I proceeded down to the computer room to check my messages. Like always, I had a ton of messages to reply to, which took up the entire thirty minutes we were allowed on Corrlinks for messaging. I responded to everyone and then made my way to the phone to call my little girl, Makaela.

Makaela Frost was my only child. She was my world, the reason I lived, my everything. My little princess was beautiful inside and out, smart, and had a bright future ahead of her. My mother brought her up to FDC Philly every week to visit me. I was blessed to have a great support system, but most importantly, to be able to still be active with my seed.

I dialed up her mom's number and stated my name into the phone. When the call went through, it only rang once before her mother, Morgan, answered and accepted the call.

"Hold on," she said as soon as the call went through.

"Daddy?" Makaela got on the phone seconds later.

"Yeah, baby girl. Wassup?"

"Nothing, I just finished eating. Mommy about to get me dressed."

"How did you sleep?"

"Good. How about you, daddy?"

"Daddy slept ard, mama. I hope you have a great day at school. I'll call you later."

"Okay. I love you," she sang happily.

Makaela was only four, but was wise beyond her years. She was observant and outspoken. She knew exactly where I was. We didn't sugarcoat shit and sell her a dream about me being away at school or for work. As a family, we kept it one hundred and told her the truth. She didn't love me any less.

"I love you more."

After we concluded our conversation, I hung up and made my way back to my cell. As soon as I rested my ass on my bed, I heard someone yelling my name.

"Frost!" a guard hollered.

I knew it was time for my call-out to medical since I peeped it on the sheet, but it was odd that someone was actually calling my last name. I was putting on my sneakers when I heard him again.

"Frost!" he yelled again, sounding even louder.

Before I could respond, I heard the guys on the unit yell at whoever the clown was that I was coming. When I finally exited my cell, I looked toward the booth and saw an unfamiliar officer.

No wonder why this fool was yelling "Frost," I thought to myself. *He's new.*

Making my way down to the bottom tier slowly, I walked over to the booth. When I approached bull, he looked at me like I had five heads or something. He looked young, even younger than me.

Ion have time for no bullshit today, man.

"Inmate Frost?" he quizzed.

I looked at him dumbfounded because he was yelling my name so damn much and I was the only person who walked right up to him. What I wanted to say was "no shit," but I just stayed calm.

"Yeah man, that's me," I answered.

"Where's your greens?" he asked, looking puzzled, referring to the nasty dark green jumpsuit they made us wear.

Yeah, he's definitely new and don't know who the fuck I am. I shook my head.

"I don't wear greens, my man. Come on, I'ma be late for my call-out," I smoothly said, walking past him.

Passing the booth, I gave the guard that occupied it a head

nod. He returned it but was quickly approached by the newbie. I overheard him telling him I was trying to leave the unit with my grays on and not my greens, but I didn't have to intervene. The newbie was checked and put into his place. He walked off toward my direction with a confused look on his face but brushed it off when he reached me.

We made our way down to the medical floor and, once there, the doctor took me right in.

"Good morning, Manic," Doctor Gannon greeted me as I walked into his office.

"Morning, doc. What's up?" I hopped on the examination table.

He went into his hidden cabinet in this office and pulled out a duffle bag. Resting it on the table, he unzipped the bag and showed the contents inside. I nodded in acknowledgement and hopped off the table. Inspecting inside, I made sure every-thing that was supposed to be there was there.

"We all good," I told him.

He zipped it back and placed it back in his hiding spot. Doctor Gannon been one of the key persons bringing in the drugs and whatever else was needed inside the detention center. He was lowkey and moved shit well.

"I'll get it to Grace," he stated.

"Ard, cool. See you when I see you." I left out his office and requested to see Lieutenant Grace.

"Ughhh, mmm, yesss," LT Grace moaned softly.

I had her bent over the desk, fist full of hair in my hand while I penetrated her from the back. Her ass was so fat, it mesmerized me, and there was nothing stopping me from trying to dig deep and seeing her ass jiggle with every stroke.

"Manic, oh my—" she whispered, not able to complete her sentence.

When I pulled out and slid the condom off, she got on her knees and wrapped her pretty lips around my dick. I let baby girl do her thing while she sucked the nut out of me. As usual, she let me dump my load in the back of her throat.

"Mmmhmmm, shit," I hissed.

"You never cease to amaze me, Manic," she said breathlessly.

If it was one thing a nigga was blessed with besides a big ass dick, it was a wicked sex game. I gave her a smirk and smacked her ass before she pulled her uniform pants up, but the way it jiggled made me want to go again.

"Brown to Lieutenant Grace," her walkie chimed.

We both looked at each other. She rolled her eyes and pressed the walkie. "Lieutenant Grace, go." She went back and forth with her co-worker for a moment.

Most people would've thought me fuckin' the lieutenant was wild. Nah, I was smart. Not only did I have a nice piece of ass to hit when I wanted to, but she was the head lieutenant right under the captain. She allowed everything to move with no problems. I had a two-in-one package deal.

"Listen, I know we got right to it. But you know we gotta' talk about the shit that you needed me to handle. Like, what the fuck man? You gotta choose your guys wisely," she went off.

I knew it was coming; I saw it written all over her face when I first came into her office. That's why I bent her ass over immediately to avoid hearing her mouth, but I knew it was gon' come up.

"I know, I know. I'm just glad I found out before that nigga started doing goofy shit and I would've had to put him down myself," I stated, referring to Reef and him getting high off my shit instead of selling it.

She went into a drawer and pulled out a clear plastic bag full of pills, strips, cigarettes, and coke. Reluctantly, she handed it to me with a smug look on her face. "Give it to someone smarter next time and not a fuckin' junkie." She shoved it into my chest.

"Mmmm, understood. I got it handled. Don't even trip."

"You better." She shot me a stern look.

Her walkie chimed again with calls, breaking our intense stare.

"Alright, I'm about to get you taken back to the unit. I have to deal with something. Everything went good at medical, right?" she asked.

"Yeah, everything cool. Doc got the shipment that was supposed to come in, so everything straight. Go handle that for me." I slapped her on her ass and grabbed her close to me, planting a kiss on her neck.

We were in an old office in the back of medical where they barely used. That part of medical was used a little while back to house the infamous Kaboni Savage after he sent countless hits from inside the facility. One of them was a major hit that caused multiple deaths. He was the first ever.

I hid the drugs she gave me in different places on my person before we left out the office. As we walked and made our way to the front where Dr. Gannon's office was, we ran into a few of the female inmates sitting in the waiting area. I paid their gasping for air asses no mind and kept it pushing. That was, until I accidentally bumped into someone walking out of the office as I was passing by the door.

"Shit, sorry," she yelped, reaching her arms out as if I was about to fall.

"You coo—"

My sentence got cut short when I saw who it was. It was the thick, long hair jawn that caught my eye in R&D. The one that kept creeping her little way into my thoughts here and there since she crossed my path.

"Back away," LT Grace raised her voice at us, prompting us to separate instantly.

LT Grace didn't waste another second getting me out of there. She moved a little sloppy not knowing the women were there, but other than that, I believe she saw how the jawn had me stuck for a moment.

Once out of the visibility of the females, I was handed over to a CO to take me back to the unit. The entire way upstairs, I wore a smirk as I thought about how soft her hands were and how much prettier she was up close.

Why the fuck am I on her like that? I asked myself.

CHAPTER FIVE

U.S Department of Justice
Federal Bureau of Prisons

75816-066

MILAN
KEILANI

Eye: BR   Ht: 5'03"

INMATE

Vending

KEI

*O*ut of all the fellas I already saw behind the walls, only one kept catching my attention. I was walking out of the doctor's office back into the waiting area when I bumped head first into the green-eyed handsome dude from R&D. To begin with, I didn't know it was him so, as a reflex, I reached my hand out to prevent the person from falling.

When our hands touched, I felt a wave of electricity run throughout my body, making the hairs stand up. Looking up into his pretty ass green eyes, I got stuck in the moment and totally forgot where I was. While I wanted to stay there just a while longer, the Lieutenant wasn't having it. She quickly separated us, escorting him out of the medical area.

"Damn, you got to touch Manic," a female inmate scoffed.

"Who?" I quizzed.

"Manic, the nigga you just bumped into. You don't know who he is?"

Am I supposed to know who the fuck he is? I thought.

"No." I shook my head.

Just when she was about to open her mouth again, the same CO who took us to medical walked in the door.

"Come on ladies, let's go," she announced.

Everyone stood to their feet and shuffled out of the room. We made our way to the huge elevator and upstairs back onto the unit.

I was anxious to set my phone up, so I went in search of Lena to see if she was up yet. The CO called us to go to medical first thing, so I wasn't able to activate my account. Lucky for me, when I walked up to Lena's cell, she was lying down reading a book.

"Hey," I opened the door and greeted.

"Hey, hun. How was medical?" she inquired.

"It was cool, normal shit for the most part. Can you show me how to set my phone up and to check my balance?"

"Yeah, let's go." She placed the book face down on her bed so she didn't lose her page, then followed me outside of the cell.

We went to get on the computers first to see if any money was on my account before attempting to make a call. My family had already made it clear they were going to make sure I had everything I needed and wanted my entire bid. I just prayed they could figure out how to put the money on my account.

After checking my account on the computer, I discovered it was money on there, a lot at that. While helping me navigate everything, Lena peeped at the amount and told me to not tell people how much support I had and how much money was on my books. She informed me they would befriend me for ulterior motives and it wouldn't end well. I took note to take heed of her warning.

Since I knew the money was there, we proceeded to the phones, which were in the rear of the unit. To set up the phone, you had to make a recording of yourself saying your full name. And whenever you dialed a number, in order for it to go through, you had to say your name the same exact way you said it in the recording. It was a way the institutions kept inmates from using each other's phone accounts.

After what felt like the hundredth time, my call to my

mom finally went through, which went unanswered. I felt defeated and felt like giving up, but the will in me didn't allow it. I quickly gathered myself and tried the phone system again. After about ten attempts, it finally picked up my voice and made the call; that time, my mother answered.

"Lani, are you good?" my mother said as soon as the call connected.

"Hey, ma. Yeah, I'm aight, I guess," I answered lowly.

No matter how I was truly feeling, I wasn't going to tell her because I didn't want to have her worrying about me. My mother took on all of her children's feelings, whether we were sad, angry, depressed, or even happy. Bad as it was, she had her own feelings to channel.

"It's good to finally hear your voice."

"Yeah, same. I miss you, I miss y'all." I started to cry. "I don't know if I can do this."

"Lani, don't say that. You got this. If it's anyone capable of handling anything thrown their way, it's you," she spoke, trying to give words of encouragement.

"I thought so, but I don't know, ma. It's a lot of wild people with fucked up stories in here. I don't belong here."

"I know, I know. Just keep in mind, it's only temporary, and before you know it, you'll be back home with us."

"Right," I said above a whisper. "Where's Brix?"

"He's right here. Hold on."

"Bae, what's good? How you holding up?"

Hearing my man's voice took me to another level of emotion. I felt my ears tingling as a lump formed in my throat.

"Bae?" he called out to me again.

I sniffled, then wiped away my tears and snot. "I'm here," I finally answered.

"Talk to me, wassup?" he went on.

"I'm good. Did you get my email request? Tell everyone to check their inboxes. When y'all approve it, we can email back and forth," I explained, trying to change the subject away from him asking about my state of mind.

"Yeah, I did already."

"Okay, bet. So, how long you staying at the house?"

I was surprised he was still at my place since it had been two days since I'd been gone. Brix was always on the go and bussing moves. He would drive back and forth to New York from Pennsylvania just to handle business, party, then come back and be with me. Half the time, I was right with him.

"I needed to hear from you before I went anywhere," he confirmed my assumption.

"Got it. Thanks a lot, baby."

"You got shit off commissary yet?" he went on to ask.

"No, I just saw the money, so I'll ask about it."

"Aight. Get everything you need. We got you."

"Thank you."

"I love you, Lani."

"I love you more."

The phone got passed around quickly for me to at least say

hi to everyone that was there before it hung up. I felt a little better that I finally spoke to them, but it also pained me deeply that I couldn't be next to them.

On my way back to my cell, I ran into Trouble. Since I came in, I hadn't seen her and didn't notice until we crossed each other's path.

"Oh, hey," I greeted.

"Keilani, right?" she asked with squinted eyes.

"Yeah. And it's Trouble?"

"Mmmhmm."

"I haven't seen you since. Where you be hiding?" I pried.

She started to laugh as if I said a joke.

"I'm a low-key person. I stay to myself and don't mingle much. I really be with my girlfriend and on business for real," she explained.

"Oh, I see. As you should."

"Them niggas been asking about you," she revealed.

"What niggas?" I cocked my head back.

"All the niggas in this building, what you mean, what niggas?" she chuckled.

"Oh, right. I wouldn't know, and I don't care. I have a man."

"That's wassup. I hope he sticks by you and doesn't run off like muthafuckers usually do."

"Nah, not mine," I defended.

Ring! Ring!

The loud bell to our unit went off, indicating someone was

by the door. Both Trouble and I looked toward the entrance to see who it was.

"Milan!" a lady yelled as she walked in holding two mesh net laundry bags.

"Oh, that's yo shit, go get it," Trouble informed me.

I went and approached the woman and told her I was Milan. She handed over the laundry bags and just walked away without saying a word. Peeking inside the bags, I saw it was clothes, so I went into my cell to investigate further.

When inside, I pulled the contents out of the bag and saw it was the same tan uniforms I saw all the ladies wear, brown t-shirts, brown sports bras and underwear, socks, and huge gray nightgowns.

"This is it?" I asked myself out loud, looking at the items.

"Yup, that's it," my cellmate spoke like if I was speaking to her.

It was a long way from Gucci and gold; it was rags, not riches. On the bright side, I was happy to have shit to change into. For the first two days, I had been wearing the one green raggedy jumpsuit with only the nightgown Lena gave to me to sleep in. Since I only had one underwear at the time, I washed it and let it air dry until I could put it back on.

"You wanna play cards or something?" my bunky, Shannon, asked out of nowhere.

Knock! Knock!

My head snapped in the direction of the door. I saw Noelle peeking through the window, so I waved her in.

"Hey, boo. Just came to see what you were up to," she spoke once inside.

"Oh, shit. Just got my laundry. I was finna shower and chill."

"I know yo ass happy to get out of that jumpsuit. When you're finished, come fuck with us," she invited.

"Aight, bet. I'm finna go shower now."

"Ard."

She left out, leaving me to get myself ready to hit the water. I gathered my things and left out the cell. There were three showers, plus a handicap, one on the bottom tier while three were on the top tier. All of them were open, giving me different options. They faced the day room, out in the open with just a shower curtain to block our naked bodies. If someone wanted to be wicked, they could've just simply snatched the curtain and the person's whole pussy would've been out for everyone to see, including the people watching the cameras.

After handling my hygiene, I went and joined the girls, who were just talking, playing cards, listening to music, and watching TV. They started to prepare dinner ahead of time while we chilled, giving me a glimpse of how they cooked behind the wall, which was utterly impressive. It was crazy what a microwave could do.

THE FOLLOWING MORNING, I woke up feeling agitated. My bunky was on the toilet bowl all night shitting. I wasn't sure what the hell was wrong with her, but I knew for certain whatever it was ran through her. Every second, she was jumping off her bed with her fast ass and running to the toilet. She kept flushing, which was considered the courtesy flush, to keep the room from smelling. She even had a small nasal spray bottle that was filled with water, dish soap, and smell good oil mixed together, spraying it in the air like an air freshener.

When the guard unlocked the door for the morning, I flew out of the cell with the quickness. I hurried over to the computer room but I saw it wasn't yet open, so I decided to go back and grab my things to handle my hygiene. On the call-out sheet, I was scheduled to go see the psychologist, which I knew was eventually coming.

I got myself dressed while Shannon snored her life away on the bottom bunk. The moment I was ready, I grabbed my ID and exited out the cell with plans of not returning until I came back from my call-out. By that time, the computer room was open, so I hopped on to check my email, which I had many of, making me smile.

After I replied to everyone, I sat in the dayroom and watched a silent TV since I didn't have an MP3 to connect to it. But it wasn't long before a CO came into the unit and called for me and a few others. We all made our way downstairs to the psych department.

"HOW ARE YOU FEELING TODAY, Ms. Milan?" Dr. Reese questioned me.

He was an older, fat Caucasian man with gray hair and beard, who came off sincere about his job, unlike the other staff I had met.

"I'm okay, I guess," I answered.

"Okay? That's it?" He looked at a file in front of him. "I just received your file from your doctor and therapist you've been seeing. I also noticed that it was court mandated and will be in here as well."

I nodded in acknowledgement. When I caught my case, I became not only depressed but suicidal. With everything slowly slipping from my fingertips and my life crashing down on me, I felt there was no reason for me to live. My mother knew me so well. She went as far as to get my gun out of my room and away from me until she knew I was a bit more stable mentally.

My first court date after being arraigned, the judge was notified of my actions and thoughts, then asked me if I wanted to stay incarcerated for the safety of myself. Since I rejected, he made it mandatory that I went and saw a therapist twice a week, which resulted in me seeing a psychologist who diagnosed me with severe depression, anxiety, PTSD, and borderline personality disorder. I was placed on medication to help me cope.

"Have you taken any of your medication since you been here?" he asked.

"No, they told me I'd get a fresh batch here," I answered. At that time, I hadn't taken my meds for over a month.

"It's Zoloft, I see. Do you think it helps you?"

I nodded.

"Okay, so we'll stick with the same dose and go from there. But tell me, what are your thoughts about being in here as of right now?"

I looked at him blankly because it didn't take a rocket scientist to know it wasn't an ideal situation. Instead of being a bitch about it, I thought maybe the session would help, even if it was just a little bit.

"I shouldn't be here. I blame myself for even getting involved with someone who didn't even love me. I hate that I put men before myself, all to be loved. But in the end, I get the shit at the end of the stick and got hurt."

"You feel the reason you're in this predicament is that you love too much or love easily?" He looked at me intensely.

"I do."

"Was it one particular person who has you in this position or multiple?"

"Multiple but mainly one. If only I hadn't run into him, none of this would have ever happened. I wouldn't be here talking to you."

My thoughts quickly drifted back to the night I ran into the reason my world got flipped upside down.

December 2016

"Hurry up, I'm two seconds away from pulling off, Lani," my homegirl, Lala, threatened. *She was downstairs waiting for me, so we could go to the club.*

"I'm coming, damn."

I abruptly hung up the phone. Grabbing my clutch for the night, I poked my head in my grandparents' bedroom to see if they were still awake. "Goodnight, granny, goodnight grandpa. I'm out," I told them as both their heads turned my way.

"You have the spare keys?" my grandmother checked.

"Yes, don't wait up. I'll be fine," I assured them.

I was in town for the weekend because of a toy drive I conducted at my old elementary school, C.S. 21. Whenever I touched down in Brooklyn, I stayed at my grandparents' place on Malcolm X Blvd in Bed-Stuy. It was where I knew since I was a kid and it was better than paying for a hotel or Airbnb.

Swiftly making my way out of the apartment and down the steps, I finally made it outside to see Lala double parked. The weather was biting cold, almost had made me regret putting on a freak 'em dress. There was frozen snow on the ground, so I carefully made my way to her car and got inside.

"Damn, you took forever and a day," Lala exaggerated.

"Hi to you too, hoe," I retorted. We hugged each other tightly.

I hadn't seen Lala in a while since we both played college basketball. Our schedules were hectic and, not to mention, I moved out of Brooklyn my senior year of high school to Chester, Pennsylvania.

"I missed you," she expressed as she pulled away from the curb.

Lala was one of my fake big sisters. We met through the basketball world. It was a handful of us in our circle who all hooped at different universities and colleges. Whenever time permitted, we would link up and have a good time.

"You know I missed yo light skinned ass more." We both giggled.

She turned up the music as she moved in and out of traffic to the city. We got in the mood and rapped our asses off the entire ride.

By the time we reached the Meatpacking District, we were so hyped and ready to hop out the whip. We peeped the line at the club we were going to, but Lala knew the promoter, thankfully.

"He said come on," she told me. She parked properly, cut the engine, and exited the car. I grabbed my phone and clutch, then followed suit.

Meticulously, we walked across the brick road to the front of the club. Straight to the front of the line we went and met her connect, who led us right inside. Of course, we caught stares and grills from the ladies, who were unfortunate to stand in the cold weather, freezing their cats off.

Once inside, I surveyed the place to see it was already lit, and it was only minutes after midnight. We followed her folks to a section where he told us to get comfortable. There were already bottles on the table with a few other people occupying the place. Lala wasted no time pouring us some drinks. The only thing that was left to do was party and enjoy ourselves.

TWO HOURS LATER, and we both were feeling tipsy. There was not a care in the world for me at that moment. I didn't think about the new university I was about to start, the fact I decided to quit hooping, or that I was single around the holidays once again. The liquor was my best friend and knew exactly how to make me smile.

"I'm done because I still have to drive," Lala spoke in my ear. I nodded at her in agreement.

"I gotta pee, I'll be right back," I told her as I scanned the room for the ladies' room sign.

Slipping out of the section, I twisted and turned to make my way to the washroom, but only to be met with a long line. My piss was so hot, I couldn't hold it any longer. The men's bathroom was clear, so I swiftly made my way inside and, luckily, no one was inside. I dashed into a stall, pulled down my thong and relieved myself.

"Ughhh," I moaned out in relief. "Thank God," I whispered.

Just as I was wiping, I heard the door to the bathroom open. My eyes popped open as I got paranoid. I didn't think this through, I said to myself. Thoughts of a weirdo showing his true colors when he saw me alone plagued my mind. No, everything would be fine girl.

I flushed the toilet and fixed myself. Unlocking the stall door, I stepped out and saw a guy using the urinal. From the angle he was standing in, I saw his dick and almost choked on the saliva I was swallowing. At first, I didn't see his face, but I noticed he was tall and well built, as if he went to the gym. His threads were fly as fuck and the jewelry on his neck almost blinded me. As I was admiring him, he turned slightly to face me and a heavy weight settled inside my stomach.

"Tavian?" I asked in disbelief.

"Keilani?" he asked, then quickly turned and fixed himself before returning his attention back to me.

Tavian was my old childhood crush. His family and mine were close for years. My older brother and him ran the streets together as young boys while our moms were good girlfriends. My mother barely allowed me to go anywhere as a young girl, but whenever Tavian's mom threw a party for one of her kids, I was able to go.

"Long time, it's been forever," I expressed.

"Word, fuck you doing here? Wait, what are you doing in here?" He looked around the bathroom.

"Listen, I had to pee, and that line for the ladies' room was ridiculous. So, I quietly slipped my ass in here."

"Crazy ass." We both laughed.

We moved over to the sinks and both washed our hands in

silence and reached for the tissue at the same time, resulting into us shocking one another.

"Damn," he blurted out. "That's a sign, I gotta stay away from yo ass," he joked.

"Nah, that's a sign to stay far away from you," I retorted.

Tavian was an alright looker, but his swag and sex appeal was through the roof, making it hard to not wonder how he was in the bed. He'd always been that way since we were kids. All the girls would throw themselves at him, and he always caught them, being the lady's man he was.

"Yeah, aight," he chuckled as we made our way out the men's room.

It still had a long line of females waiting to use the ladies' room. When they saw us both walk out together, their eyes bulged. Some had grins on their faces while others shot me a stink look. I knew they thought Tavian and I were in there fucking, but that wasn't even the case. Good thing I wasn't the type to explain myself to people I didn't give two shits about.

As I was walking off to go back to meet Lala's hyped ass, Tavian pulled my arm and brought me close to him. My hands landed on his chest and slipped down a bit, allowing me to feel how firm and tones his abs were.

"Come fuck with me in my section," he spoke in my ear, loud enough to hear over the music.

"I'm with my sis though."

"Bring her ass too."

I looked over and saw Lala with a drink in the air and her ass swaying. As long as there was liquor and a good vibe, I knew she wouldn't have cared that we switched places. Besides, I wanted to stay next to Tavian so I could inhale the sweet smell of his cologne.

"Where you at?" I asked.

He pointed to where his section was, and I nodded in acknowledgement. We parted ways, as I fought through the thick crowd of people to get to Lala.

"Come on." I grabbed her hands as I reached her.

"I don't wanna leave yet," she pleaded.

"We're not leaving, we're just going to another section!" I yelled over the music.

"Where?"

I pointed at Tavian's section and, after she surveyed who was in there and what was going on, she smiled and obliged. A minute later, we were entering Tavian's space with his homeboys. Right away, we were handed drinks and blended right in as we were there with them the entire night.

"Nobody haffi know seh me and you a fuck. Nobody haffi know seh yuh a give it up. Nobody haffi know seh yo come over mi yard. Baby take off your drawers," Kranium's lyrics to Nobody Has to Know blurred through the speakers.

Tavian found his way behind me, as I moved my waistline in a circular motion. I bent over a little and pushed my ass onto him as he thrust back, matching my energy. Grabbing my hand, he held it in the air while I continued to grind on him in sync with the music.

"Keep throwing ya shit back like that and I'ma have to take yo ass with me," he spoke in my ear, sending chills throughout my body.

The way he gripped my waist as I danced sent me crazy. It was firm but yet gentle. The liquor I consumed didn't help the lustful feeling I had over him. At that point, I was ready to go home with him. In my eyes, he wasn't no stranger, and I always wanted him. I was single, and it had been a while since I got any action.

I turned around and grabbed his neck, making him lower his head since he was so damn tall compared to my short frame.

"Maybe I want you to," I spoke in his ears.

He pulled back, hovering over me with a wicked grin that turned me on more. Pulling my chin up with his finger, he came close to my ear, "Fuck it, you leaving with me then," he demanded.

When it was time to leave, we all walked out together. Lala and I were holding hands as we passed the threshold of the club into the cold winter air.

"You good to drive, right?" I asked her. Once I made my mind up that I was going with Tavian, I informed Lala, who was more excited for me than I was for myself.

"Yeah, girl. I do this shit. Besides, I ain't drink shit but water that last hour," she assured me.

One of Tavian's boys walked her to her car while I hopped in the passenger seat of his Audi. As soon as I had my seatbelt on, he sped off from in front the club, making a skidding sound for everyone to hear. His driving was reckless and dangerous, but I loved it. It was something about New York niggas and the way they drove and carried themselves.

The music thumped the entire ride back to Brooklyn. When we drove down Atlantic Avenue, I knew we were headed to his block. I wasn't sure why I thought we were going to a hotel or something. But then, I remembered he must've not only liked me but trusted me since our families were close.

Hopping out, I hurriedly followed him inside the house to dodge the brisk wind. We entered his room, where I immediately kicked off my heels and coat. Plopping down on his bed, I watched him as he undressed himself. Once down to his draws, he went into his dresser and pulled out a t-shirt, tossing it my way.

"Thanks," I spoke shyly, then proceeded to get undressed.

I turned around, having my back facing him as I unzipped my dress, letting it drop to the floor, only having a thong on. As I was putting the t-shirt over my head, he came up behind me and wrapped his arms around my waist. Instantly, I felt butterflies in my stomach at his touch.

"You want something to drink?" he asked, tugging at my earlobes with his mouth.

Yeah, you, I thought, but didn't let it come out of my mouth.

"Some water is fine, thanks." I turned and smiled.

He grabbed the remote to his TV, turned it on, and handed it to me.

"Go ahead and get comfortable, I'll be right back." He left out the room.

Climbing on the bed, I got under the covers and comforter. I flipped through Netflix and just picked any show I saw. I knew it wasn't going to be long before the show and us traded places, making us the spotlight.

Moments later, Tavian returned with two cold bottles of water. He handed me one while he cracked one open and took a huge gulp. Resting the bottle on his nightstand, he slid into the bed, grabbing me close to him.

"Fuck is this you watching?" he quizzed.

"Some African show I be watching," I answered with a little giggle.

"Y'all girls be watching anything, man."

"Whatever." I pushed him playfully.

We both laughed.

"Watch yo hands before I put my hands on you. But you might like it."

"In that case…" I shoved him again.

That time, he grabbed ahold of my hand and grabbed me on top of him. Straddling his lap, he gripped my waist as he bit down on his bottom lip. I felt his tool rising underneath me, touching my perfect place between my legs.

"Come here," he spoke in a low but authoritative tone.

I leaned down toward him as he grabbed the back of my neck, making our lips connect. Our tongues danced around each other's mouths as I savored the taste of Dusse he possessed.

Tavian's hands roamed around my body, making me wetter by every touch, grip, and caress. While still kissing, he pulled down his drawers and flipped me on my back, never pulling his lips away. Positioning himself between my legs, he slid my thong to the side and placed his dick at my opening. He rubbed the head around my clit, slid down, and finally into my love canal.

"Ughhh," I moaned out in pleasure.

"Oh fuck," he huffed, closing his eyes tightly.

Taking one of my legs in the crook of his hand, he penetrated me deeply, sending me into a frenzy. It was only a minute or so into our sex session, and I was already flowing. Tavian was the right size and fit for me. The way he moved his hips and touched my body only made me submit to him more. He was everything I could imagine he was.

We had the best sex, which resulted in us going round for round. There were sleep breaks, but as soon as I moved an inch in the bed, waking him up, he slid his way right back in me. I wasn't sure if it was the liquor or if it was chemistry, but we couldn't get enough of one another.

The following morning, I woke up with him on my chest and body between my legs asleep. His arms were wrapped around my body, holding me tight. I smiled and blushed at the sight, not wanting to wake him, but I had a hot pee that couldn't wait for him to wake up when he wanted to.

"Tay," I caressed his head.

"Hmmp?" he groaned, moving his body a little.

"I have to use the bathroom."

He took a moment to flip over and land on his back. I grabbed the t-shirt from off the ground and threw it over my head. Remembering where the bathroom was, I hurriedly left out the room and raced to it.

Finally releasing my bladder, I washed my hands, then my face, and returned to the room. Tay was sitting up on his phone. Once I got in the bed, he snatched me back in his embrace as we laid down cuddled up.

"You good?" he asked, rubbing his nose onto the side of my face.

I nodded, then looked up at him and smiled. *"What time is it?"* I inquired.

It was a Sunday, which meant I had to drive back to Pennsylvania to get prepared for work the following day.

"One-forty-two," he answered.

"Ughhh. I gotta get ready to hit the road."

"Damn, why? I wanted to chill with you some more."

"Chill or fuck me?" I raised a brow as I sat up facing him.

"Like I said, I wanted to chill with you."

"I'd love that, but I have work tomorrow. I'll check my schedule and see my next off days to link with you."

"Okay, miss hard working lady. Where you work at anyway?"

"I'm a teller at a bank." I smiled at his compliment.

Tavian's eyes opened wide as if he hit the jackpot when I told him my occupation.

"Dead ass?" He raised his eyebrows.

"Yeah, why?" I was confused.

"Wassup, what if I said it's a way to make a whole lot of money?" He grinned.

Money made the world go round. While I was comfortable with my earnings, I always wanted to make more to do things I wanted to do and buy things I'd always wanted to buy. Even the rich people wanted to make more money, so who was I?

By the shit Tay wore and cars he drove, I knew he was making paper. If I even wanted to be around him or be with him, I had to look the part and be on the same type of timing.

"I would tell you to put me on how to." I returned the grin.

From that moment on, Tavian and I became business part-ners, amongst others, doing the same thing. I quickly fell down the rabbit hole into the world of scamming.

"Do you blame him for your current position?" Dr. Reese asked.

I thought about his question for a second. In the beginning, I did when everything popped off, but as time went on, I saw it wasn't him at all.

"No, I blame myself. I got myself here. I should've been stronger. I should've loved myself more."

CHAPTER SIX

MANIC

ith the new shipment that came in, money was on my mind, heavy. LT Grace sorted and got it ready to be distributed amongst the team. Dr. Gannon would put everyone on my team on the callout to see him and give out the product. I had a smooth system runnin but was thinking of new ways to do things, just to switch it up. It was never a smart idea to get too comfortable and keep the same routine, even if it worked.

With a lot of other shit going on in my head, I couldn't understand why I wasn't able to shake the thought of the jawn. It wasn't like I knew her on the streets or even had a use for her within the walls. I knew nothing about her yet, she stayed on a nigga mind.

"Aye, who's the guard right now?" I asked Touch. We were just on some chill shit in my cell.

"Ummm, Tansland," he answered.

I sat up on my bed and slid my feet into my Crocs. "I'll be right back," I told him.

Touch looked at me suspiciously but didn't bother to ask me where I was going or what I was about to do. He knew if he was entitled to know, I would've told him.

Making my way down the steps to the bottom tier, a bunch of niggas sitting around doing various shit all shot me a head nod. I returned the gesture as I walked to the officer's booth. It was no denying that I was well respected and feared in FDC Philly, but for the most part, I just wanted to be respected; it was better than being feared. When muthafuckers feared you, they'd also do anything to refrain from feeling your wrath. If they respected you, they'd do anything to make sure you're good in every aspect.

"Tans, wassup?" I greeted the middle-aged man.

Tans was one of those cool ass guards that knew when to look the other way. He was Caucasian, but acted black, or should I say tried to act black.

"Manic, what's good?" he addressed me.

"I need you to look someone up for me."

"An inmate?" He raised a brow.

"Yeah, a female."

The COs would look up people within the building for us. Most of the dudes would ask that of them when they were on the toilet bowl talking to the jawns. They wanted to see how they looked if they never ran into them in traffic, which was the halls. I used it when I needed to locate certain people or find out certain shit. This act was prohibited, but it was still done on the regular.

"What's the name or number?" he inquired.

Fuck, I said to myself.

"That's the thing, I don't know. I saw her twice, never spoke to her though. Is it a way you can see who just came in?"

"Matter fact, it is. When she came in?"

I recollected when I had court because that was the day she first came in. "Tuesday," I told him.

He immediately started searching the database and, within a few seconds, shorty's mugshot popped up.

"Keilani Milan, twenty-three, from Chester, PA," Tans rattled off the information.

Chester? That was my hometown before I started staying in Philadelphia. It was crazy I never saw her ass in the city. She either had to be new or one of those homebound kind of bitches.

I zeroed in on her mugshot and admired the full, long hair she had. She was pretty despite the photo not being the normal selfie the chicks would take. Observing the information on the screen, I took note of a few things. I had a photogenic memory.

"Good lookin', Tans," I told him before tapping the glass on the booth, then making my way back up to my cell.

ALL THE MALE inmates that occupied the cells of FDC Philly were all on pre-trial, meaning they were still fighting their case or they were back on an appeal. No male stayed in the building once sentenced; they were shipped out to their designated prisons across the country. With ten units in the building, excluding the SHU floor, which is the "Special Housing Unit" aka the hole, all units housed men, only leaving one unit for women.

While some women were on pre-trial, some actually completed their time there, if it was a short sentence or close to the end of their time. The better jobs went to them since it was considered their prison. They ran the best-paying jobs, the kitchen and commissary, while the men handled laundry, the warehouse, and all the maintenance jobs like painting, plumbing, and electric.

It was a rule, if you were sentenced, you had to have a job and actually work. If not, they would give you a shot, which could cause you to either lose a privilege or be sent to the SHU, whatever the lieutenant or counselor felt like doing at the time. If you were pre-trial, you had the option to not work. If you didn't need the lil' chump change they paid, nobody worked unless it was for the fun of it or an ulterior motive. Who the fuck wanted to work hard labor for only sixteen cents an hour?

I ended up taking the lil' bullshit orderly job in the halls, only to see the females and mess with 'em and get off the unit. There were times I had opportunities to take some of the bitches down with their thirsty asses. I didn't give in because I was getting good pussy from LT Grace. Besides the female inmates throwing cat, it was a boatload of female staff members tryna buss it wide open for a nigga, but I didn't want shit to get messy and fuck up my business. Plus, LT Grace had a lot to bring to the table. I was content.

I was in my cell reading *A Saint Luv'n a Savage: A Philly Love Story* by P. Wise, when I heard the CO on duty yell on the mic, "Frost!"

I was lowkey tight because I was at a good ass part in the book. Annoyed, I got up and walked to the entranceway of my cell to look down at the booth, hoping he saw me and just told me what he wanted instead of me walking all the way downstairs to potentially having to go back up to my cell to put on my sneakers or something.

"Work, lace those tennis shoes up," he announced.

See, just as I thought, I would've been even hotter if I had to make an about-face. I was already interrupted while reading some fire. I had on my gray sweats and a gray t-shirt but had to throw on my green jumpsuit. I slipped off my Crocs and threw on my Nike running sneakers, grabbed my ID and turned to leave out my cell. As I was about to close the door, I saw the CO coming to lock it. *Good shit bull,* I thought. Touch was on the orderly crew with me and my boy, Zain, so there was no reason for my door to be open while we were off the unit.

When we got outside in the hallway, the supervising CO told us we were going down on the third floor to clean, which was the floor the girls were on. As we walked to the elevator to go down, Touch looked at me with the biggest grin on his face. He was a whole character when it came to the ladies. That man had about ten bitches on his top and they all knew about each other. They would fight and try to out-do one another to get the most attention from him. It was pure comedy from where I stood.

As soon as we reached the third floor, we immediately got the cleaning supplies out of the orderly closet. The CO wasn't paying us no mind. As usual, he was busy flirting with the floor unit secretary. Quickly, before I swept my area, I pressed play on my work playlist on my mp3 player to hear Meek Mill's thorough lyrics. Him and Moneybagg Yo were my go-to artist to listen to, to get through my day.

"Yo bro, did you ever holla at the jawn that came through my line lookin' for you?" Touch asked Zaine.

"Yeah, I looked her up too, she nice as fuck," Zaine replied with a big ass smile on his face.

"Y'all niggas and that bowl, man," I cracked.

"You need you a lil' jawn through the pipeline. It gets lonely nigga, you can't front," Zain tried to persuade me.

"Yeah, yeah, yeah. I rather get my dick wet than have a stiff one fuckin' with them bitches through the bowl."

Which was the God given truth. Some of those girls knew what they were doing and would have you hornier than you were reading some of those urban books. Just like a nigga, they knew how to spit game and get what they wanted out of you, plus more. Some would even have their pictures sent into niggas, knowing good and well mutha fuckers been in for a while and any attention they got from the opposite sex, they were open and vice versa.

The elevator door slammed open, letting us know someone reached the floor we were on. An older female CO stuck her head out. Once she saw we were there, she turned around and told the females she had in her custody to hold on.

"Aye, fellas, you know the deal. Step to the back of the wall over here." She pointed to the wall at the end of the hall.

We dropped our mops and walked toward the wall. In order to get to the wall she wanted us against, we had to pass the elevator where she had the women so, of course, we looked in their direction. And there she was, Keilani mutha-fuckin' Milan.

CHAPTER SEVEN

U.S Department of Justice
Federal Bureau of Prisons

75816-066

MILAN
KEILANI

Eye: BR   Ht: 5'03"

Vending

INMATE

KEI

$\mathcal{M}$y feet were stuck and felt heavy, as if they were cemented to the ground. I stood there, unable to move after locking eyes with the green-eyed stranger for the third time. We looked at each other intensely, ignoring the fact we weren't even supposed to be looking at one another in the first place. In that moment, everyone disappeared, including the pale, depressing walls of the detention center.

"Move it, Frost!" the CO yelled at him.

At first, he didn't move an inch, making her place her hands on her pepper spray. He sized her up and down with a menacing stare before finally walking off.

"Let's go, ladies." She stood in between us and the guys.

Getting off the elevator, I couldn't help but look his way. He stood there, eyes trained on me without blinking. He was truly an art, one I had no business being drawn to.

"Milan, keep it moving."

I quickly turned and followed the other ladies through the door that separated us from the guys and into the unit.

"You know, Manic?" one of the girls that went to psych asked.

"No, why?" I shot back, scrunching up my face.

"The way that nigga was stuck staring at you, would've thought he knew you from somewhere," she observed.

"Nah, I don't know him," I spoke before walking off to the computer room.

That was the second time one of those broads asked me something about that nigga. I had no clue who he was or what kind of status he had in FDC because it was apparent he held some kind of weight, and I must admit, I was a little intrigued.

Checking my emails, I saw there weren't any from Brix. I sent him a message a whole twenty-four hours prior. There was no way he didn't respond yet while everyone else responded multiple times since then. I sucked my teeth at the computer as if it did something to me and logged off.

Making my way to the phones, I dialed Brix's number and stated my name a few times before it picked up my voice, putting the call through. It rang out with no answer. I called again, but after one ring, it went to voicemail. I tried again, ending in the same result, one ring, then voicemail. I slammed the phone onto the hook and stormed off towards my cell, but before I went in, Lena called out to me.

"Keilani!" she yelled from the top tier.

Looking up, I saw her motioning for me to come to her. I rerouted and made my way up the steps to her.

"We gotta get a nickname for you. Can't have me hollering your government all loud and shit," she joked, making me crack a smile.

"Everyone home calls me Lani," I informed her.

"Nah, don't mix the two. In here, we can call you something different. Something like Kei."

I nodded slowly as the corners of my mouth dipped. "Hmmm, that'll work. Kei it is."

"Cool, now that's out of the way. What's this I'm hearing you caught the eyes of the infamous Manic?" She eyed me closely while wearing a huge smirk on her face.

"Who the fuck is he?" I blurted out.

I was about tired of hearing that man's name and noticing the admiration the women had for him. Granted, he was fine as fuck, but what else was so fascinating about him?

Lena started laughing whole-heartedly like I told a joke. I knew I was out of my element and I had a lot to learn, but they were making me feel like I should've known who the nigga was.

"Makhi Frost, aka Manic, is that nigga, baby girl. He runs shit in here and on the streets," she briefly explained.

Makes a whole lot of sense now, I thought.

"Where he from?" I questioned.

"I think he's originally from Chester, but Philly been his stomping grounds. He run shit from New Jersey to DMV though. You really never heard of him? Wait, aren't you from Chester?"

"I'm from Brooklyn boo, just moved to Chester during my senior year of high school. I don't be out in them streets though; I be in Philly. I went to high school and college in Philly," I revealed.

"Oh, okay. Then, that explains it. Y'all just didn't run in the same crowd."

"Right." I nodded in agreement.

"If that nigga checkin' for you, you better check back," she stated with a chuckled.

"I have a nigga. But why you say that?"

"Mmmhmm, he ain't in here with you. You gon' want some company while you walk this time down. But Manic don't really be on the bowl like these other niggas. Bitches always called for him but he never entertained them. So, if he checks for you, it's something he saw in you that peeked his interest."

"The bowl?" I raised a brow, leaning up on the banister.

"Out of everything I just said, that's the only thing you heard?" She rested her hands on her hips and scolded me playfully.

"Girl, I heard you, but for real, what's the bowl?"

"The toilet bowl, Kei."

I tilted my head to the side and knitted my eyebrows in confusion.

"We talk through the toilet bowl."

"But how?" I questioned.

"Once all the water is out, you can hear whoever is on your line. Don't worry, I'll show you one of these days." She waved me off.

"Yeah, no thanks."

We chopped it up for a minute, jumping from topic to topic. Lena was cool as fuck and down to earth. She was easy to talk to and had a genuine vibe. I just prayed it stayed that way and she didn't switch up.

CLICK! Click!

Another day to live through my worst nightmare. I slept a

little better the night before since I was put up on game about the hot water bottles to go to sleep with. It was February, which meant the winter weather seeped into the metal and steel-filled building. FDC Philly didn't know what heat was or, if they did, it wasn't on our unit.

Noelle and the girls taught me to fill used water or soda bottles with hot water, then advised to put them in socks so I didn't get burned. They would place them around their bodies on the bed while they slept to keep them warm. I did just that, and it was the first night I didn't shiver uncontrollably while trying to rest.

Since I had nothing to do that day, I got up to just eat breakfast and check my emails. Still, there was no message from Brix. I told myself I'd try to call him later in the day. I refilled the bottles with hot water and returned to my bed. I lied down and read a book I got from Kali, one of the girls that hung with Noelle.

After reading a chapter, I heard the bell to the unit ring loudly. Moments later, the guard announced, "Pill line."

Minding my business, I continued to read, or at least I thought I was going to be able to.

"Milan!" I heard my name being called on the speaker.

I rested the book down on my lap. *What now?* I thought. As I was getting down off the top bunk, Zaara, another one of Noelle's girls, came in my cell.

"Kei, they calling you to take your meds," she informed me. "Make sure and bring water."

"Thanks, I'm coming," I told her.

Grabbing my cup off the small metal table, I proceeded out my cell and saw a Caucasian nurse in scrubs with a cart at the unit's entrance. Walking over, she eyed me.

"Milan?" she questioned.

"Yes," I simply answered.

She looked at a piece of paper she had on the cart and signed off next to what I assumed to be my name. She then opened a draw of meds and dumped a pill in the small cup the nurses in the hospitals would give you the meds in. I took it from her hand, tilted my head back as I took the pill, then drunk some water.

I started to walk away but was quickly halted by the on-duty CO.

"Aht, aht. Let me see," the nurse stated.

"See what?" I asked in an irritated tone.

"Your tongue."

"You're serious?" I looked at the guard, who gestured for me to open my mouth for her. I rolled my eyes and opened my mouth.

"Wider, raise your tongue," she demanded.

This bitch can't be for real, I thought.

I did what she said, wiggling my tongue all about to show her I did indeed swallow my medication.

"Thank you," she stated.

"Mmmhmm. I ain't no junky," I spat before walking off finally.

Racist ass bitch.

I went right back into my cell and went to sleep.

I WOKE up to the sound of continuous flushing.

This bitch again, I thought. All my new bunky did was eat, shit, and sit on her fat ass to speak about people's business. I made a mental note that I had to get out of this cell as soon as I could.

As I sat up, I felt weird and the room seemed to had been spinning. I flipped over to place my foot on the ladder to come down but almost lost my grip. Holding on tight to regain my composure, I took my time coming off the ladder. Once my feet were planted on the ground, I felt like I was too weak to stand. My vision was blurry, I was lightheaded, and my body felt like it was floating in the air.

"Yo, you good?" my bunky asked.

I was still holding onto the bed, trying to keep myself from falling. The whiff of her shit made me nauseous to a whole other level. I wobbled my way quickly to the sink and threw up, feeling like I emptied my entire insides.

"Ahhh, what the fuck, man," she chided. "Why would you do that?"

She was on the toilet, still shitting, so it was either the sink or the floor. The small trash bin we had was filled and too far away to get to. While I wanted to explain that to her,

I didn't have the energy to. Besides, it was the disgusting smell that seeped out from her ass that had me hurling my guts up.

I ran the water and, thankfully, my throw up went down the drain and it didn't clog up. She started to clean herself, so I quickly bypassed her to exit out of the cell, but I fell to the ground as soon as I touched the dayroom, causing everyone to look my way. Thankfully, Noelle and the girls were out there chilling, so they quickly ran to my aid.

"Kei, what the hell? Are you okay?" Noelle asked, grabbing one of my arms while someone else grabbed the next. I felt someone behind me holding my back as they sat me down at one of the tables.

"I don't know what's wrong with me. When I got up, I felt crazy," I slurred, leaning on Noelle.

"Did you eat something? You pregnant?" one of the girls started asking question after question.

"I doubt it. I was on birth control until I came in here."

The girls started speaking amongst each other, trying to figure out what the hell was wrong with me.

"Wait, she took meds this morning," Zaara pointed out.

"What they gave you?" Noelle questioned.

"Zoloft," I answered.

"You been taking it for a while or this your first time?"

"I was taking it but stopped for like a month now."

Noelle started laughing out of nowhere, which confused the fuck out of me.

"What the fuck is funny Nollee?" Gia asked, calling her by her nickname.

"This lil' baby is high, y'all." She continued to laugh.

"You fuckin' right," Zaara agreed, laughing as well.

"Y'all serious?" I quizzed, barely able to open my eyes since the light was irritating me.

I'd never felt that way before in my life, not even when I was sick with natural colds or flus. When they said I was high, I understood why I felt like I was floating or some shit. The only thing I did on the outs was drink here and there. I tried smoking weed once when I was a teenager, but it wasn't for me. So, being high like that was a whole new level unlocked in my life.

"Yeah, boo. They should've started you off with a low dose. You'll be fine," Zaara explained.

"She ard?" I heard my bunky ask.

"Yeah, she will be," Nollee answered.

"Okay, good. Because she needs to come and clean up in here."

"Girl, please. You clearly see she's fucked up right now. You on some real weird shit," Kali spat.

"For real though," Gia added, surprising me since she always seemed to have had a problem with me. "We'll clean it up, don't worry."

"Come on, you need to get in the shower. It will help," Noelle suggested.

They helped me to my cell to get my shower things. I

wasn't able to walk on my own, so Noelle and Kali helped me wherever. When we reached the shower, Noelle literally had to help me get undressed and hold me in the shower while I slowly washed my body. I was so high, I squeezed the toothpaste on my hands, thinking it was the body wash and started to rub it on my skin. Once I felt it wasn't getting soapy, I looked down and saw what I had done, quickly correcting my act.

When I was finished showering, Noelle took me back to my cell and helped me get dressed. The cell smelled and looked clean, letting me know they kept their word. I was grateful for Noelle and the girls. They really came through when I needed them, and they didn't have to. I was a complete stranger, but in a place like where we were, the environment tended to bring people together.

CHAPTER EIGHT

U.S Department of Justice
Federal Bureau of Prisons

90056-066

FROST
MAKHI

Eye: GR   Ht: 6'03"

INMATE

MANIC

$\mathcal{I}$f only I had a little more time, I might've had to get at shorty. She was still looking gorgeous despite her situation. That told me, on the outs, she was a bad jawn. It's funny, some people looked their best in prison while others looked their worst. But for her, she had to have the blessing of looking good anywhere possible, and I was willing to bet my last dollar on it.

"Bro, I know you saw shawty breaking her neck to look at you." Touch walked into my cell after count all hyper.

"Yeah, I peeped her. It ain't nothing. If she was thirsty and like the rest, she would've already been calling up through the bowl, but she ain't."

"I hear you, man. Listen, can I holla at Noelle on ya' line? Nigga Zain on mine talkin' to somebody," he asked, referring to the toilet bowl.

The toilet bowl was a fast and easy line of communication to the other floors in the building. We had to push the water out of the toilet bowl by forcing it through the exit hole with our hands, making a motion as if we were telling someone to come here with our hands. In order to hear the next person clearly, all the water had to be out. We used an empty shampoo bottle to suck up the remaining water. Afterwards, we'd place a garbage bag over the toilet so no nasty smells or splashes from other people on the line using the toilet would get out. To hear the other person, we made a mic out of soda bottles or creamer containers, cutting the ends off and stacking them together, so it's long. That way, our face wasn't in the bowl itself.

"Yeah, go ahead. I'm 'boutta just lay back until Abdullah

finishes with the food," I told him, speaking about our in-house cook.

While he went ahead and popped the bowl, I placed my headphones in and laid back on my bed, allowing my thoughts to consume me.

DINNER WAS GOOD. My boy, Abdullah, made us some pizza on the iron. I hardly ever ate from the kitchen, unless it was Saturdays for brunch when they gave us French toast and eggs. Abdullah was a Muslim brother who was a chef on the outs, so he knew what he was doing, even with the limited resources we had inside. He was my personal chef for me and my team. We would get the girls that worked in the kitchen to send up fresh vegetables and other things from the kitchen for him to cook with; everything else, we got off of commissary.

Touch was love jonesing on my bowl so, after I ate, I decided to just stay out in the dayroom and watch the game while he did his thing. The Sixers were playing the Bucks, and it was a good ass match up; so good, I started to place bets on the table, starting a whole uproar on the unit.

"I'm tellin' you, bro, Giannis gon' keep bringing that pressure Embiid way." Zain jumped up out of his seat.

"Facts, he ain't lettin' up my nigga," my boy Bodhi, a nigga on my team, agreed.

"Ard, ard, just watch. It's still the first half, y'all niggas drawin'," I spoke up.

I had a good feeling the Sixers were going to pull through. Ben Simmons was getting warmed up, and the rest of the team was falling in line. It was a whole lot of game to be played; I wasn't worried.

When it was all said and done, my predictions came through. The Sixers took the win, and I came up on some more commissary, even though I didn't need it. I enjoyed being right; I loved when I made niggas swallow their words. If it was one thing us men took pride in, it was having a big ego.

"Aye, y'all make sure and have all my shit next week. I'll give y'all a break this week. I don't wanna hear no goofy shit 'bout y'all limits either," I boosted.

They all swatted me off, annoyed, but I didn't give two shits. I meant what I said.

"Yooo, Manic!" Touch yelled from the doorway of my cell.

"What nigga?" I shot back.

"Come! Come quick and listen to this shit."

After a few seconds of debating if I wanted to see what was so interesting to Touch, I got up and went to my cell. As I thought, he was still on the bowl fooling with those girls.

"Man, what the hell you want?" I quizzed.

"Listen to this," he said as he handed me the mic to listen.

When I placed my ears to the mic, I heard a guy's voice

yelling through the bowl, "Yooo, caramel shawty that just came in, come to the bowl!" He was tryna get at the new jawn, Keilani, that I saw in R&D and in the hall. She was the newest female in the women's unit and the description fit her.

When fresh meat came in and niggas saw them, they acted thirsty as fuck. They would send kites and call for them through the bowl in hopes of a response. Depending on the female, they would either get lucky or their calls would go unanswered.

I continued to listen for a little while longer to see if the jawn was going to come to the bowl, but she didn't. *Smart girl, she ain't easy to crack*, I thought. Part of me was happy she didn't get on and speak to the bull. I lowkey wanted her to myself. When the time was right, I told myself I would make the move. Until then, I was gon' make sure no one got to her, but from what it looked like, she wouldn't even had budge if they tried.

"They on shawty heavy, that's like the eighth nigga to come through hollering for her," Touch chuckled.

"She ain't come on at all?" I asked.

"Nah, not at all. They even went and told her. They came back and told the niggas she said she was cool."

"Hmmm," I hummed as I was about to walk back out of the cell.

"Yo, Gia keep asking for you, nigga."

"Oh, okay. Well, let her keep asking. A nigga ain't interested."

Gia was a jawn that been in FDC for a little over a year. She was in for pimping some little ass girls. If it was one thing, I made sure to do my homework on everyone, especially if they were in my circle or tried to be. Gia been tryna get at me since I landed back within the gray walls, but I never paid her ass any attention. She wasn't bad looking either, but her ways were ugly, just like her charges. I didn't condone pimping out underage girls. That shit just wasn't cool. And to boast about it was on some next level weirdo shit.

"You know she hard of hearing," Touch laughed but was stating facts.

Even though I repeatedly shut her down, she still tried to get in my good graces. She would send me kites with pictures, even send me shit up from the kitchen. I gladly took the food from the kitchen, but I handed off her kites and pictures to the niggas on my unit that were lonely. They had better use of it than I did.

I went back downstairs, but before I returned to the table, I went to the computer room to check my emails. I had a boatload of them, so I got comfortable in the seat and replied to all. Some read:

Kayla: Wassup handsome, I was missing you something crazy; I wish I can come and see you, but meantime, you'll have something nice coming in the mail.

Tiffany: Manic baby, I miss that dick deep in me when you coming home???

Kam: Aye dawg, what's the word? When's ya next court date? I just dropped some bread on your account.

Mom: Hey Baby, I hope you have a great day. Keep your head low. Don't forget to pray.

Morgan: Makaela said goodnight, and she loves you!

That was just a few emails. Every time I logged on, I had a ton of them. A nigga was loved and missed. Being away from your loved ones could take a toll on you. Some people would act like they're hard about the situation and it didn't faze them, but deep down inside, they were missing at least one person on the outs.

Besides my mother and the rest of my family, the main person I missed was my beautiful daughter. At that time, baby girl was young, which was a sensitive age to be away from her. My mother made sure to bring her, if not every week, every other week, for me to see her. We had phone conversations all the time and sent letters, drawings, and pictures back and forth. She was my favorite pen pal.

Anytime I heard her pretty little voice or saw her adorable face, I reminded myself that I had to do everything in my power to get back to her safe and sound and soon. Being locked up wasn't a punishment for me, being away from my seed was.

CHAPTER NINE

KEI

A few days had passed, and I was finally back feeling like myself. While experiencing the high of Zoloft, it was scary as fuck, but I laughed at it when everything was done and over with. I refused my meds until I requested to see Dr. Reese again, so he could reduce the dosage until my body got back used to the medication.

When Lena found out what happened, she died laughing. Initially when I first started tripping, she was at work. By the time she came back in the unit, I was resting, but Noelle told her what happened.

The crazy part was, I was informed it had a boatload of women in there getting high off those same exact psych meds. I didn't see what the hell was so comforting about that feeling. I felt like I was about to die. But to each their own.

Knock! Knock!

The person at the door woke me out of my mid-day nap.

"She's asleep," I heard my bunky tell the person.

"I came to check on her," I heard Lena say.

"Okay, but she's sleeping," my bunky stated again with a hint of irritation.

"I'm up, I'm up," I spoke groggily as I sat up in my bed. "I'm finna come out."

I saw Lena shoot my bunky a wicked look, then rolled her eyes at her before walking out. Climbing off the top bunk, I went and brushed my teeth and washed my face. Just as I was about to leave out the door, my bunky grumbled something under her breath, halting my steps.

"What you said?" I snapped my head in her direction.

"Nothing," she quickly stated.

I stepped towards her. "Nah, what you said?"

She looked up at me while she toyed with her MP3 player. "You always quick to run when one of them calls for you."

"Fuck is that supposed to mean?" I took another step closer.

"I'm just saying. You never chill with me or nothing."

I knew she felt some kind of way. But in all honesty, she wasn't the type of bitch I would've chilled with on the streets, so why would I sit with her because we were in prison? I held myself to a certain standard, and she just wasn't my taste of crowd.

"Just because we stay in the same space doesn't mean we're supposed to do anything together. Chill with that possessive shit because I'm not the one," I spat before walking out.

I need to get the fuck out of this cell, I thought.

"You cool?" Zaara asked, as I walked up to the group.

They were just chilling between two tables. Looking around, I saw all different kinds of cliques. For the most part, all ethnic groups stayed together. The Spanish mamis stuck together, whites hung out, and us blacks rocked out as one. And the weirdos stayed with the weirdos. It only confirmed what I was thinking and what I told my bunky. Although she was black, she wasn't my cup of tea.

"Yeah, I'm good. What y'all over here chatting about?" I brushed off the question.

"We just speaking about how we all caught our cases and how the law pulled up on us," Noelle stated.

Some of the girls were still fighting their case and got no bond, while some were sentenced and finishing their time.

"I knew I was caught when the manager at the store asked me to come to the back with her just to verify the card. By the time my ass turned around, a guard was standing behind me," Kali revealed with a chuckle.

It got me to thinking about the day leading up and the day of when things got real for me.

February 22, 2016 (My Birthday)

My stomach was doing backflips and cartwheels as my heart rate sped up with every second that went by that I was trying to memorize information at a rapid pace.

"Is everything alright?" the customer asked me through the drive-through microphone.

I worked at one of the top banks in the country and was processing a deposit for someone. While in the account, I tried my best to grab as much information from it as I could. It wasn't my first time doing this, but every time I did it, I couldn't help but have an uneasy feeling. What I was doing wasn't just illegal, but it was ethically wrong. Nevertheless, I did it all for the attention of a nigga and acceptance within society.

"Ah, yes. Just one moment. The system has been moving slow all day," I responded, stalling for more time.

Swiftly, I got what I needed to get or what I could get before it became alarming, then shot over the information to where I stored it, or at least that's what I thought. When I doubled checked, I accidentally copied and pasted the information to a chat with one of my co-workers.

"Shit," I spoke in a hushed tone. Thankfully, I was the only one in the drive-through banking area, so I didn't look off to anyone.

Wasting no time, I shot her a message, letting her know it was a mistake. She was a new bank teller, so I figured she wouldn't have thought too much about it and just brushed it off.

"Okay, here's your receipt. I'm so sorry about that. Is there anything else I can do for you today?" I asked professionally.

"No, that's all, thank you." She grabbed the paper from the drawer and pulled off.

Another car pulled right into her place while two more drove up to the distant lanes. It was a Wednesday, but it was a rush hour for us since it was lunchtime for everyone else. Most people came to the bank either during their breaks or right after they got off. As usual, I tended to the customers at a fast pace and got them out of there.

"Keiii, happy birthday, boo," one of my favorite co-workers bussed in the room and sang.

I spun around and saw her standing there with balloons and a box from Edible Arrangements. It was my twenty-second birthday.

"Awwwhhh, Janelle, you didn't have to boo," I told her.

Once someone got you something for your birthday or

whatever occasion, it was an unwritten rule you had to return the gesture when it was their turn. Who said I had money like that?

We hugged each other happily like two school girls when my manager walked in.

"What's going on here?" he quizzed.

"Nothing," I quickly spoke up.

"It doesn't look like nothing." He looked at the balloons, then the arrangement on the desk.

Seconds later, my assistant manager and supervisor walked in with a cake and started singing happy birthday to me. I blushed so hard and couldn't refrain from smiling as if I had won the jackpot. It was the small things that made me truly fuck with people.

"Thank y'all so so much," I beamed.

"You're welcome, sweetie," my assistant manager spoke. "Wishing you many more years."

I hugged everyone; then, they quickly disappeared to get back to work. Returning to my station in time, a customer pulled up, and I greeted them, diving right back into my routine.

A few hours later, it was time for me to clock out and get out of dodge. I had to drive all the way from the county in Pennsylvania to Delaware to coach a college basketball game. I landed a dope position as a student coach and basketball operations personnel at the same school I went to. After hooping for two years at my previous school where I earned my associate degree in Sports Management, I decided to hang up my kicks and took the sidelines.

Gathering my things, I quickly made my way from the back of the bank to the lobby.

"Keilani!" my manager called out to me.

I looked over and saw him sitting at his desk with a client. I click clacked my brand new YSL heels towards him and noticed the customer sizing me up and down. Looking closer, I noticed who the person was. She was one of the profiles I snagged and automatically tensed up because her demeanor wasn't satisfying at all. It was a white middle-aged woman who had multiple accounts with the bank, which all were loaded heavily with cash.

"Yes, Charles?" I asked when I reached his desk.

He grabbed an envelope from on top of his desk and handed it to me. It had my name on it, along with happy birthday.

"I can't take anything else from y'all. Look, my hands are full," I told him. I already had a rack of shit I was holding from what everyone got me.

He stood up and stuck the envelope in my open bag.

"There you go. Now, enjoy the rest of your birthday."

"Mmm, nice heels," the customer complimented with a hint of sarcasm. "Y'all must be getting paid well here for that kind of name brand," she added.

I let out a light laugh as I looked down at my feet. My

salary could've afforded it, but it wasn't what bought it; my dude did.

"Thank you," I simply responded.

I shot them both a smirk, about faced, and made my way out of the bank, into my car, and to the university for the game.

"WHERE WE GOING?" my mom asked, as I took a sharp turn off Fulton. She noticed I drove off route from our destination.

"I have to make a quick stop," I told her.

It was me, my mom, and her boyfriend in the car, with my brother and his girl following us. We took a drive from Pennsylvania to New York to celebrate my birthday. I was having a party later that night with Bryson Tiller as the host. It was my twenty-seconded birthday.

When I pulled up to Tavian's house, I dialed him up to let him know I was outside.

"You here?" he asked as soon as he answered.

"Yeah."

"Aight. I'm coming."

As I was opening the door to get out, I peeped my brother also doing the same behind my parked car.

"Why didn't you tell me we were coming here?" my mother asked all surprised.

"Because we're not staying. I'm just picking something up," I told her.

"From whom?" She raised a brow.

"Damn, ma, chill."

I closed the door, leaving her nosy behind in the car with her man. By the time I turned, my brother and Tavian were clapping hands and exchanging words. My brother had a little idea of what I was doing but not the full-on details of it. He also didn't know how involved Tavian and I were.

Ever since we reconnected that night, we started dealing with one another hard. Every chance I got, I was speeding down the New Jersey turnpike to see him. I would always go out my way and tuck in my scary ass ways and got him hella profiles from work, which I got paid for each one.

"Let me holla at Lani right quick," Tavian told my brother, prompting him to walk back and get in his whip.

Turning to face me, he wore a big smirk as he hovered over me. Inhaling his scent, I was ready to snatch him and go inside. But I quickly remembered who I was with.

"Happy Birthday, beautiful," he flirted as he bit his lip.

Handing over two Louis Vuitton bags, I took them in my hand. "What's this?" I quizzed.

"You'll see when you open it. But look..." He pulled out two huge wads of cash. "Good lookin' on the pros." He handed one stack in my hand. "And happy birthday." He placed the second stack in my other hand.

My eyes opened widely at everything in my possession. I knew Tavian was swimming in money, but what I didn't expect was for him to be so generous to me for my birthday.

"Thank you, baby," I cooed.

Surprisingly, he leaned down and pecked my lips for everyone to see. In my mind, I figured things were moving to another level since we were letting our family's know we were dealing.

"Go have fun tonight. Your section and bottles already booked," he told me.

"I wish you'd come out." I curled my bottom lip down, giving a sad expression.

"Nah, you know the club scene ain't always for me. We'll do something else."

"Okay. Let me go then."

He walked me to the car, helped me inside with the bags, and sent me on my way.

TWO DAYS AFTER MY BIRTHDAY, *I was due back to work. I rested the entire day before after partying like crazy. The club was wild lit and everyone had a great time, including my moms, who came through with her dude. Tavian definitely made sure my night was well spent, and his presence was felt as if he was there.*

Pulling into the parking lot of the bank, I parked and hopped out of my whip. I had about three minutes to clock in, so I moved my tiny feet as fast as I could. Greeting everyone as usual, I went ahead and logged in my computer and punch the timer. Followed by my normal routine of getting my drawer out of the vault and setting up, I was up and running in no time.

Finally settled and able to take customers, I looked over and noticed that there were two men in suits speaking with my manager, Charles, in the conference room. The room's walls were glass, so we were able to see right through it.

"Who's that?" I asked my co-worker, nodding in the direction of the conference room.

"Ummm, I'm not sure. But they've been here almost two hours now," she answered.

My head teller was passing by while we tried to figure out things.

"Ruby, who's that?" she asked her.

"Oh, that's corporate," she answered uppity.

From her response, it seemed to had been a friendly visit, so I didn't pay it any mind. I also thought it could've been for me since I had caught some fake checks the week before, earning the Guardian Angel award.

I took a few more customers until I saw Charles exit out the conference room and walk in my direction.

"Hey, Keilani, close up for a second. Some people want to speak with you," he informed me.

I immediately froze up, unable to swallow the huge lump that formed in my throat. Staring past him and into the room, all kinds of things crossed my mind. Shit, they know, I thought.

"Keilani!" Charles called out to me again.

"Yes." I snapped out of my trance. "I'm coming." I locked my draw and computer.

With every step I took, my feet felt like they were chained to an anchor. Part of me just wanted to take off and run out of the bank without looking back while the other part told me to keep calm, that I might've been overacting.

Reaching the door of the conference room, one of the gentlemen came and held it open for me to enter. Both of them were middle-aged Caucasian men that looked like assholes, but I gave them the benefit of the doubt.

"Ms. Milan, thanks for meeting with us. On the phone is your HR rep, Kelsi, who will guide you through everything," he explained.

"Ms. Milan, I'm Kelsi, how are you doing today?" she asked.

"I'm fine, thanks."

"These gentlemen would like to ask you some questions. You do not have to answer anything if you don't want to, but your corporation would be appreciated. If at any time you feel you may need a lawyer, you may state so."

"Okay," I simply answered, wearing a confused face.

"Ms. Milan, where are you from?" one guy asked.

"I live in Chester."

"Is that where you spent your whole life?"

"No, I was raised in Brooklyn."

"You still have family there?" he went on to asked.

"Yes."

"You visit frequently?"

And that's when I knew where the line of questioning was leading to. That meeting was not about me being no damn guardian angel. My heart sunk to the pit of my stomach as my freedom flashed before me.

More questions followed and, once they weren't satisfied with my answered, they slammed a huge folder in front of me and started to flip through the pages. There were tons of pictures and information inside. Pictures of my social media posts, of Tavian and his friends doing transactions in the banks and ATM, pictures of me on camera at work, all kinds of shit.

"I want a lawyer," I simply stated.

Following the small interrogation, I was suspended without pay pending an investigation, which only lasted for a few days. The following week, Charles and the assistant manager called me and fired me. I was told I'd be contacted from corporate and that was the last I heard from them.

A month later, while I was out getting my hair done, my mother called me all hysterical.

"Lani, get home right now!" she screamed.

"What's wrong, ma?" I started to panic.

"Can I speak to her?" I heard an unfamiliar voice say in the back. "Hello? Keilani?"

"Yes, who's this?"

"I'm U. S. District Attorney Calvin Deen. I'm here with

FBI agent Boyd Fritz, in regards to a grand jury investigation related to your old job."

The moment I heard U.S. district attorney, I knew exactly who they were and what they wanted. The past month, I tried to act normal and forget about what happened or what was to come. I prayed they'd just forget about me and let me be.

"Okay?"

"I'm giving your mother a letter for you. You must get an attorney within the time permitted in the letter. If you can't afford one, reach out to me using my contact and I will connect you with the public defender's office," he explained.

"What are the charges?" I asked.

"I can't speak with you about anything as of right now until you get a lawyer. All I will say is, think long and hard about what's about to happen. Put yourself first and let us know about everything and who's involved. If not, you'll be going away for at least two years."

Two what? I thought as my eyes bulged. My homegirl was doing my hair but stopped once she saw how serious the call was. She looked on, as my facial expressions changed and got more intense as the conversation continued.

I didn't respond, I didn't know how to.

"Talk soon," he said before passing the phone back to my mom.

"Come straight home once you're done," my mother scolded me as if I was a child.

The last place I wanted to go was home. Although after about two weeks, I sat my moms down and told her what happened, I was scared of her wrath. I couldn't face her after the embarrassment of federal persons had come to her front door.

On my ride home, I contemplated if to drive off the Girard Point Bridge or if to simply take the safety off my gun, place it to my head, and squeeze the trigger. Either one would've been ideal because prison wasn't a place for me.

CHAPTER TEN

MANIC

"Yo Manic, you comin' out?" asked Touch from my open cell door.

I was in the midst of going over my books,

checking on payments from the fiends. My team and I collected funds in all sorts of ways. People's folks would link with mine on the outs and give cash, use Zelle, Cashapp, or any electronic finance app to make the payment. Some used the money on their books to send out checks to some of my holding companies, to keep things untraceable. And, of course, they paid with commissary, which I had a few stores running in each unit.

"Yeah, gimmie a min'," I told him, raising up from my bunk.

I had to get out of my funk, so I decided to go meet the guys out in the rec yard for a lil' bit. But before I headed out to the yard, I went to request a legal call; I needed to hear what my lawyer had to say about this new evidence that was discovered. As quickly as I requested the call was as quick as I got it.

"It's Manic, what's the word on the evidence they got?" I asked.

"Hi Mr. Frost, well, to keep it straightforward, from what I briefly read while in court, someone is talking. I haven't fully examined the evidence. Once I have, I will be up to see you as soon as possible," he explained.

"Say no more. Keep me posted." I hung up and headed to the rec yard.

When I got out there, they were running a three-on-three basketball game. Everyone gave me a head nod while I dapped up some of my guys. Touch was on the court thinking he was Kobe. Little did he know, he needed to just stick to selling drugs; hooping wasn't for everybody. Within a few minutes, the game was over. Touch and some of my most trusted soldiers came and sat with me.

"What's good yo?" Touch's tired and out of breath ass asked.

"I had to holla at my lawyer for a second, but yo, Wright told me that new CO been overly doing his job. You heard anything about him?" I inquired.

Earlier that morning, I had a quick run-in with Wright, who told me the new CO who I had the quick encounter with was a robo cop. He actually did things by the books, which most of them did when they first came onto the job. But after some persuading, they fell in line.

"Nah, I ain't hear shit about him," he answered.

"Mmmm... I gotta get that nigga in line before he even thinks to start fuckin' my shit up. What's his name again?" I quizzed.

"I think Jones or some shit."

I nodded and took in the information. "Ard, bet."

As I stood up to walk away, Touch followed. I went back into my cell to just relax and read. But Touch had a better idea. He brought up shorty, Keilani. Funny thing was, when he was talking about her, I had this weird feeling of defending her, as if she was mine or some shit, even though he was only complimenting her. In a sense, I felt like she was, though I didn't know her. *Fuck around, I just might make her mine,* I thought.

"I wonder what she got hemmed up for," he stated, which

shook me out of my thoughts because I was wondering the same thing.

A girl like her didn't belong in a place like FDC Philly. I know they say, *don't judge a book by its cover*, but I just had that gut feeling she wasn't meant to be booked. Either way, I knew I would find out.

"I don't know, but it had to be some shit to end up in the feds," I responded curiously.

"Nah dawg. She really a jawn though, sheesh," he went on.

I looked at him with one eyebrow up and a smug face. "Ard yo, I heard you the first time," I snapped back, getting irritated again.

He caught on and laughed it off while walking out of my cell.

Right move, dickhead.

USUALLY RIGHT BEFORE the 4 p.m. count, the guards would change shifts. When they were conducting the count, I saw the new CO, Jones, pass by my door, letting me know there was a change, and he was going to be on duty that evening. I found it so ironic that Touch and I literally spoke on him earlier that day and, turned around, he was on our pod.

Once the count was done and cleared, I heard the cells doors being unlocked. Finally reaching my cell, I saw it was indeed Jones as the guard on duty. *Just my fucking luck*, I thought. He shot me a weird look as he passed by, leaving me wondering what the fuck type of timing he was on.

Touch ran his ass in my cell and sat in his usual seat, propping his feet up. We started chopping it up about the operations.

"Yo, you don't think it's time we get work back on the girls' unit?" he came out and asked.

I looked at him with a raised eyebrow because I didn't know where the hell that question came from.

"That's a serious question, dickhead?"

Once upon a time, the girls' unit was flooded with my product. But some white girl was a straight up fiend and fucked everything up. She mixed so many different drugs at once, she overdosed. Shit was hot on their unit for a while, so we pulled all drugs from it and stayed clear from the women. Plus, those hoes ran their mouths too damn much.

"Yeah. It's a lot of money to be made down there. At least let us have a trial run to see what's up," he suggested.

Touch was a smart nigga, and I valued his opinion on mostly everything. Hence the reason he's my second in command. While I was hesitant about the idea, I couldn't see why we couldn't do a test run to see how things would've went.

"This shit goes south, it's on you, nigga."

"It won't."

"Who we gon' get to hold shit down besides Trouble? The

bitches we were fuckin' with left. One went to another prison and the other went home."

"Gia," he blurted out.

Okay, now this nigga is just on some bullshit, I thought.

"Gia, nigga? Gia?" I stared at him.

"Yeah. She would do anything for you. You know that shit."

"Exactly the reason I don't think it's a smart move to make. Now, if that bitch start being on some nut ass shit? That's yo bitch friend and all, and I'd hate to have to do something to her."

"Nigga, you drawin'. Just relax and let's try shit out."

I looked at Touch, who had the most serious facial expression.

"Ard, nigga. We gon' try this shit out," I agreed, putting emphasis on the word try.

The conversation continued with how we were going to move forward. I knew in my mind that a lot more money was going to be made; I was more so just worried the women fucked up the bag as a whole.

Just as we're wrapping things up, CO Jones barged into my cell.

"Ahmed, you're not supposed to be in here. Let's go," he demanded as he stood by the door, waiting for Touch to get up and leave.

In the rule book, no other inmate should be in a cell that's not assigned to them. It was considered being out of bounds, which resulted in a shot.

"Man, you serious right now?" Touch asked, still sitting down.

"Does it look like I'm playing?"

Touch looked at me for a second. I gave him a head nod, gesturing to just leave because I was seconds away from snapping on bul. He finally stood to his feet and walked out of the cell, making sure to size Jones up.

The moment Touch was gone, Jones' eyes shifted back into my cell and started looking around.

"Oh, so you be on this shit talkin' to those girls, huh?" he asked sarcastically as he walked into my cell and grabbed my mic.

I couldn't even answer him; I just simply chuckled because that nigga clearly ain't know about me.

"What else you got in here?" He started looking around again.

I stood up from my bed and took a step towards him. Instantly, he placed his hand on the panic button all COs had on their person. That button and the pepper spray was their life savers behind the walls. Sometimes, they couldn't get to them fast enough and, in my case, I would've had that nigga in a headlock before he was able to even blink.

"You got yourself a token from me, now leave and find something safer to do," I spoke sternly, looking him dead in his eyes.

I noticed his breathing picked up, but he tried to wear a poker face as if in some kind of way, I didn't intimidate him.

"Don't have nobody in here," he stated as he back-peddled out of my cell.

I walked to my door and kept my eyes trained on him. As he walked down the steps and to the booth, he continued to look back at me. My gut told me he was going to be a problem. That's when I knew I needed to get intel on him and figure out how to move forward; it was either I had to get rid of him or put him on the team. Whichever way, I was going to get my way.

I WAS WOKEN up in the middle of the night from my cell door being unlocked. My hands passed to the side of my bed and gripped my shank. I kept my shit close at all times because being in a place like that could be deadly at any given moment.

Wiping my eyes, I quickly looked at the time on my G-shock and saw it was one-twenty-seven in the morning. The flashlight was flashed in my face, making it hard for me to see who it was.

"Who the fuck is that?" I asked.

"It's me, bul, come walk with me," I heard Wright state.

Once I knew it was him, I calmed down just a little bit, but I was still curious to know what the fuck he wanted at that time of the morning. Only one thing came to mind, but until I saw her with my own two eyes, I was still on edge.

After I slipped my Crocs on and placed my shank in my basketball shorts, I followed Wright out my cell and to the kitchen area, which was at the front of the unit by the guard booth. The door was already open, letting me know someone was there. As soon as I walked in, I saw LT Grace standing there with her uniform shirt open and exposed.

I smirked while looking at her with hooded eyes. Grace was a sight to see. Not only did she have a nice ass body, but she was also beautiful. No matter the connections or what a bitch could do for me, I couldn't stick my dick in no ugly ass hoe or one that wasn't worth shit. While Grace was the reason I got my way around FDC Philly, she was good peoples and good company. Not to mention, the pussy was fire.

"You just had to wake a nigga up, huh?" I asked as I approached her and grabbed her by the waist.

"I saw the opportunity, so why not? Plus, I been craving you," she cooed in my ears.

I took my shank out the side of my basketball shorts and rested it on the metal counter. She looked over at it but didn't budge. Grace knew what it was; it would've been the same on the streets with me, but instead, the shank would've been replaced with a gun.

She descended to her knees and pulled my shorts down. My dick had already started to brick up, so she started to stroke it while she played with my balls. Her hair was down, so I grabbed it in one hand, as I anticipated what was next.

When I became hard as fuck, she kissed the head of my dick before wrapping her lips around it. Inching down, she sucked until I was sitting in the back of her throat.

"Oh, shiiittt," I whispered.

She worked her mouth like it was a wet vacuum. The shit felt so good, I ended up with my back against the wall to support my weak knees.

After slurping and sucking the shit out of me, I motioned for her to get up. She grabbed a condom out of her pants before slipping it off completely. While she got undressed, I placed the rubber on. That was one of my conditions when dealing with her.

Protection was imperative every single time; I didn't know what the fuck she was out in the streets doing and I didn't care. We both agreed no babies, that would've ended her career and sent her ass to prison if it got out we were fucking.

Lifting her up onto the metal counter, I positioned myself between her legs and at her opening. Slowly penetrating her, she slid back some, giving me full access.

"Mmmm, Manic," she moaned lowly, as I started working my way in and out of her.

Wrapping one hand around her neck, I used the other to grip her waist. When I thrusted into her, I helped her to slam down on me. She squeezed her walls, as I tore her shit up.

With an urge to scream out loud, she covered her mouth and shut her eyelids tightly.

Taking one leg into the crook of my arm, I held onto her mid area tight while bringing her down on my tool. Grace was so wet; I felt her cum cascading down my thigh.

"Ma... man... Manic," she whimpered.

"Mmmhmmm, take this shit. You came for it, right?"

I pulled out and turned her ass around. Bending her over, I slid right back in but made sure to touch her g-spot on my first thrust. Grace arched her back deep and poked her ass out. Taking a firm stance, I drilled my dick in and out of her. I loved to see a bitch ass jiggle anytime our bodies clashed.

Starting out at a moderate pace, I quickly sped up when I saw her throwing back her ass. Moments later, I felt myself reaching my peak.

"I'm bouta cum," I groaned. I sunk her back in deep as I pulled her hair like I wanted to remove it from her scalp.

"Ugghhh, fuck," I spoke in a hushed tone as I emptied my load into the condom. "God damn."

Grace leaned over the counter trying to catch her breath while I leaned my back against the wall. Eventually, we started to get ourselves together. I always kept the condom on to take back to my cell to flush.

"Jones gave you a shot," she blurted out.

"He did?" I quizzed.

She nodded her head and started to laugh.

"That nigga gon' make me fuck him up."

"No, no. Don't do anything to add onto your already wild charges. Don't pay him any mind. Besides, I threw the shot out; it was bullshit," she assured me.

"Good lookin'. But on some real shit, I got a feeling that muthafucker gon' be a problem, Tiff," I spoke sternly, addressing her by her first name.

"Then, we'll just have to take care of him one way or another." She looked at me with raised eyebrows.

"As long as you know."

CHAPTER ELEVEN

KEI

nother day, I thought as I heard the cell door unlock. Ever since I'd been inside, I always woke up when we were allowed out, so I carefully got off the top bunk. My bunky was still sound asleep, snoring. She didn't have to be up early to go to work. Since she was still fighting her case, she had no obligation to have a job assignment.

After relieving my bladder, I brushed my teeth and washed my face. Changing out of my nightgown, I threw on the one gray shirt and shorts I had gotten from one of the girls. I couldn't wait to get my own shit, and that day had come.

Finally, the day for our unit to go to commissary had arrived. The night before, I sat with the girls and filled out my slip and handed it in. Just like on the streets, I was ready to buy every single thing on the sheet. The only thing that held me back from doing just that was the limit they placed on how much money we were able to spend. For the most part, I got all my necessities, clothes, and even a MP3 player. Music was a big thing for me, and I also needed it to listen to the TV.

Knock! Knock!

Sherell was at the door, peeking in. Sherell was in the crew with us. She was a Jamaican chick with a strong ass accent. Because I myself was born in the Caribbean, Trinidad and Tobago to be exact, I understood her very well, while other people had a hard time figuring out if she was cursing them out or simply just talking.

"Yuh haffa geh ready fah mainline, gyal," she spoke.

"What the hell is mainline?" I raised a brow as I approached her.

My bunky was still asleep, and I didn't want her to wake up on no bullshit. We took our conversation outside.

"That's when de people dem cum and inspect de place. Make sure ya yard clean and in line," she explained.

"It's every Monday or something?"

"Yeah."

"Okay, bet. Thanks, boo."

I went back in the cell and woke my bunky up. For the most part, all my things were put up and neat. Her, on the other hand, had a way of just being messy. I wasn't about to fail my first inspection because of her ass.

Surprisingly, she woke up and sprang into action cleaning the cell. That told me she knew how important this day was because the bitch was lazy as fuck. When it was all said and done, our cell was spotless and ready to be seen.

That morning, everyone was up bright and early cleaning. The orderlies were scrubbing the showers, sweeping and mopping the dayroom, and helping anyone who needed help.

When the cart with lunch reached the unit, a line of suits followed. From the looks of it, the people were of high ranks in the building.

"Who are they?" I asked the girls as we sat down to eat.

"Those are the head of each department," Kali answered. "That's the unit secretary and manager, that's the chaplain of course, he's the head of food service, she's the head lieutenant, that's the captain, and that right there is the Warden." She pointed out.

I looked over each person as they all stood in a line against the wall just looking at us eat. *Are we a fucking show or some-*

thing? I thought. Ignoring them, I continued to munch on the taco salad we were served.

By the time we were finished eating, the suits had made their rounds around the entire unit, going inside of the cells and checking out enclosed areas as well. After they were finished, two huge carts with red netted bags were brought onto the unit.

"Commissary!" someone yelled.

Everyone started to scramble, running to their cells and leaving back out with their IDs in hand.

"Go get your ID and come on," Noelle told me.

I went in my cell, grabbed my ID, and returned right back out. We went to the front of the unit by the kitchen and waited for our names to be called. After a few people got their things, my last name was called. I showed them my ID and was handed over a huge ass red bag.

"Take it to your room, go through it and bring them back the bag," Noelle told me.

I did as she instructed and was so happy to know I got my own shit finally. Although I knew I had money on my books, I felt like a bum having to ask for things or even accept anything from anyone.

After packing everything away, I ran to the computer to activate my MP3 player. Noelle showed me how to search, preview, and buy songs. Then, she proceeded to show me how to connect to the TVs in the dayroom. I was good to go.

While on the computer, I noticed I still hadn't received any messages from Brix, which stung badly. I made my way over to the phones to try calling him. When the call went through, it only rang once before he picked up. My eyes got wide with excitement, but I quickly remembered what type of timing he was on.

"Bae, what's good?" he answered so nonchalantly.

"You tell me because you been on bullshit," I went right at him.

"I'm sorry, baby. I been on the move," Brix pleaded on the other end of the phone.

It had been days since I'd heard his voice. Anytime I called, it went straight to voicemail or just simply rang out.

"So, your phone wasn't moving with you?" I retorted.

If he thought I was stupid, he had another thing coming. Brix knew better than to try to get over on me. After multiple times of catching him cheating and lying, he knew I knew him too well. And since I was locked up, it was even easier for him to do what he wanted.

"Bae, don't even start with that shit, man. You know how hectic shit can get."

"Nigga, I don't want to hear that. I know for sure when them hoes texting and calling down your phone, you're answering. All yo ugly ass have to do is listen to this white lady talk for a few seconds and press five. Damn," I snapped.

The line went silent, making me wonder if he had hung up.

"Hello?" I called out.

"I'm here, man."

"I don't understand why the fuck you have an attitude. You have your freedom and can do as you please. I'm expressing how much I miss you and you giving off a wild vibe. Brix, get your shit together, brah."

"I'm gone, Lani. I ain't got time for this," he spoke before hanging up.

It was no, *I love you, keep your head up,* and *I'll see you soon* for me. It wasn't the first time Brix hung up on me while we had an argument, but I must admit that this time around, it hit me different and harder due to the position I was in. I couldn't pull up on him and wild out; I couldn't defend myself.

Tears started to fall as I made my way to my cell. Some of the girls called out to me on the way there, but I ignored them and went inside. I dropped myself on the plastic chair and just cried.

All I thought about was why the fuck did I do what I did. I started to blame myself and thinking about the what ifs. What if I didn't run into Tavian? What if I just told him no and continued to earn my honest dollar? What if I had ran when they first questioned me? What if I would've told and got myself off the hook instead of taking the whole wrap?

I knew shit was going to be hard, but I didn't know it would've felt even worse when the people I loved weren't exactly trying to be there for me.

"Kei," I heard Noelle's voice from the door.

"Just leave me alone," I told her.

When I heard the cell door shut, I thought she listened and left. But when I felt someone's presence coming closer, I looked up and saw Noelle approaching me.

"I can't do that. Not with you like this. You don't have to tell me anything, I'm just gon' sit here," she voiced.

Immediately, I broke down crying because a complete stranger was supporting me and showing more affection than my own man was. Nollee came and hugged me while allowing me to just release all the hurt and pain I had built up. It was a lot inside of me, but at least I let some out, even if it was just a small amount.

"He don't love me no more," I cried.

"Who, baby?" she asked, wiping my tears away.

"Brix. He's already on bullshit. Not answering my calls, not emailing back. His ass just hung up on me and all," I ranted.

Nollee didn't say anything. She just hugged me and kept wiping away my tears as they flowed down.

"I don't know what to do. Should I just let him go completely? I think I should, it'll make things easy for both of us, right?" I asked.

"You want my honest opinion?" She pulled away, looking me in my eyes.

I nodded because I wanted to know what to do. Noelle had been in for at least a year, leaving behind people she loved, so I know she had some good advice to give.

"Learn to separate from your life outside these walls and

adjust to your surroundings. It'll make your stay easier and faster," she started. "Find things to do in here that would help you escape from the reality that you're really here, if you know what I mean."

"Like what, Nollee?"

"Well, for me, after my dude starting doing the exact same thing Brix is, I blocked him out and got myself a bowl dude. Now, we built a solid ass relationship and really fuck with each other. He helps me forget about all my worries and even got me studying Islam. I think I'll take my Shahadah soon."

"You talkin' about a dude through the toilet bowl?" I raised a brow.

"Aye, don't judge me."

"That ain't even in me to do, boo." I lifted my hands up in surrender, causing us both to laugh.

"Nah, but real shit, get in tune with your surroundings and allow time to pass. I also read a lot. You may have other things you do or want to do, start now," she pushed.

Noelle made a lot of sense with everything she was saying. I understood what she meant about separating from my life. It was almost as if I shut off my emotions about it, I wouldn't be able to feel any pain. It was the best option for me because while everyone said they loved me and was going to walk down the time with me, I was the only one physically doing it.

"You're right. Thanks so much for not leaving when I told you to," I stated.

"You're welcome. I'm here boo."

That was a defining moment for Noelle and my friendship. Time and time again, she proved to be someone I wanted around. Along with the other girls in her crew and, of course, Lena, I believed I found my team.

After Noelle and I talked some more, I went ahead and made my way to Ms. Walsh's office. Noelle told me about the visiting process, which my mother had been asking me about. When I went to see Ms. Walsh, she gave me the form I had to mail out for everyone individually to fill out and sign. Since I wasn't designated to FDC Philly just yet, I was only allowed visits from my immediate family members; everyone else had to wait.

The rest of the day was calm. I kept running to the computer and buying more music as the songs popped in my head. I kicked back, watched TV and did some reading as well. It wasn't the kind of day I wanted at all if it was up to me, but I was content about it.

After dinner, the bell to the unit rang and in walked a CO with an inmate. She looked just like I did on my first-time walking on the pod. All the ladies started hollering the same thing they did when I came in. It sounded like they were saying chulo and, when asked about it, I was told it meant fresh meat. *Whatever*, I thought.

It was a full African American woman. She was directed to go in the back of the unit to get a mattress just like I was. A few people approached her and eventually some of the girls from our crew went and spoke to her. I said hi and kept it pushing. It wasn't much for me to say, I was still adjusting myself.

Not long after, the guard started calling out names for mail. The call-outs also got posted, so I went to check to see if my name was on there for anything and it was. "What this mean?" I asked out loud to no one in particular.

"Oh, they put you in the kitchen to work," a girl spoke.

"Kitchen?" I smacked my lips.

"Yeah, they always put everyone in the kitchen." She shrugged and walked off.

I know this a muthafuckin' joke, I said to myself.

"You handle sanitizing while I wash, and she rinses," a white chick stated.

The following day came fast as hell. Right after lunch, I was off to my first day at work. Looking around, everyone started to work their part of the kitchen. There were line workers, dish room, the cooks, and where I was, pots and pans. *This ain't no fuckin' joke*, I thought as I looked down at my hands in a pair of huge gloves.

People like me went to school and worked to gain experience just so we didn't have to work jobs like the one I was assigned to. After graduating with two college degrees, there I was washing pots and pans for a measly nineteen cents per hour. I told myself I was grateful that I didn't have to depend on that check to survive. My mind quickly shifted on those who didn't have the support like I did. It was heartbreaking.

As I was placing a bowl on the drying rack, I almost slipped and busted my ass. "Shit!" I hollered, catching everyone's attention.

I held onto the sink to brace myself, quickly regaining my composure. "These boots are supposed to be non-slip?" I asked the girls I was working with.

They all looked at me and shook their head.

We were working in an area that was constantly wet and slippery from the soap. The CO who gave me the boots told me it was non-slip, but that shit was a lie. Let me had hurt myself, the first thing I was doing was calling up my lawyer.

I went back to work as I tried to block out what I was really doing. Before I knew it, it was time to go back to the unit. We were patted down and searched on the way out. Some girls were caught with food, vegetables, and, apparently, letters from the guy inmates.

Once all that was sorted, we were taken back upstairs to the unit. All I wanted to do was get out of the wet clothes I had on and take a nice, hot shower. Before I went to speak with anyone, I went and handled my hygiene; I felt so nasty.

When I was finished taking care of myself, I went and looked for the girls. They weren't out in the dayroom, which told me they had to be in one of their cells. Checking room to room, I finally located them in Noelle and Zaara's room. Literally, everyone was in there.

"What the hell going on in here?" I quizzed.

They all jumped at my voice since they were so tuned into what was going on in the toilet bowl.

"Shhh," Zaara spoke.

Noelle's ear was in the mic listening, while Kali had her ears near trying to listen. Sherell, Gia, and Zaara were sitting around just watching and listening.

"He said he need someone for his brother," Noelle jumped up and stated to no one in particular.

"But everyone here already has someone in his unit," Kali pointed out.

"That's true," Zaara chimed in.

"Aht, aht, Kei don't," Gia blurted out.

My eyes popped open wide. I turned quick on my heels and tried to exit, but they all started shouting my name.

"Fuck," I whispered lowly.

"Come on, Kei, take one for the team and talk to his brother," Zaara pleaded.

"I don't know y'all. I wouldn't know what to say, how to act."

"Girl, just be you, be normal. Just don't speak about your personal business on there. It's all fun and games," Zaara explained.

I looked at Noelle, who wore a smirk on her face, and our conversation replayed in my mind.

"Ughhh, okay," I gave in.

Noelle waved me over. "Okay, my friend here. Where your brother?"

"Right here," I heard a man's voice in the distant say.

I took the mic that was made of soda bottles in my hand and took a deep breath, then let it out.

"Hi," I spoke.

I can't believe I'm doing this shit.

CHAPTER TWELVE

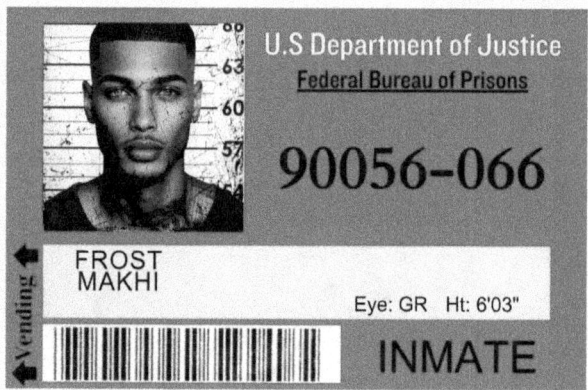

MANIC

*A*fter bussing a good nut the night before, I woke up feeling like a new man. It was a new week, which meant new goals and a harder grind. We were going to send some work down to the women to see how things would go. And we also had a new person to look out for who could easily try to fuck up business.

As we were let out of our cells, I did the usual and went to the computer room to check my email. After, I got on the phone and called baby girl to talk to her before she went off to school. I didn't get to see her that weekend because my moms was feeling under the weather.

As soon as I hung up the phone, Touch approached me with a concern expression.

"Man, go open up, some nut shit happened last night," he informed me.

I sighed while rubbing the back of my head, a habit I had when I was stressed. "If it's not one thing, it's the next. Ard yo, I'ma go deal with it."

Just when I thought I woke up in a good mood and was optimistic about the day, I had to deal with some bullshit first thing in the morning.

Dreadfully, I headed back to my cell, closing the door shut with annoyance. Immediately, I pushed the water out of the toilet bowl by forcing it through the exit hole. In order to hear the next person clearly, all water had to be out, so I used an empty shampoo bottle to suck up the remaining water. A soon as I got the last of the water out, I heard, "Ayeee yooooo!"

"Yo, what's the word?" I yelled back, using the new mic I had someone make out of creamer containers.

"Key caught a nigga stealing his work out his cell. Long

story short, the bus came to pick bull up," he informed, referring to an ambulance.

What the fuck was all I thought.

"So, where Key now?" I questioned.

"SHU, you know they took him right up. Big mutha fucka put up a crazy fight, took damn near ten guards and pepper spray to tame him."

"Ard, stay low, this ain't gon' be no SIS situation if bull condition ends up real bad, the big boys gon' be coming in," I told him.

SIS stood for Special Investigation Supervisor, where they investigated all incidents and determined the consequences, which sometimes led to a new charge or something small as a privilege being taken away.

"Ard, sayless."

Before any other exchange was made, I flushed the toilet and went to find Touch and Zaine to discuss what the hell went down.

LATER THAT DAY, I had to get back on the line to find out more things regarding the incident. When I opened up the bowl, I heard a nigga talking to a female. I wasn't sure who they were and didn't give a fuck, so I intervened.

"Aye, take that shit to another line," I demanded.

At first it got quiet, then another female got on.

"Who the fuck is this?" she asked.

"It's Manic. I said to get the fuck on."

"Oh, my fault Manic. It's Noelle, my girl was just using my jawn to talk. Go ahead."

"Bet. Close up," I told her, referring to her flushing her toilet bowl so she didn't hear my conversation.

Whoever the dude was got gone in a heartbeat; he never even responded when I first got on. I went ahead and called for anyone on my team that was on the same floor Key was on. Finally getting onto someone, they put me on to whatever else information they had received. I took note and went about my business, but before I was able to flush, Touch came in and said he wanted to get on the bowl with his jawn.

"Yo, ask Noelle who that was on her bowl earlier," I told him.

"What you mean?" he asked, looking confused.

I briefly told him about a jawn and a nigga having a conversation on the line earlier. He said he was going to ask her about it. While I exited my cell and went to check my email, Touch went and told another dude who was on the bowl with his bitch to tell Noelle to open up again.

By the time I went back to my cell, Touch was comfortable on the chair and mic in hand, talking.

"Bro, you wouldn't believe it," Touch said in a hushed tone.

Sometimes, without speaking into the mic, the other person could still hear what was being said if loud enough.

"What happen?" I quizzed.

"The girl you heard on the line, it was the jawn you been checkin' for," he revealed.

"Who, Keilani?" My eyes opened wide.

He nodded hesitantly. I guess he noticed my reaction and told Noelle he was going be right back and flushed the toilet.

"What's good, bro?" he asked in a serious tone.

I went and sat on my bed, just staring at the wall. Keilani wasn't my bitch; hell, I didn't even know her, but for some reason, I felt some kind of way. For once, someone caught my eye and attention in FDC Philly and, now, she was potentially about to be sucked into that bowl life with another nigga.

"Who was she talking to?" I inquired, already know Touch asked Noelle.

"Some new nigga on four-south. He's Dami's family."

"Oh yeah?"

"Mmmhmm."

"Tell him that shit dead. Don't call for her no more. I don't care if you tell him directly or Dami," I instructed.

Touch looked at me, then put down his head and shook it. Out of nowhere, he started to chuckle.

"Bro, what you doing, man? You gon' get at the jawn or just block her from doing her?"

What am I doing? I asked myself.

"I don't even know, nigga," I voiced honestly.

"Why don't you just say fuck it and see wassup with

shorty? The worst that can happen is she doesn't wanna check for you," he joked, but I got his point.

I never took any of those hoes seriously on the bowl. If I ever spoke to any of them, it was for pure entertainment purposes only. There was a funny feeling in me that it wouldn't have been the case with shorty. Part of me wasn't trying to be on that timing with so much to be dealing with, while the other part wanted her.

"Now, if she fucks around and have a nigga hooked? If she turns around and breaks my heart, you have to kill her, since it was your idea for me to pull up on her," I half-joked.

"Fuck it then. That's gon' be on her." He shot me an evil grin and shrugged.

"Nah, on some real shit, I'll probably fuck that girl life up more than it's already in the hole."

"Or maybe you'd be just what her ass need," he countered.

"Like you and Noelle, huh?" I side eyed him.

Touch was Muslim and, ever since he started dealing with Noelle, he had her wanting to study Islam more and more to the point she was eventually going to take her Shahadah. I was happy for my nigga that he caught a good one, but I wasn't sure if that was in the same cards for me.

There was a rack of bitches on the outside waiting for me to get free. Some I spoke to on a daily while some were once in a blue. It wasn't a bitch that I came across that wasn't ready to risk it all for me.

"Yeah, dickhead, like me and Noelle," he spoke sarcastically.

"Throw the bone and see if she bite, but I ain't pressed, bro."

Touch smiled so wide, as if I told the nigga I wanted to marry the jawn.

"Say less," he sang happily, making me crack up.

"Dickhead." I shook my head.

CHAPTER THIRTEEN

KEI

ho the hell was that?" I quizzed.

While I was having a calm conversation

with the dude Noelle put me onto, Reem, someone rudely interrupted.

"Manic." Noelle raised her eyebrows.

"Why did you just let him do as he please? That nigga is rude," I went on.

"Uh, uh, not that one girl. That's my dude's big homie, and Manic ain't somebody to play with. Just let that shit go and you'll talk to ol' boy another time. Yo ass finna go to work, anyway."

"Fuck that nigga too. His weak ass didn't even say shit back to Manic when he came on the line. I know it's all fun and games, but I won't waste my time with no pussy ass nigga," I expressed.

Noelle and Zaara bussed out laughing at me, but I was dead ass serious. How a whole grown ass man let another man come and rudely interrupt what he got going on?

"I mean, you got a point," Zaara agreed.

I shot Noelle a matter of fact look.

Just when she was about to say something, the bell to the unit rang.

"I'm out y'all, let me go to this wack ass job," I told them and exited out their cell.

All the ladies for the p.m. kitchen were walking out the door by the time I reached it. We piled onto the huge elevator, which let us off right at the entrance of the kitchen. Everyone dispatched and went to their assigned work area.

When I rounded the corner to where pots and pans were,

my eyes grew wide like golf balls when I saw the mess that was left behind. It was a ton of shit to wash and it was only one other person working alongside me that day. Without complaining, because it was no use in that, we got right down to business and started to knock things out.

About two hours later, we had completed the mess that we met there; then, a load from the current shift came our way. My feet and back were killing me; I just wanted to cry, but I knew it wouldn't have done me any good. I put on my big girl panties and finished the job.

We were finished with our work before the rest of the girls. I tried my hand at asking our supervisor to go back to the unit early. Usually, everyone had to wait until the shift was finished and all areas were cleaned up. We were assigned to the same CO supervisor as the cooks, and they were also finished, so it worked out in our favor. He took us up early, with, of course, the other women being mad.

I rushed and jumped in the shower before it got taken by those who went back to the unit with me. Picking the shower that got the hottest, I stood under the showerhead as the water beat down on my body, relaxing my muscles. I was so tired and hurting, all I wanted to do was lie down and relax.

"Kei!" Noelle called out to me, poking her head in my cell.

"Hey, boo," I greeted her. "Wassup?" I applied lotion to my legs.

"So, I was told to show you someone to see what you think."

"What you talkin' 'bout, girl?" I was confused.

She held a picture in her hand, but from the angle, I only saw her dude in the picture. I remembered his face from the previous pictures she'd shown me.

"What you think about him?" She handed me the picture.

When my eyes landed on the green-eyed stranger, my heart skipped a beat.

"Why?" I looked up at a smirking Noelle.

"Don't worry about why. What do you think about him?"

"Isn't this the Manic dude?"

She nodded.

"He's disrespectful as fuck. That's what I think about him." I shoved the picture back into her hand.

"Okayyy then. How was work?" she asked, trying to change the subject.

"Exhausting. I'm finna take a nap."

"Did you eat?"

"I'm good. I just want to sleep."

"Okay, well, I'll make sure and bring you something to eat later," she volunteered.

"Thanks, boo."

As Noelle left out the cell, my bunky walked in.

"I don't want people in and out of here as they please. Before you moved in, no one came in here," she scolded.

Who the fuck is this bitch talking to? I thought.

"Bro, I don't know who the hell you think you are, but you

don't fuckin' run me or run shit around here. I been nice to you, but you working my last fuckin' nerves," I snapped.

"I said what I said." She quickly turned and left back out the cell.

That's when I knew I had to get out of that cell with her. I knew how I could get and it was no way in hell she was about to tell me who could and couldn't pull up on me.

Quickly shaking off her weird ass vibe, I climbed the ladder and got on my bunk. I placed my headphones in my ears and pressed play. Within minutes, I was knocked out.

My nap turned into sleeping for the entire night. Noelle came and brought me food to eat, which I tore up and went right back to sleep. The dayroom didn't see me at all. I didn't even bother to go and check my email.

When I woke up the following morning, I felt refresh, although my body felt sore. That kitchen was getting the best of me and I knew something had to give. I went and checked my emails, knowing they were backed up. The usual people had reached out: my mom, aunt, who was my best friend, and a few of my friends. Of course, there was no email from Brix.

After replying to everyone, I walked outside into the rec yard for some fresh air. It was freezing but stimulating since inside felt like it was choking me sometimes. The rec yard was concrete, with a basketball court on it and benches. It was closed up with the upper part as bars, allowing us to see the sky from an angle. Since there were units above us, the top was completely covered.

"What you doing out here?" I heard Lena ask from the doorway.

"Just getting some fresh air," I responded.

She eyed me as she placed her hands on her hips like a mother would.

"Come see me when you're done trying to catch a cold." She closed the door and walked off.

I stayed outside for a few more minutes before finally going back in. As I walked through the door, an inmate was happily walking past me with a few other girls following her.

"Don't forget to write to me. We're gonna miss you," one girl stated.

The others fell in line and spoke similar things to her, which told me she was being released. She smiled so brightly and seemed so happy to be going home. I thought about the day my time was going to be up, but it quickly faded away once I remembered I literally just started my bid. Nevertheless, I was happy for shorty, even though I didn't know her.

One less hoe I have to deal with in here, I thought.

I made my way to Lena's cell as she requested. When I got there, she was on the bowl talking to someone.

"Wassup with you, you good?" she pulled the mic away from her mouth and asked.

"Yeah, I just need to get a new job and get the fuck out of

that cell," I expressed.

"The kitchen ain't no joke. I'm a cook, so I know. But wassup with you and your cellmate?"

"That bitch weird. First, she was upset I'm not hanging with her. Now, she talking about she don't want people coming and going. The bitch always eating, shitting, and talking smack."

Lena bussed out laughing hysterically. Her laugh was so contagious, I started laughing too.

"Yo, Kei, you something else," she spoke in between laughing.

"I'm dead ass, Lena. I'm just over everything."

"Well, this white girl just got released today. She was in a cell by herself. The one right by the phones. You better go and ask Ms. Walsh if you can get up in there," she put me on.

"You serious?" My eyes bucked.

She nodded.

"I'll be back." I dipped out her room and hustled over to Ms. Walsh's office.

No one was waiting outside of her office, granting me access right away. When I knocked on the door, she waved me in.

"Milan, everything okay?"

"No, I need to get out of my cell and out of the kitchen," I jumped straight to the point.

She started laughing at me as if something I said was funny.

"I know the kitchen can be tough, but I can't place you anywhere else right now until I know if you're staying here or not. And as for your cell, what's going on?"

Instantly, I felt defeated when she shut me down about the work reassignment, but I understood.

"We're just not a good match," I simply stated. I wasn't the type to snitch, so what did I look like telling this woman anything?

"Find a cell and get back to me."

"I already found out. It's completely empty. Someone just left today."

"In order to refrain from getting someone in there you wouldn't want, go and find someone to move in there with you," she directed.

I jumped up out of the chair with the quickness and flew out the door. Before I even started to walk around, my eyes landed on the woman that recently came in after me. She seemed chill and normal in the head. I went ahead and approached her about moving in with me and, luckily, she was looking to get out of her current cell, so it worked out.

Returning to Ms. Walsh, she did the change without hesitation.

"Y'all can move after count," she instructed like last time.

"Thank you," I told her and left out her office happy despite not getting everything I wanted. I had a way to finesse people into giving me what I wanted, so I knew I was going to have to work my way around the kitchen.

After I packed up my things so it would've been an easy process to move cells, it was already time to head to work. I placed my belongings in Lena's cell until I returned. I wasn't sure what type of time my cellmate was on since she knew I was leaving.

Walking off the unit and getting into the elevator, I took a deep breath and let it out. The doors opened, and I saw the entrance to the kitchen. Immediately, I felt my body aching. I continued in and went over to my section. My supervisor, who was a middle-aged Caucasian man, was resting a mixing bowl in the sink.

"Ladies," he greeted when we walked up to him.

Remembering I had a mission to accomplish and he played a valuable role, I acted according. "Hey, Williams," I spoke with a little more excitement than I wanted.

He nodded his head at me and walked off, returning his attention to the cooks. The other ladies and I got down to work. There were four of us that day, so the workload felt lighter than usual. We took turns doing things and taking breaks, which worked out in everyone's favor. While we were the ones that always had a load of shit to do, being the last to finish between us and the cooks, they were behind.

"Hey, you need help?" I asked the pretty Dominican who was the head cook.

"Yeah, sure." She smiled. "What's your name?"

"Kei, and yours?"

"Isabella, call me Bell."

She seemed sweet and down to earth. Her body was stacked in all the right places, giving that exotic look. When Williams saw me on the cook's side, he asked what I was doing there, but Bell quickly told him I was good. That's when I knew she held weight and was the right company to keep.

Bell showed me what she needed help with, and I got right down to business. Cooking wasn't a foreign thing to me since I loved doing it, but it was a different story when having to prepare a meal for over a thousand individuals. It wasn't normal sized pots either. There were huge heavy duty cooking kettles that were five times my size.

"Kei?" a girl called out to me from behind an oven.

I was stirring the beans at the time. "Yes?" I looked at her suspiciously.

She walked around the oven and came close to me, so I stepped back. I didn't know what she wanted. But when she extended her hand, I saw she had a piece of paper folded up.

"This is for you. I just caught it from the five-south cart," she informed me. "Put it away. Make sure the guards don't see it or feel it when they pat you down."

"Thank you," I told her, even though I was totally lost in what the hell was going on.

After completing everything Bell told me to do, curiosity got the best of me and I went to the bathroom to check the mysterious paper. When the door was locked and secured, I dug in my sports bra, pulled out the paper, and unfolded it.

It read:

If you thought I was disrespectful, then you should think that nigga you were talking to was corny as fuck. You had no business talking to him in the first place. I'm not your average nigga, Keilani. And I didn't take you to be an average woman, but I could be wrong. Am I wrong?

Keep your head up and stay ten toes down.

-M. A.

It didn't take a rocket scientist to know who the note was from. What surprised me was that he actually sent me one. I blushed at the gesture and his arrogance.

Knock! Knock!

"Kei, come on, Williams taking us up early again!" I heard someone yell from the other side of the bathroom door.

I quickly folded the paper back and tucked it between my breasts. "Coming!" I hollered back.

I went and flushed the toilet with my boots. Exiting out the bathroom, I washed my hands and met the girls by the entrance. Williams was still in the office doing something, so we waited patiently at the elevator, talking amongst ourselves.

Moments later, the elevator opened on both sides and in walked Manic with a CO. My breath got caught in my throat as butterflies fluttered in my stomach. The way he stared into my eyes, it was like he was trying to see my soul.

"So, I'm disrespectful?" he asked, taking a step towards me.

CHAPTER FOURTEEN

MANIC

K eilani's mouth opened as if she wanted to say something, but her words got stuck in her throat. Her facial expression looked like she saw a ghost as she stood there frozen, looking at me. The rest of the women that were around her threw all kinds of words my way, seeking attention, but my focus was on Keilani.

"Alright ladies, get searched and let's go up," a CO announced, walking out of the kitchen.

If it wasn't for him, Keilani would've been still staring at me.

"Come on, man," Wright told me, making me finally peel my eyes away from her.

Although she looked exhausted from what I assumed was a hard day at work, she wasn't any less beautiful than when I first laid eyes on her. Her long hair was pulled into a ponytail, giving me a full view of her face. She was nothing but radiant.

"You know shorty?" Wright pried.

"Nah, but find out what you can about her. Keilani Milan," I told him.

He nodded, then opened the door to LT Grace's office. If I said I didn't know what she wanted, I would've been lying.

"Thanks, Wright. I got it from here," she told him.

Once the door was shut behind me, she started up, wasting not a second.

"What the fuck, Makhi?" she snapped, calling me by my real name.

Yeah, this ain't no dick appointment, I thought.

I took a seat because I knew she was finna chew a nigga apart as if I was the one that did anything. It cost to be a boss though; whatever your team did fell back on you. In that case, what Key did was on my hands.

"What Tiffany?" I spoke unbothered.

"You serious right now? This shit could turn out real bad."

"I know, I know, I don't know what the fuck he was thinkin' yo. Now, he might have another potential body added to his list of murders he's already sitting in for. But what happened to the work that was in his cell?"

"It's secured. Luckily, Ramone was on duty and got it," she revealed.

Ramone was another CO on my payroll. I had a good amount of them, especially the ones that stayed on the units a lot and a few in visiting.

"I need it to get to Tahira in the women's unit," I ordered, speaking about Touch's sister.

"Ard, but it better not be no bullshit with these girls, neither." She eyed me.

"I got chu'. But what the heat lookin' like?" I was curious about how shit was gon' blow back on business.

"Well, in the meeting this morning, we were told the suits are coming in to investigate. It shouldn't be a long, drawn-out process if he just tells them they got into an argument and it became physical. Of course, he shouldn't mention the guy was in his cell stealing drugs. That would open a whole other can of warms we don't need around here." She let out a long sigh.

"Mmm, ard." I nodded slowly, taking everything in.

I knew I had to get word to Key in the SHU. He should've

known better than to speak on shit, but it didn't hurt to assure he didn't.

As I got up to leave, I remembered to ask her something. "Oh yeah, you found out anything about that goofy ass nigga, Jones?" I inquired.

"Yeah. So, apparently, he's from up Broad and Olney. He some square ass nigga. He used to hoop, got hurt, and here he is now."

"Ard. Let me know if you find out anything else."

When I opened the door, Wright was right there waiting to take me back to five-south.

"FROST," I heard my name being announced loudly through my headphones.

Touch tapped me on the knee, which confirmed I did hear what I heard. We were just chilling in the dayroom. I looked over to the guard booth and saw the unit secretary, Ms. Ellis, standing there, so I got up and went over to her.

"Your lawyer's on the line," she informed me.

I followed her out of the unit and into her office, which was located right outside the doors. She motioned for me to sit down, handed me the phone, then stepped outside of the office, making sure to close the door behind herself.

"Hello?" I answered.

"Makhi, it's Hash. I just received a new court date for you.

After fully analyzing the evidence with my team, I have a very strong feeling I can get the charges dropped," he exclaimed.

"Man, don't bullshit me. I don't want no false hope or empty promises," I responded.

I know I should've been happy to hear him say that, but until the judge banged his gavel, it meant nothing to me.

"I totally understand why you feel that way. I just thought I'd let you know. But we'll be going to court this week."

"Good to know. Anything else?"

I didn't ask what day because it fucked with my nerves. When they came and got me was when I would just have no other choice but to go. All I needed to know was around the time I was supposed to head across the street.

"No."

"Ard. I'll holla at you then." I hung the phone up.

I opened the door and saw Ms. Ellis standing there toying with her fingers. When she saw me walking out, her eyes landed on my grey sweats and stayed there for a minute.

"You like what you see or something?" I asked.

Ms. Ellis was a nice-looking jawn. By the looks of her, she was in her thirties. I wouldn't have mind bending her ass over. She always threw me looks, but I didn't pay her any mind because she never acted on it.

"Ah, I—"

"It's written all over your face. You ain't gotta lie to me." I bit my bottom lip as I checked her out. I kept my distance because I knew we were on camera.

She started to giggle and fix her clothes, which didn't even need any fixing. Nervousness was written all over her face.

"I can't—"

I back-peddled into her office and, once out of camera, pulled my dick out. Her eyes popped wide open and her body moved in a motion that let me know she liked what she saw.

"Call CO Wright and tell him I said to come to your office now," I demanded.

Slowly, putting one foot in front of the other, she came in the office, now out of the camera's vision, and did what I told her to do.

"What's he coming for?" she questioned.

"Don't worry about it."

She sat behind her desk, as I sat across from her. Underneath the desk was completely free, giving room to do whatever. I sat there staring at her intensely, wondering how inside of her felt. She couldn't keep eye contact and kept fidgeting in her seat. When Wright finally made it to us, her eyes shot to him.

"What you need?" Wright asked when he opened the door.

"Look out for me," I stated without removing my eyes off her. She kept looking between me and Wright.

"Ard. Don't take forever," he spoke, already knowing what was up.

"By the way she looks, I don't think I will."

Once he shut the door, I motioned for her to get underneath the table. The office didn't have a traditional wall. It was a window, allowing anyone in the hall to see right through. With the way I positioned myself in my seat under the desk, it was hard for someone to see what was going on. Wright also stood in a way to block their view.

Ms. Ellis crawled up to me, placing her hands on my knees. She tugged at my sweats, pulling out my manhood. Almost immediately, she swallowed my dick whole.

"Oh shit," I hissed, grabbing her head as it bobbed up and down.

She was sucking the shit out of my dick, not even coming up for air. I started to wonder why I never came at her sooner.

Hitting the back of her throat continuously, I looked under and saw she had tears in her eyes. Lil' mama was doing the damn thing and was one of the best to top me off. Once she spat on my shit and slurped it up, I knew she was a mutha-fuckin' freak and I wanted all parts.

After fucking LT Grace for all those months, I was happy to get some action outside of her. It wasn't hard for me to fuck anyone. I just didn't. The ones that were throwing cat was either not worth touching or weren't my type. I only hit two other women in the facility: a nurse and a female inmate.

I felt myself about to reach my climax. Palming the back of her head, I shot my kids down her throat, making sure she caught every drip. Surprisingly, she obliged and sucked a nigga dry.

"What the fuck is this?" LT Grace burst through the door.

Oh my fuckin' God, I thought as I threw my head back.

Ms. Ellis came from under the desk wiping the side of her mouth. She wore a worried expression while I had a huge smirk on mine. That was the second time Grace caught me fucking around with someone besides her, and I knew an earful was coming.

"Wait, it's not what you think," Ms. Ellis started to plead.

"Nah, it's exactly what I think. You just got done sucking his dick," Grace spat, sounding territorial.

I looked outside the office window and saw Wright standing there shaking his head.

"Please, I don't want to lose my job."

"Oh, you gon'—"

"You're not losing your job," I spoke sternly as I hovered over Grace.

Ms. Ellis looked between me and Grace, trying to figure out what the fuck was going on. The way I approached her, any other inmate would've got put down already.

"Please give us a minute," Grace looked at Ellis and stated.

She hurriedly left out of the office, leaving me and Grace to have a standoff.

"What the fuck is your problem? I thought we were past this?" she started.

"Fuck is you talkin' 'bout? You're not my bitch, Tiffany. Where I stick my dick is none of your fuckin' business." I got low in her face. "Get that shit through your fuckin' skull, man."

"That's crazy as fuck, Makhi. After everything I've done for you, this how you treat me?"

"You sound like one of them bitches off a movie," I shot her way. "Tiffany, our business relationship is mutually beneficial to me as it is to you. We spoke about this shit already. You play your part, and I got you always. All this other shit won't do nothing but make me not want to fuck with you at all on any level."

Her hard exterior softened with defeat as those words left my mouth. I wasn't into worrying about bitches' feelings, especially when you knew what it was when we got involved. What Grace and I had was mainly business, with a splash of occasional fucks.

"Can you handle that?" I asked since she hadn't said a word.

She nodded. "Yeah, I got it."

"Good. Now, you ain't see nothing today, right?"

"Right."

She turned, opened the door, and walked out. Walking past Ms. Ellis, she sized her up and down before exiting the door that separated the units and the elevators.

"Everything good?" Wright questioned.

"Yeah, everything straight," I answered, looking at Ms. Ellis.

CHAPTER FIFTEEN

KEI

"*H*e said what?" Zaara questioned with goggle eyes, making me giggle. I was in Noelle and Zaara's cell putting them onto Manic and my encounter.

Once Williams came and interrupted our stare down, I couldn't help but think about him. I wanted to say something, but the boss aura that seeped off him intimidated me; it had me nervous as hell.

"The nigga practically walked up to me and pressed me on what I told Noelle." I side-eyed her. She was the only person I told that to, not to mention, she was the one who asked me what I thought about him.

"Hey, I just relayed the message." Noelle raised her hands up in the air.

"Mmmhmm." I curled my lip up.

"So, what you gon' do, girl? That nigga checking for you," Zaara asked.

"Who's checking for who?" Gia asked, walking in on the conversation.

"Manic," Zaara answered happily.

"Manic? What the hell he want with you?" Gia asked, creasing her forehead.

"He wants her, period," Zaara spoke.

Gia stared at me as if I stole something from her, making me wonder if they had anything prior to him trying to shoot his shot.

"Nollee, can I get a pack of noodles, please?" Gia turned and asked, trying to change the subject, but I already caught onto her weird ass energy.

She took the ramen noodles from Noelle and left out of the cell as fast as she came. The whole mood in the room shifted when she first entered, but once gone, it went back to how it was.

"I'm about to go check my email and hop on the phone," I told them before exiting the cell.

I made my way to the computer room and patiently waited in line to get in. All the computers were being used, and I was the third person in line. By the time I reached the front to go in, Zaara came speed-walking towards me with a huge smile on her face.

Oh lord, what now? I thought.

"Come, come," she spoke quickly and grabbed ahold of my hand.

I tugged back because I was next to go in. "What happen?" I quizzed.

"Just come." She yanked the shit out of my arm, pulling me in the direction of her cell.

When we entered, Noelle was on the bowl talking to someone.

"He's looking for you?" Noelle stated.

"Who?"

"Who else?" she piped.

My eyes grew wide like saucers as my stomach started doing cartwheels. Nervousness crept into me, making me feel like I wasn't equipped to speak to him. After everything the girls told me about his reputation and history, I was scared I said the wrong thing and turned him off.

"I can't," I quivered.

"Girl, yes, you can. Just be yourself. It's clear as day it's something about you that he liked. Come on," Noelle persuaded.

Zaara pushed me to the bowl and handed me over the mic.

"Hello?" I said, barely above a whisper.

"Bitch, now you know ain't nobody hearing that shit," Noelle blurted out.

I cleared my throat, took a deep breath in, and let it out. "Hello," I spoke with more confidence and volume.

"Wassup shorty?" I heard his voice boom through the bowl and into the mic, sending shivers throughout my body.

"Nothing, what's good?"

"Cat cut ya tongue earlier?"

Cocking my neck, I looked at the mic and then at the girls. *Oh no, he didn't*, I thought.

"I mean, you just caught me off guard, that's all," I answered.

"Mmm, I hear you. Let me find out yo ass scary acting."

"Me, scary? Nah," I replied, smiling hard.

"Ard, then. Where you from though?" he went on to ask.

"Brooklyn, but I live out Chester," I revealed, quickly wondering if I said too much.

"Where in Chester? That's where I'm from."

What a small ass world.

"I live on the west side, on Eighth street. How about you?"

"Same, not far from you. But I live in Philly now," he disclosed.

"Oh okay. I have a spot out there as well."

"Crazy how I never ran into you. I guess you were Chester's best kept secret."

"I guess so," I replied, blushing.

"I ain't gon' hold you. I don't be on this bowl shit. You have a text app?" he questioned.

"What's a text app?" I moved the mic and asked the girls.

"It's a way to text people through the email," Noelle briefly explained.

"Nah, I don't."

"Take my number down. Get one and text me," he demanded.

I motioned for a pen and paper from the girls, who quickly scrambled to get it to me. It was funny as hell but cute how they were rooting for the connection between me and him.

Jotting down the number, I confirmed it with him and tucked it in my sports bra.

"Don't have a nigga waiting," he spoke with authority.

"I won't."

"Ard. Now, get off this bowl. I don't want to hear you have your face in this shit if it ain't for me."

Who this nigga think he is? I asked myself. I couldn't front though, I melted under his aggression. He was forward as hell, something I respected and took a strong liking to.

"Aight, say less," I responded calmly, not showing my complete eagerness to submit.

I stood up on my feet with the biggest smile on my face as I felt a burst of excitement.

"Check you out." Noelle smiled.

"Girl, whatever." I waved her off.

"Now, tell me about this text app," I inquired.

The girls ran down how to sign up and how it worked. Once they told me I'd have direct communication with him, I was all for it. I ran off to the computer with Noelle in tow. She helped me send a message to my aunt, Kayla, who happened to be my best friend too. She was my go-to person for everything.

Once I emailed her to set everything up, I jumped on the phone and discreetly told her to get on it. The text app was illegal due to it being a third-party communicator, but everyone still had them. If the system caught on to it, they'd just make a new account with the app.

The night was winding down, and it was about to be lock down. I said my goodnights to my crew and retired to my new cell with my new bunky, Tamara. We'd only been cellmates for about a day or so, and everything was smooth with us. She was clean and very easy to get along with.

"How was your day, hun?" Tamara asked while flipping through a magazine on her bunk.

"It was—" I paused. "Interesting." I smiled.

"Interesting, huh?"

"Yeah." I nodded. My mind quickly drifted off to the

moment the elevator door opened and I saw Manic's fine ass just standing there. In another world, I would've just jumped on his tall frame and seduced him.

"How was yours?" I turned and asked.

"It was cool. Just trying to adjust."

Everyone I dealt with came together and had been helping Tamara get settled, like they'd done for me.

"Yeah, it's something we just have to do until we no longer have to. If that makes sense," I spoke, mostly trying to convince myself.

"That's true. I just still can't believe I'm in here. Everything just happened so fast," she voiced.

"That, I can agree with."

I automatically started thinking about the day the feds came and officially indicted me.

January 20, 2017 (After the feds arrested me.)

The entire ride was quiet, or at least to me it was. Both agents that rode with me spoke, but it was murmurs. I sat back still since every movement made the handcuffs tighter. Staring out the window, I looked at all the city's landmarks, like the Philadelphia International airport, the Wells Fargo center, the Lincoln Financial Field, and the Citizen's Bank Park, thinking when I was going to be able to see them again.

I had no clue what waited ahead; all there was to do was go with the flow at that point. My anxiety was so high, my heart raced with every mile we drove.

Finally reaching the city of Philadelphia, we pulled into a driveway that led to an underground garage. Once parked, they took me out of the car and carried me into a building, up an elevator and into a room. There, they started to ask me simple questions about my background, nothing pertaining to the case. After finishing up with the FBI agents, I was handed off to the United States Marshal. The same kind of questions the FBI inquired were asked again; then, I was placed in a holding cell until it was time for me to see the judge.

"Milan," a Marshal came to the cell and called out to me.

"Yes."

"Let's go, you're up," he spoke, undoing his cuffs.

I walked to him and waited for the cell door to open. Once there wasn't a barrier between the two of us, he motioned for me to stick my hands out in front of me, so I did just that. He cuffed my hands and locked it, then walked me to an elevator in the back of the holding area. We bypassed cells filled with a bunch of male inmates. All sorts of cat calls came my way, making me feel uncomfortable.

We got onto the elevator and finally to the floor our destination was on. Walking off, we stood at a door that was opened by another Marshal, which was the courtroom. When I walked in, my eyes landed on my family right away. Front row was my mother, brothers, sister in laws, and a few others.

I felt tears welling at the looks on their faces. My body started to feel weak; thankfully, I was seated just in time *before my knees gave out. We all sat there while we waited for the judge to present themselves.*

"All rise for the honorable Judge Casen," the court officer announced.

I stood to my feet and eyed the older white woman who wore a black robe. She sat down in her seat and opened a folder without looking my way at all. I tried to read her, but it was hard. All I thought to do was pray she was in a good mood that day and allowed me to go home with my family.

"We're going to see the matter of Keilani Milan vs. the United States of America, case number..." her words started to fade as I heard my name.

The officer helped me from where I sat, alongside other defendants, and took me in front the judge. I was seated next to a white woman I'd never saw a day in my life, which I had assumed to be my attorney.

"Hi, I'm Kelsi Reyes. I'm just standing in place for your attorney for today," she introduced herself.

"Hi, okay," I simply answered.

"Please state your name for the record," the judge requested.

"Keilani Milan."

Moments after, the proceedings began with the judge reading off the alleged charges. The U.S. attorney started to speak back and forth with the judge in regards to bond and requirements. When I heard there weren't going to be any opposition to me being released, my anxiety calmed just a little.

"Ms. Milan, you will be released on OR, which means on your own recognizance. You will follow the following require-ments. You are to be present for each and every court date, you are to attend counseling as often as the doctor sees fit, you are to surrender your firearm, and you are to follow all rules laid out by the office of pre-trial. If and when you do not comply with any of these, you will be remanded into custody pending the outcome of your case. Do you understand?"

"Yes, Your Honor," I answered.

"Good. This case is due back in six days, the twenty-sixth of January for your arraignment." She banged her gavel.

Although the sound of the gavel banging was only in my head, it sounded as if it was real and happening. It pulled me from my deep thoughts.

When I attended my arraignment, I pled not guilty and was preparing to go to trial. I fought my case for an entire year, going back and forth to court, counseling, and pretrial sessions. It was mentally and emotionally exhausting.

THE FOLLOWING MORNING, I woke up in a content mood. Of course, I wasn't happy about my position, but I was grateful I still had life and my health. Thanking God for another day, I got off my top bunk and did my normal morning routine: brush my teeth, wash my face, and race to the computer.

Bypassing everyone's email, I went straight to the email from the text app. I saw everything went through after I did what I had to do, as well as my aunt on her end. Manic's number was in my bra, so I pulled it out and added him to my address book. Returning to my inbox, I went ahead and replied to all messages. The email from my mom stood out the most.

Mom: Your birthday is approaching. I wish you were here to celebrate it.

I was turning twenty-four years old and, while I pictured my Kobe year being lit, I had to settle with the fact it was going to be non-existent.

Not quite sure how to respond to her email, I changed the subject and asked how she was doing. Anytime I thought about things I wasn't able to do, I replayed Noelle's voice in my head and remembered to enjoy the small things I did have and what I could do.

That morning, I returned to my cell and rested until it was lunch, which work followed right after. Before leaving off the unit, I went to check the computer to see if they had added Manic to my address book. When I saw that they did, I felt exhilarated as I opened a new message and typed his name in. I save his contact under BDE, which meant big dick energy. It was what he gave off, so it fitted him perfectly.

Me: Hey rude boy. I hope your day is going well.

Reaching out because you told me to and because I don't want no smoke. -Kei.

When I hit the send button, I cringed, knowing I sent a corny message like that. It was undoable, so I had to live with it.

"Milan, let's go!" I heard Williams yell from the guard booth.

I logged out of my account and went to meet the rest of the ladies to go downstairs to the kitchen.

CHAPTER SIXTEEN

MANIC

$\mathcal{A}$ big smirk appeared on my face when I read the message Keilani sent me. I was surprised I even had something from her in my email. It only showed me she wanted to talk to a nigga after all. She handled what she needed to in order to communicate with me and didn't stall. By the looks and vibe I got from her, I already had a mind it wasn't going to be a one-sided thing between us.

Me: You better had because I was willing to give all smoke. But my day going good. Better now that you reached out. How you feeling? You ard? I hope nobody not on no nut shit with you.

I responded to everyone else's email and jumped off. There were a few things I needed to take care of. Walking out of the computer room, Touch was walking in my direction.

"Shorty hit a nigga line," I revealed.

Touch grinned so hard at the news. For some odd reason, he was pressed on having me talk to someone from the women's unit. He felt I was always working, worried about the bag. While I had to deal with shit inside the facility, I still had motion going on in the streets. I thought LT Grace was going to be my escape from everything, but she started acting too possessive, so I had to fall back.

"I knew she would've softened up. Noelle told me she spoke to her."

"That's wassup. Tell ya girl I said good looks," I told him. "Oh, shit. That reminds me, I need to holla at your sister, like now."

We both turned and walked off towards his cell. He was on the same pipeline as Trouble, which was perfect for business. We had direct contact with her.

Once inside his and Zaine's cell, he went ahead and popped the bowl, making sure to get all the water out. Placing the garbage bag over the toilet, he stuck the mic in and called out for Trouble. We sat there for a few minutes before she finally came in.

"Ayooo!" she yelled.

"Yo, sis," Touch spoke.

"Yeah, wassup?"

"Here go Man," he shortened my name.

"Ayo, Tee."

"Yeah, bro."

"I need you to put in for a sick call for tomorrow," I instructed her.

Trouble was already hip to how things operated, so it wasn't much that was needed to be said. The less we spoke through the bowl, the better. Wright was already told to send Dr. Gannon a message about seeing Trouble. Once he saw her request to see him, he'd accept and handle everything else.

"Ard, I got you."

"Aye, holla at Gia for me too. Once she with it, put her on," I added.

"Bet."

I jumped off the bowl and went about my business while she and Touch rapped to one another about family shit.

213

LATER IN THE EVENING, I laid back on my bunk, and thoughts of Keilani invaded my mind. When I was free of stressing, I caught myself always thinking about her. I wanted to know how her day was going, how she was feeling, what she was thinking, was she adjusting alright to the inside. Not many people were able to penetrate my thoughts the way she did, especially if it wasn't about making money. I took it as a sign that I should dig deeper and really see what's up with shorty.

I sat up and swung my legs around, landing my feet on the ground. Slipping into my Crocs, I exited out my cell and made my way to the computer room. I was barely on it all day, so I figure there should've been a message back from her, amongst other emails. When I logged on, I saw her name at the top.

Keilani: You most likely would've gotten some smoke back. And I'm good, thanks for asking. I wish a bitch would try me. I'm sweet as hell but deadly when necessary, so don't get on my wrong side.

I chucked at her message because I didn't know who she was trying to play tough with.

Me: I just want to see you stay sweet, keep that tough shit away. Let a nigga see you for real, for real, all of you. It's something about you, I just can't put my finger on it yet.

As usual, I wrote back who sent me messages; then, I went and made a quick call to my baby girl. It was getting late, and I knew her bedtime was approaching.

After speaking to Makaela for a few minutes, I went and hollered at Touch, who was on his line with Noelle.

"What's good, bro?" We dapped each other up.

"Shit, what you on, dickhead?" I asked.

"Fuckin' around with this girl. I was tryna get her folks and them to get out the room, so I could get some pussy, but them hoes cock blockin' like a muthafucker."

"Here you go nigga. Tell her stop playing and give the real box up, not that bowl shit."

"Soon, nigga, soon. Yo jawn was just in there too," he blurted out.

"Where she at now?" I inquired.

"Aye, baby, where Kei at?" he asked Noelle, then places his ear to the mic to hear her response.

"She on the rec yard getting air."

"In this cold weather?"

Touch shrugged and returned back to his conversation with his girl.

I walked over to one of my boys' cells and told him I had to check something out. Of course, he didn't ask me no questions; he gave me the green light. The way his room was, we could look down into the ladies rec yard during the night and see them at certain angles.

Looking through the slim rectangular window, I saw Keilani pacing the basketball court back and forth. I just stood there watching her, wondering what the hell was going through her mind to be doing what she was doing.

For another ten minutes, she paced, and I watched. I started to feel like a stalker or creep just preying on someone. Just when I was about to finally leave, she walked off and left out of the rec yard. I exited my boy's cell, returned to my own, and got ready for lockdown.

Why the fuck I can't shake this girl?

"PUT ON YOUR GREENS FROST, you got court," a guard informed me as he unlocked my cell.

It was no surprise about court that day, although Has didn't tell me the exact date. I kept strong on my prayers, and it was either going to be good news or some more bullshit. Either way, I was prepared for the worst and hoped for the best.

They had bagels for breakfast, something that was actually edible, so I grabbed a tray and munched on it before getting ready. I didn't even have time to check my email; they had already called me to go down to R&D.

Within two hours, I was across the street in the Marshal holding cell waiting for my time to go in front of the judge. I placed my utmost trust in my attorney to figure shit out and get me right. Most details of the case I wasn't aware of, only the important parts. Thoughts of my case made me angry because I really didn't do shit. I'd done a lot of shit like push weight, distribute, kill, and hurt people, but what they tried to get me for, I was truly innocent.

The night of my arrest...

"Yo bul crazy as fuck," I cracked.

I was tipsy as hell leaving a lounge with my guys and this jawn I was fooling around with. Inside was an ol' head who was drunk off his ass and was break dancing; the shit was hilarious.

"You better chill. Where you think Michael Jackson got his moves from?" my boy, Jig, joked.

"Aye, I ain't even fuckin' with you right now. Clownin' ass nigga. I'ma holla at y'all later." I dapped everyone up and walked to the driver's side of my Range Rover. Shorty hopped into the passenger side and got comfortable. I turned up the music and pulled off to my destination.

About ten minutes into the ride, I saw flashing lights behind me, followed by police sirens. "What the fuck they want?" I asked out loud to no one in particular.

I was calm and wasn't worried because I didn't have shit in the whip, not even my gun. A few cars back, I had my bodyguard, Teddy, following my every move. It was random stops like that one that made me start moving smarter. All they wanted was to catch me slippin' with a piece.

Pulling over, I placed the car in park and lowered the music as I waited for the law to approach my vehicle.

"Cut the engine. License and registration," the officer demanded in a harsh tone.

From the way he asked for my shit, I already knew what

type of timing he was on. I slowly reached in my armrest and pulled out my documents, then handed it over to him.

"What did you pull me over for?"

"You swerved a few times." He looked at me blankly.

"You sure?" I knew he was bullshitting.

"I'm positive."

Just as he was walking away, he back-peddled and looked at me and shorty.

"Is that marijuana I smell? Are you driving under the influence?" he asked.

"Sir, —"

"Step out of the vehicle," he ordered.

I know this nigga ain't serious, I thought.

They also had the jawn I was with to get out. We both leaned up against the hood of my truck. We were in a residential area at the time, but everyone was inside asleep, being as though it was three o'clock in the morning.

One officer started to search my truck while the other one stayed put in front of me, not allowing me to even look back. I felt confident as hell that they weren't going to find anything, though, so I had a smug look on my face. But it was quickly wiped away.

"Look what we have here," the officer boasted as he walked up with a medium-size duffle bag in his hand.

I'd never saw that bag a day in my life, so it was either one of my boys slipped up and put it in my truck, which was unlikely, or those goofy muthafuckers planted it there.

"That shit ain't mine," I gritted, as he pulled out five kilos of cocaine, resting it on the hood of my Range.

"So, whose is it? Hers?" They looked at shorty, who had a frightened facial expression. I wasn't worried about her talking because the bitch knew nothing.

One officer walked away and got on his phone out of earshot. He spoke to whoever was on the other end for a few minutes before coming back our way.

"The feds are coming," he told his partner while looking at me.

"Y'all got me fucked up. This some nut ass shit," I snapped.

"Wait, what's going on?" the jawn cried.

"Man, be quiet, that's all you need to do," I told her.

She quickly shut her mouth and leaned back on the truck.

The two white fuckers in front of me just kept talking shit; it went in one ear and out the other. A few more minutes had passed before two black SUVs had pulled up with federal agents hopping out.

"What we have here?" a husky white man asked. He looked to be in his early forties.

The cop passed him the bag they had of the drugs, and he observed the contents inside briefly. All the legal formalities were spoken, but half the shit they were saying, I wasn't listening to. But one thing caught my attention.

"Yeah, 'bout time this nigga got put down," one of the agents spoke with malice in his voice.

"What the fuck you just said?" I raised off the truck.

"You heard me."

"Nah, what you just called me?"

"What? Nigga?"

My ears burned at the sound of that word falling from the lips of a white man. I lost all control I had in that moment and snapped. I landed one good blow to his face, breaking his nose in one hit. I quickly sent another blow to his eye, fucking up his eye socket.

By the time the other officers were trying to restrain me, I had my arms around his throat, squeezing tight. I was already livid I was put in a fucked-up position, one that I didn't do myself. If I was going down, I was going to go down for a good reason and without a fight.

Bang! Bang!

"You've set a motion to dismiss the charges. On what grounds, counselor?" the judge asked.

The sound of the gavel and the judge's voice brought me back to my reality. I looked around the courtroom and everyone occupying it and still felt alone. My family was in attendance, including my daughter, but not any of my friends or workers.

We had a rule to stay far away when someone was indicted or into it with the law. We didn't need everyone getting wrapped up in things and having eyes on them. They still played a valuable part of my operation on the streets, and that I was grateful for.

"Yeah, I can't wait to hear this," I overheard the U.S. attorney mumble under his breath.

"At this time, I'd like you to focus your attention on exhibit A. Here is a camera footage of the night my client was pulled over for an apparent traffic stop. Watch closely at the encounter," my lawyer stated.

We all watched the footage closely and, when we saw the officer go in his car, grabbed a bag, then place it in mine, the courtroom went into an uproar. I sat back in my seat and felt the most at peace than I ever had before.

Bang! Bang! Bang!

The gavel came crashing down repeatedly.

"Both of you, approach, now," the judge snapped.

My lawyer and the U.S. attorney both went and approached him. I couldn't hear what was being said, but I had a pretty good idea what it was.

From the moment I was locked up, my lawyer continuously fought hard to get all evidence, but kept getting the runaround. That night, the officers didn't have on their body cams or their dash camera, which made all the sense. I knew it was a setup, but it was hard proving that at the time.

Moments later, my lawyer walked back to me with a smirk on his face, which told me things were working in our favor. I couldn't believe I was about to be a free man.

"I have no other choice but to dismiss the charges. Motion granted," the judge stated in an irritated tone.

"Your Honor, we request that the assault charges stay. Yes,

this has all been a complete mess, but he did severely injure a federal agent, knowing he was one," the U.S. attorney pushed.

"If your agents didn't set him up, he wouldn't have been in the position to do such a thing," my lawyer retorted.

Bang! Bang!

"That's enough!" the judge yelled. "The possession and intent to distribute charge will be dropped. Mr. Frost, you will still be charged with assault on a federal officer. Counsel, be sure to file with the court your client's plea. This matter is adjourned."

Bang!

"Let me sort out some things and I'll be in to see you," Hash told me as the court officer came to take me back to the holding cell.

Before walking off, I turned around to see my moms smiling while holding onto Makaela's hand.

"I love you, daddy," she sang.

"I love you more, baby." I blew her a kiss.

The officer led me out of the courtroom, but I felt much more confident about everything than I did walking in it.

CHAPTER SEVENTEEN

KEI

𝓜anic: I'm sending something your way. Look out for it.

I logged on to the computer and saw that short message

from Manic. Putting two and two together, I figured he was talking about a kite. So, when I got to work, I told the girls in the dish room to look out for something for me.

We spoke through the bowl the night before; he had given me some good news but didn't want to speak too much on it. He informed me his case was looking great. I couldn't have been happier for him. I didn't wish jail or prison on my worst enemy. Besides, Manic was growing on me fast. The way we vibed off only a few conversations, I knew we would hit it off, whether it would be as friends or lovers.

"Kei, I think she wants you," Bell informed me, as I was stirring the food.

I was back on the cook side helping out again when Bell noticed one of the dish room workers was trying to get my attention. Automatically, I knew what she wanted. I dropped the large paddle that we used as a spoon to stir and discreetly went over to her. When I passed by her, she handed off the letter and I slipped into the bathroom. I was eager to read it, so I quickly locked the door and unfolded the taped letter.

It read:

Wassup with you? Hopefully, everything good. As for me, I'm great. I went to court yesterday and the main charges were dropped. I'm still fighting this other bullshit charge, but it won't hold any weight or crazy sentence. I won't be surprised if I get out soon. Besides my boy Touch, only you know about this. Keep it between us. I don't like people in my business. Too many hating goofy ass niggas.

I told you because I got the vibe I could trust you. A nigga wants to still get to know you no matter if I'm here now or gone tomorrow. You can kind of say I'm low-key invested. I read you from the moment I laid eyes on you, but I just want to make sure I read you correctly. Talk to you in a minute.

-M.A.

I blushed and smiled the entire time I read the letter. Folding it back up, I secured it in my sports bra and headed back outside to finish work. That day, Manic wasn't the only person to make me smile. Williams did as well. He offered to switch me to the cook side permanently, and I happily accepted. It was more work, especially since we had to cook for over a thousand people, but it was right up my alley.

When I returned to the unit after work, I raced to the computer to check my messages. I saw I had one from Manic and beamed.

Manic: I hope your day is going well, beautiful. When you get settled in from work, make sure and call for me. I'll be waiting.

"Damn, what got you smiling for damn hard?" Lena asked, walking into the computer room.

I motioned for her to read the message Manic sent me, and she started smiling her damn self as if the email was for her.

"Okayyy, I see you," she sang.

I waved her off as I blushed and returned to looking at my emails. There was one from my mother, so I clicked on it next.

Queen: I sent in all the forms for your brothers and me. Can't wait to see you. Love you, Princess.

No matter how old I got, my mother always called me Princess, and I called her Queen. Certain things just didn't change, no matter how much time had gone by.

I replied to her and the other emails, then went and got myself cleaned up. Only one thing was on my mind, that was talking to Manic's fine ass.

"Push it like this," Zaara instructed as she showed me how to pop the bowl open.

I stood there looking at her with wide eyes. Anytime I saw them talking on the bowl, it was already set up. That was the first time I witnessed how the process was to get the water out.

After I got dressed, I went and told Noelle what Manic said. Not to my surprise, she already knew he was expecting me to come holler at him. He had access to my line so, after I asked Tamara if it was cool to talk to him, out of respect, Zaara came to assist me.

"Use this bottle to suck the rest of the water out and just pour it in the sink. And you're all set." She stood to her feet.

"How am I supposed to talk to him?" I quizzed.

"Oh, right. We gon' have to make you a mic, but for now, I have one you can use." She left out the cell quickly.

A minute later, she came back with the mic broken into two hidden under her clothes. She stuck the mic in the bowl and started yelling.

"Five-south!" she hollered.

Seconds later, someone came on and yelled back.

"Get Manic for me."

We waited about three minutes and then heard his voice boom through the bowl. A mic wasn't needed to hear him.

"Ayooo!" he yelled.

"Well, have fun." She passed me the mic and disappeared out of the cell, leaving me alone with the person who made my heart race in the bowl.

"Heyyy," I sang, instantly regretting I did that. I covered my mouth with my hand in a childlike way. *Eeew, I know I sounded crazy*, I thought.

"Wassup with you? You good?" he asked.

"Yeah, you good?" I retorted.

"I'm always good. How was work?"

"Good, I'm a cook now," I revealed.

"Ah, shit. We really finna die now," he joked.

"Ohhh, that's crazy. You gon do me like that?"

"You just better know how to cook, man."

"And that I do know how to do," I assured him.

"Ard, then, we gon' see. Aye, you know a young bul named Kadir?"

"From Chester?" I quizzed.

"Yeah."

"Yeah, I do. How you know him?"

Kadir was my little brothers' close friend. He was like my little brother himself. They all played basketball together and did teenage shit like go out and fool around with girls.

"That's my nephew. He told me about you and your family," he exclaimed.

What a small fucking world. My eyes got wide at his revelation.

"Seriously?"

"Mmmhmm. He told me you are a hot commodity. All the niggas be on yo ass."

"Oh, my God. What else he said?" I needed to know.

"He told me you get the bag, you fly as shit, and got a lot going for yourself. You just graduated college?"

Damn, Kadir told it all.

"Yeah, I did. Two days before I came in."

"Oh, so you a smart jawn. I like that."

Manic and I spoke for the remainder of the night. I didn't move from the bowl at all, not even to check my email. Our conversation bounced around to different topics, flowing endlessly, and didn't feel forced at all. Our chemistry and connection were undeniable. It was crazy it took for us to be incarcerated to meet when we roamed the same streets.

I knew niggas loved to talk that sweet jail talk when they were locked up, but I didn't get that vibe from Manic. Since he told me about his charges being dismissed, I really didn't see why he would sit around and want to talk to me. From what I got from his letter, he wasn't expecting a long time, so a pen pal wasn't needed. Only time was going to tell his true intentions. Until then, I decided to just let things flow and enjoy things.

A WEEK LATER...

"Happy birthday to you, happy birthday to you..." the girls walked in my cell and sang.

The whole crew, including Trouble, was present and singing while holding three cakes they'd made for me. Everyone seemed so sincere to wish me a happy birthday. It was my twenty-fourth birthday and, while I was upset that I was spending it behind the walls of FDC Philly, I was grateful I still had life.

"Make a wish," Sherrell said in her thick Jamaican accent.

It was no candle or anything on the cake but some pudding used as icing. I walked up and blew on all three cakes, and the girls erupted in cheers.

"This is from us and from Manic," Noelle stated with a big smile plastered on her face.

Manic? I asked myself. I never recalled telling him my birthday, nor the girls. While I was appreciative, I was completely surprised.

Zaara popped my bowl and sucked the water out. I thought she was about to talk to her dude, since we all used one another bowls. But when she asked the person who was on for Manic, my head snapped in her direction.

"Yooo," I heard his voice travel down to us.

"She right here," Zaara told him, then handed me the mic.

Everyone started to leave out the cell one by one.

"We're out here waiting for you when you're finished," Lena spoke before shutting the door.

"Hey love," I greeted him.

"Happy Birthday, gorgeous."

I blushed at his voice and even more after finding out he was behind what the girls did. "Thank you. I appreciate what you did, but how did you even know it was my birthday?" I wondered.

"I make it my duty to know things about anyone I encounter and everything about someone I'm interested in."

It was like Manic had all the right answers when a question was thrown at him. He would never answer straightforward, but if you paid close attention, you'd figure it out.

"Mmm, okay. Thank you again. You're too sweet. You didn't have to."

"I know, but I did. Just wanted you to feel the love on your special day, even though you in this nut ass place," he expressed.

The fact he went out his way to find out my birthday and do something for it showed me what kind of man he was.

Small gestures always won me over. I was never the type to be hooked on material shit, trips, money, or none of that. Granted, it was all lovely and I didn't decline those things, but the simple things were what moved me.

"Yeah, true. I just wish I could see my family. I'm still waiting for them to get approved to visit."

"It'll be soon."

"Praying it is."

We talked a little longer before he let me chill with the girls. I was off that day from work, so I balanced my time between Manic, the crew, and hopping on and off the computer and phone. It wasn't the ideal birthday, but everyone played their part in making it a good one under the circumstances.

The best birthday gift was when I received mail and it was an approval letter for my family to come visit. *God works in mysterious ways*, I thought as I read the paper. Earlier in the day, I expressed to Manic how much I wanted to see them, then turned around and got what I prayed for.

MONDAY CAME AROUND, and it was the day my mother and brothers were visiting. I washed my hair and got it flat ironed. My uniform was ironed neatly, and I put on light make-up. Once dressed, I sat at one of the tables in the dayroom, patiently waiting for them to call my name to go down to the visiting room. I was already alerted that they were in the building.

Keeping my eyes trained on the door and then my watch, my legs shook from excitement and my anxiety rose through the roof. When the bell to the unit sounded, my legs stopped as my eyes darted to see who it was.

"Milan!" a woman CO called out to me.

The guard in the booth popped his head out and motioned for me to go to her. When I reached the door, I saw the woman had on a white shirt, which meant she was a lieutenant. Her shirt read Grace.

"You ready?" she asked.

I nodded and followed her out of the unit and onto the elevator. We took it down to the first floor. When the door opened, another female CO was standing in the doorway of a room. We entered the room, and I was handed off to her while LT Grace proceeded through the room and exited through another door.

"Stand right here and get undressed," the officer instructed me.

I slipped my body in between the brick cubicles and took my clothes off. I left on my underwear and sports bra but was told to take those off as well.

"Turn around, squat, and cough," she ordered as she searched my clothes.

I turned and did what I was told, feeling humiliated.

"Get dressed." She placed my clothes on the top of the brick wall.

You're getting to see your family. Just chill the fuck out, I told myself.

Once I was dressed again, I ran my fingers through my hair and followed the officer to the same door LT Grace went through. When she opened it, allowing me to pass through, my eyes landed on my mother right away, holding my nephew. My heart skipped a beat as I speed-walked over to them.

"Mommy," I cried as I embraced her and the baby.

"How are you?" She pulled back and started to observe me.

"I'm okay." The tears started to flow down uncontrollably.

I knew I was going to get emotional seeing them for the first time, but the shit hit differently when I physically got that hug from her. Her touch calmed me. It made me feel like everything was going to be alright.

"Where's his dad?" I asked, referring to my brother.

"They wouldn't let him in because of the color he's wearing. It's certain colors we can't wear. He sends his love though and said he'll come see you next week," she explained.

I felt cheated not being able to see my brother, especially since he was the only person other than my mom that could see me. The other twin was away at college and my older brother had to get special permission to come and see me since he was on probation.

"That's bullshit. But I guess I have you." I took my nephew in my arms and kissed him on his head.

"How are you? How are things?" my mom asked. "Wait, before you start, let me get you some stuff from the machines." She held up a Ziploc bag with quarters.

While I played with KJ, she went and bought me a ton of shit to eat, snack on, and drink. It was junk but a whole different ball game from the shit we were fed or able to access on commissary.

When she returned, we picked up where we left off regarding her questions. I broke down everything to her, not holding anything back. My mother was a person I learned to open up to while I was a teenager. At a point, it was hard to speak to her, but as we both grew and matured, we built an amazing relationship.

"Wow, you're really strong, Lani. I don't know what the hell I would've been doing if I was in your shoes," she commended.

"I didn't know either until I was in this position. I guess people don't know what they're capable of until their backs are against the wall and have no other choice but to deal with things."

"Yeah, I can see that."

"How are th—"

Oh, my fucking God, I thought as my stomach felt like I was going down on a rollercoaster ride. My words were cut short as my whole focus shifted from my moms to the most striking man I'd ever laid eyes on. The way he swaggered his way across the visiting room floor had my heart beating with every step.

Our eyes connected and never left one another's until he was placed in a room with a glass window. Inside was a man in a suit, whom I assumed was his lawyer.

"Lani!" my mother called out to me, snapping me out of my trance.

"Who's that? You know him?"

I nodded and started blushing.

"Okay, who is he?" she pried.

"His name is Mahki, but goes by Manic," I started.

I gave my mother the whole run down and, to my surprise, she loved the whole idea of Manic and me talking. Once I felt she was truly sincere about it, I decided then and there I was going to give him an honest chance at whatever it was we were doing. I just prayed I didn't fall too hard or fast and get my heart broken. I was already trying to get over Brix, which Manic was the perfect distraction.

The entire visit, Manic and I kept stealing peeks at one another like teenagers. My mother caught us a few times, so I knew other people who were watching us saw as well. I didn't give a fuck, though; he was so captivating, I couldn't keep my eyes off him.

"How was your visit?" Noelle asked excitedly.

I had just walked out of my cell after they conducted count. After my visit, I returned to the unit, showered, and went to take a nap.

"It was great. I can't wait until next week for another one." I beamed, still coming off a high of being around my moms and seeing Manic. "And I got to see Manic. He had a legal visit."

"Oh, you had one hell of a day. Yesss," she sang, snapping her fingers. "I'm happy for you, boo."

"Thank you." I smiled. "I'm finna check this computer. I'll come see you afterwards."

"Okay."

Walking in the computer room, I saw Lena's face buried in the screen and her finger moving a hundred miles per hour. I sat next to her and logged on; I saw I received an email from Manic.

Manic: You're fuckin' gorgeous. I hope you know that. Don't let no one tell you any different.

That was the shortest and deepest message I'd gotten in a while. I heard him saying it in his baritone voice.

I replied with a simple message as well.

Me: And you're fuckin' handsome. I hope I was the only female to tell you this today, though.

As I hit the send button, I heard a loud commotion outside the computer room. A new girl walked in, and everyone rushed her with open arms. From observation, she had to had been at the facility before.

"Oh, shit," Lena said above a whisper.

"What happen? Who is that?" I inquired.

She looked at me with a worried look.

"That's Briana."

"Okay, who's she?"

Lena looked like she didn't want to answer, but she knew I'd keep pressing her.

"Manic's old bitch."

My heart dropped in the pit of my stomach as I gazed in the girl's direction.

CHAPTER EIGHTEEN

MANIC

*A*fter Kei told me her folks were coming to see her, I hopped into action and got on the line with my lawyer. He wasn't ready to see me just yet, but I told him what

I needed him for and that he was being paid. Without hesitation, he pulled up on perfect timing and requested a legal visit.

The way they set shit up, legal visits were any day during the week, even when the women had their visits. I saw it as the perfect opportunity for me to see Kei and peep how she interacted with her family. The way someone dealt with their loved ones said a lot.

When I found out our families were close and connected, I felt an automatic obligation to make sure she was good at all times. All the other females went to the back of my head while she held the forefront. I was a true believer in everything happened for a reason, and there was a reason God made us cross paths.

"Aye, bro." Touch rushed in my cell looking bewildered.

"Fuck wrong with you?" I looked him up and down.

"You wouldn't believe it."

"What dickhead?"

"Bri back," he exclaimed.

"Stop bullshitting me."

He shot me a serious facial expression, letting me know he wasn't fooling around.

Briana was my old flame. She was the one other person I actually fucked besides Grace. Bri also held shit down with Trouble in the women's unit for me. That was my muthafuckin' bitch, but I didn't like all of her ways. I saw what she was good for and used her for it. Once she was sentenced, they shipped her ass to a women's prison in West Virginia.

"Trouble just came through and told me," he confirmed.

I dropped my head and ran my hands to the back of my neck as I took a deep breath in and let it out. Bri was one of those ghetto, loudmouth, and shit talkers. With Keilani and I building, I wasn't sure what the fuck was about to transpire. Plus, all those bitches that fuck with Keilani were all Bri's friends. My gut was telling me some nut shit was about to happen.

"Where Kei?" I asked, knowing Touch already inquired.

"She's with Lena. Noelle and the other joe bitches all in Bri face."

Just like I thought, I said to myself.

"Five-south!" we heard a female voice yell through the bowl.

I usually had my line open when I was just chilling in my cell. Some of my guys would pop in and holler at me about business, so I tried to stay accessible.

"Who this?" Touch asked.

"Bri."

"What Bri?" He tried to act oblivious to what was going on.

"Briana, nigga. Where's Manic?"

Touch looked at me to see what I wanted him to say. Ignoring her would've only caused her to act stupid and keep blowing up my line. Bri was the type of person who wouldn't stop until she got what she wanted or if someone stopped her.

I got up from my bed and walked over to the bowl. Taking

the mic from Touch, I dropped my shoulders and said a silent prayer the conversation didn't go left or fuck things up with me and Kei.

"Yooo!" I called out.

"Hi, baby," she sang happily.

I cringed at her calling me that. Clearing my throat, I thought carefully about how to respond. The girls could've had Kei listening on some spiteful shit.

"Chill with all lat, wassup with you, though? You good?"

"Wow, it's like that?"

"Man, how you?" I pushed, trying to keep the conversation platonic.

"I'm cool. I'm back on a quick writ. I go to court in a few days, then I'll be going back," she informed me.

"Oh ard. I hope everything works on for you. Stay outta trouble while you here," I made sure to add in.

"Don't I always behave, daddy?"

Fuck no, I thought.

"I'ma holla at you, Bri."

Before she could get another word out, I pulled the mic and the garbage bag out, then flushed the toilet in one swift motion.

The following morning, I jumped on the computer to see if Kei responded to my message I sent her the day before. I wanted to test her temperature to see if anything had happened since Bri came back.

Kei: I know you'll receive this message the next day, so good morning. I'm good, I've just been chilling with my ol' heads. The girls been all hell bent over the jawn that just came back to our neck of the woods. I won't lie, the vibe has been off, so I'm just going to keep my distance. I don't have time for the drama.

I shook my head as I read her message because just like I predicted, everything was coming through. My whole concern was Bri didn't do no bullshit while she was here. She literally was only in the building for a few days, but it only took her a short amount of time to stir some shit up and leave.

Instead of emailing her back what I really wanted to say, I told her to look out for something. What I wanted to tell her was personal, and I needed her to feel me. Writing a letter would do just that.

I wrote:

Kei,

Wassup, love. I hope this letter reaches you in good spirits. I'm good on my end, maintaining, not complaining. Yo, on some real shit, I fuck with you heavy. It's like our conversations be it for me. I really be into them bidding and laughing. Nothing feels forced between us and that's a good ass feeling.

Listen, don't listen or feed into any of that bull-shit down there. Don't bring no negative vibes around *us, real shit. It's evident I picked where I want to be, so none of that other shit should bother you. You gotta learn how to let shit roll off your back because if those bitches see they getting to you, they'll continue until they destroy your peace and what we trying to build.*

You gotta learn how to separate the two types of niggas; the niggas that's serious and the niggas that's just bidding. Me, personally, I don't got no bid to be bidding. So, me feeding you some jail talk is a waste of me and your time, and I don't know about you, but I value my time, Kei. Life's too short to waste time. With that being said, I just hope you're as serious as I am.

P.S. enclosed are some pictures of me for your keepsake. My sister went on your IG like you said and got some of your pictures off it. She sent me in some, they should get to me any day now.

I folded the pictures in the letter and used the labels we used to send out mail to seal everything. Handing it over to the kitchen orderly, he placed it on one of the empty trays and slid it into the cart. She would get it when she went to work.

I hope she takes heed, I thought to myself.

Just as I was heading back to my cell, the bell to our unit went off. I turned to see who it was and in walked LT Grace. I barely spoke to her since she caught me getting my shit sucked from Ms. Ellis.

"Frost!" she called out, knowing not to call me by my nickname because I'd be hot.

I about face and went up to her. "Wassup?" I asked.

"Your little girlfriend is back in the building, but I'm pretty sure you knew that," she spoke sarcastically.

Grace hated Briana. She felt she shouldn't have had to share me with anyone. At the time, I was fucking both of them; I didn't give a fuck.

"That's not my girl. Chill with all that shit. You drawn."

"Mmmhmm, whatever you say. Don't do no stupid shit," she warned.

If it was one thing she didn't have to worry about, it was me trying to get at Bri and trying to fuck. "You got it." I nodded and walked away, letting her feel like she did something.

"And I saw you eyeing that girl in the visiting room. Let's not go there," her voice rolled off my back.

Instead of turning around to respond, I continued to walk away. I couldn't feed into her and let her know I did have a thing with Kei. All Grace would do was wreak havoc for sure.

Bitches man, I shook my head.

BEFORE OPENING up the bowl to talk to Kei, I wanted to get a response from the letter I sent her. Depending on what she wrote back, I'd know where her head was at and how to move.

I went to hop on the computer to check if she wrote back and saw she did.

Kei: M.A. I will never allow another person to stir my judgement or what I want to do. I'm a grown woman and I do what the fuck I want. While it has been a lot of tension in the hood, I try my best to not pay anything any mind. I just see people for who they are. I can't be mad though, their loyalty is to her, just like I thought yours was, but after receiving your letter, I assumed wrong.

Everything you've said made perfect sense about the two different types of niggas. Thank you for clarifying what your intentions are and what you want. It's no worse feeling than being led on to be dropped like a piece of shit.

As for me, I'm here and fucking with you. I'll be going home to the streets to see you and not these bitches. Shit, we're locked in by default. We're good, love.

Kei's message made a nigga smile. She was not only catching onto shit fast, but she was also a real one overall. I definitely saw myself dealing with her in the long run.

As I was getting ready to write her back, CO Tans knocked on the window of the computer room and waved a stack of mail in the air. Leaving my computer unlocked, I jogged out of the room, made sure to tell the niggas on line that I wasn't finished, grabbed my mail, and returned to the computer.

Quickly browsing through my mail, I saw it was an envelope from Pulse Check, a prison communications company that sends in letters, photos, postcards, and greeting cards into inmates from their loved ones. Knowing it was Kei's pictures, I slid the contents out of the envelope straight away.

God damn, I thought as I looked through Kei's pictures. Shorty was stunning as fuck. She was one of those women that would make the entire room stop what they were doing as she walked in, just to gawk at her. Kei had a sophisticated way about her but let off a little that she was a freak. Her body was nice, and her swag was on point. *I knew I saw a dope bitch when I first looked at her*, I told myself.

Looking at the computer screen, I saw I had ten minutes left in my messages, so I started to type out something to send back to her.

Me: Those pictures we spoke on? I got them. Kadir was right about everything he said. I couldn't help but to think about every position I want to have you in. Sorry, if I'm too forward, but there's no future in fronting. I just want to fuck you real good, physically, mentally, emotionally, and spiritually. I wanna be the one to make you smile, the one to spoil you. You gon' let me be that, Kei?

CHAPTER NINETEEN

KEI

 ou play entirely too much. Get off my line," I joked with Manic.

I couldn't stop laughing to the point I felt tears welling in my eyes. Manic was funny as hell, and I couldn't have thought that from his reputation or just looking at him.

We'd been inseparable for weeks after we basically made it official that we were fucking with each other. The whole situation with the Briana chick only lasted temporarily. As fast as she came, she left the following week. Manic stood ten toes and didn't entertain her, no matter how many times she called for him.

Noelle and the crew, except for Sherrell, showed their true colors. I was only a part of them when they decided. Granted, I knew they knew Briana before they knew I even existed, but it was a way they could've stayed neutral. I wasn't tripping though; I kept to myself and only dealt with my ol' heads, Lena, Tamara, and Stacey, someone who came into the facility right after Briana left. We met due to me going down to R&B to help take out her weave.

Manic made it clear a million times that I didn't need them and I needed to stay away. Everyone may seem nice and sweet, but in this place, ninety percent of the time, they all had ulterior motives.

"Man, stop playing with me. You know I ain't going nowhere," he shot back.

"I know, baby," I giggled like a schoolgirl.

Things between us were great. He made me forget where I was and how much time I even had to do. He was the perfect escape from everything. Our conversations were funny, deep, emotional, motivating, and more. He always dropped game on me about a lot of shit. I prayed for him while he prayed for me, and we made it our duty to pray together. It was nothing like a God-fearing man.

"I sent you some shit on the computer. I need you to go read it and respond. It should be there by now. I sent it first thing this morning," he informed me.

It was my day off of work, so it meant I was in the bowl talking to him all day. My days started to consist of waking up, checking emails, handling hygiene, talking to Manic before work, work, come back to the unit, check emails, make calls, shower, and talk to Manic until it was lock down. He wanted me to move on the same pipeline with him, so we could've talked all night and whenever we wanted, but I told him I couldn't leave my ol' head, Tamara. She was like a mom to me and we had a good thing going. If it wasn't with Lena, which was my other mama love, I didn't want to bunk with anyone else.

"Okay bae, I'm finna go check now. I'll be back." I stood to my feet.

Leaving out my cell, I saw Gia and Kali sitting at a table where I had to pass. I glanced at them, then refocused my attention on where I was going. Stepping into the computer room, I logged on and saw Manic's message at the top.

Manic: Picture me walking in the house and I come in

the room to catch you playing with your pussy, with your eyes closed, in the middle of the bed. I stand there and watch you for a minute before I suck my teeth. You open your eyes and look at me with eyes full of lust. I stand there and watch as you take your finger out of your pussy and put them slowly in your mouth. I slowly unbuckle my belt and release my dick. You continue to play in your wetness as my dick jumps with anticipation.

I walk to the side of the bed and you lean over to slowly stroke my dick while looking me in the eye. You remove your hand and spit on my tool, then slurp it down with no hands. I stare down at you with hooded eyes as you go down on my dick until you gag. You pull back off me and suck on the head real hard, causing it to pop out of your mouth with a loud popping noise.

I tell you to turn around and I smack my wet dick all between your cheeks. You look back and start to wiggle your ass. Inserting the head of my dick to your opening, I ram full force, making you yelp and run. I grab you and start long dicking you as you whimper and moan.

"Who pussy is this?" I ask you.

"Yours daddy," you cry back.

I call you all types of nasty bitches and stick my thump in your ass. You start to buck back on my dick. I'm moaning, "Yes, give that pussy to daddy."

My phone starts to ring. I jump out of the pussy and go bust my traps. Lol, my twenty minutes up, your turn.

Whew, lord. What is this nigga trying to do to me in here?
I thought as I finished reading his email. I felt between my
legs becoming warm and moist with a little tingle. It was my
turn to finish the story.

Me: Continuation…

**When you made an attempt to leave the house, I
followed you to the door in my robe giving you the sad
face. I was in need of you. I begged, grabbed your hand
before you opened the door and grabbed your dick. You
tried to push me away until I took your hand and placed it
between my legs. I whispered in your ears, "Can I take a
ride with you?" You smirked and told me to hurry up and
throw some clothes on.**

**Within minutes, I was running back downstairs in a
sundress with no panties on. When we reached outside,
you told your young boys to drive behind you because I
was riding with you. On the way to our destination, I
pulled out your dick and took all of you in my mouth. I
bobbed my head up and down. You swerved a few times,
letting me know it was good. After some time, I felt you
pulsate and shoot your load in the back of my throat. I
wasn't finished with you yet though.**

**I sat back in my seat and played with myself for you to
see, making your dick stand right back up at attention. I
kept rubbing my clit and licking my fingers after. We
pulled up at the spot and you called your young'ns to tell
them handle whatever it was y'all had to do. Once I saw**

they was leaving out of the car, I slid onto your lap and, in one swift motion, your dick was inside of me. I straddled you, gripping the back of your neck as you grabbed my hips and thrusted your way deeper in me. I tossed my head back, feeling the pain and pleasure you were giving me. I felt sparks run through my body when I was about to reach my peak.

Your phone rang, and they told you things were completed, but you told them to hold on for one minute. Holding me tight to your chest, where I couldn't move, you rammed your way in and out of me until you finally exploded deep inside of me. We kissed deeply and looked into one another's eyes intensely.

When I slid back onto the passenger seat, you received a text from you young boys. You showed me the message which read, "You really that nigga." Kissing me on my forehead then my lips, you said, "Good job, baby girl." (I was smirking writing this whole vision, lmao) (Smirk).

I hit the sent button with two minutes left in my email session. Gathering my thoughts, I left out the computer room and returned to my cell.

"Bae?" I hollered into the mic.

A few moments later, he came to the line.

"Yoo," he answered.

"I read it and wrote you back, but I'm feeling some kind of way."

"What you mean?"

I thought about what was going to come out of my mouth next. After all the nasty flirting we had done and then starting a sex thread, I saw no reason to hold back.

"I'm tryna slide down on your dick," I let blurt out of my mouth, then quickly covered my mouth and giggled.

"Oh yeah? Then slide down on this shit then," he responded.

Hearing him say those words only made me hornier. I wanted Manic in the worst way at that point. He found not only a way to penetrate my mind but also my heart. When someone could do those things and nothing physical happened, it was a definite sign things were meant to be. I felt like he was made for me.

"Bae, stop," I whined.

"I ain't even playing. Go put the sign up on your door and come back," he instructed.

When we used the bathroom or were changing our clothes, we had a paper with a small magnet that covered the window. That way, people knew not to come in, including the CO.

I got up and did what he said, then quickly returned to the bowl. "I'm back, baby," I told him.

"Ard, now, put your hand in your panty."

"Mmmhmm."

"Play with your clit and envision my tongue toying with it."

"Okay," I moaned.

"Now, insert a finger in your pussy and fuck yourself with thoughts of me penetrating you."

"Yes, baby."

"How that shit feel?"

"Good," I whimpered, grinding against my hand.

"Now, put another finger in." I did as he said. "You taking all this dick?"

"Yes, daddy," I moaned.

"Mmm, yeah, this pussy real good," he groaned.

"Fuck me, Manic."

"Take this shit, don't run."

"Ughhh," I moaned as I finger fucked myself with thoughts of him hitting it from the back. "Baby, don't stop."

"Who pussy is this?"

"Yours daddy, yours."

We went on for a few minutes until I reached my peak, and he came on his boy's cell floor.

"Aye, take that panty off and send it to me," he randomly requested.

"You serious?" my eyes grew wide.

"I'm dead ass. Send it on the cart. Make sure it's wrapped good, I want to smell you."

If it was any other person, I probably would've thought he was crazy, but that shit coming from him only made me fall for him more.

"Okay, bae. I got you. Let me go put it up and take a shower."

"Ard, me too."

I grabbed my shower bag and things, then headed out my cell to hop in the shower.

While the hot water cascaded down my body, I touched myself as I thought about Manic. It was scary how we'd bonded so tight and so fast. At times, I thought about slowing down or even falling back just a little, but my heart wouldn't let me, nor would Manic. I knew our journey behind the walls was temporary, but I couldn't wait to be free and next to him to do as I pleased.

Finishing off my shower, I dried my skin and pulled my nightgown over my head before stepping out of the shower. When I turned to walk into my cell, I saw my door was open, but Tamara was sitting at the table she usually sat at. Walking inside, I saw the CO was shaking our cell down.

"You finished yet? I would like to change," I stated in an irritated tone.

The CO on duty name was Jones. What I got from the girls was, he was a recent hire and loved to overly do his job.

"I'll take this," he ridiculed, grabbing my mic. "Stay off the bowl. This is a warning." He walked out of my cell.

I closed the door shut and leaned against the wall. My heart rate sped up because I didn't want any of the officers to know I was in the bowl at all. They tended to harass those people more. I cursed myself for leaving the mic out in the open while I went to the shower, instead of breaking it down into pieces and hiding them in varies places in the room. *What's done is done. I'll just make a new one*, I thought.

THE DAY WENT ON AND, of course, I kept my face in the bowl talking to Manic. I borrowed a mic from someone until I collected enough soda bottles or creamer containers to make a new mic.

"Milan!" I heard my name being called on the guard's speaker.

"Hold on bae, they calling me," I told Manic.

When I went to go see what the guard wanted, I was told to put on my tan uniform; I was going to the lieutenant's office. Automatically, my mind started racing miles per hour, trying to figure out why I was needed there.

I told Manic what they wanted and that I'd be right back. Dressed and walking out of my cell, I saw a guard at the door waiting for me. We made our way downstairs to the LT's office, and I saw the same woman lieutenant from the day of my visit sitting behind the desk.

"Milan?" she asked.

"Yes. What's this about?" I wondered.

"You got a shot," she revealed.

"A what?"

"An incident report. The guard on duty retrieved a mic

used to speak through the toilet bowl to the male inmates in your cell." She raised her brow.

I didn't respond. I just looked at her. She continued by reading out the report, then told me my counselor would be the one to hand out the disciplinary decision. As I was leaving out of the office, she stopped me.

"If I were you, I'd leave whoever it is you're talking to alone. Those men are nothing but trouble," she advised as she handed me a copy of the shot.

It wasn't what she said, it was how she said it that made me feel like she was being smart.

"Lucky thing you're not me," I stated and walked out.

The CO took me back up to the unit where I went straight to the bowl to tell Manic what happened. He went on to ask me who was the CO that shook me down and who was the serving lieutenant. He told me to be careful around them and try to stay far away. I made a mental note, and we carried on with our usual conversations.

THE NEXT DAY, before I left off the unit to go to work, Ms. Walsh called me to her office. I already knew what it was pertaining to since LT Grace told me the previous evening I had to deal with my counselor.

"Good morning," I greeted her, trying to be nice, so she went easy on me.

Lena told me for shots like the one I received, they usually took commissary for a short period of time. I had shit in my locker, but I had planned on shopping for the next mainline.

"Good morning, Ms. Milan. Have a seat," she motioned for me to sit. "I have an incident report here for you. I'm sure you already know that, though. After reading over it, I decided to take your commissary for two weeks only. Don't let it happen again," she spoke sternly.

While I was happy it wasn't a wicked punishment, I was still upset at the fact I received one. I wanted to have a clean slate, but that was obviously out the window.

"Yes, ma'am," I simply answered. "Is that all?"

"Yes."

I got up from my seat and left out the office. By the time I reached the bottom tier, the bell rang and Williams appeared by the door to take us to work. I rushed to my cell, grabbed the small baggie that my medication once occupied, which had my panty inside and Manic's initials, M.A., on it, and tucked it in my underwear.

"Milan, let's go!" I heard Williams yell.

I hurriedly left out my cell and made my way to him. He took us downstairs and had us jump right into work.

Things were a little different that day. Instead of me receiving something from the dish room workers, I had to give something to the line workers to put onto a tray. After asking Bell about a few of the line workers, I found someone who I thought I could trust to get it on there for me discreetly.

The entire time I was working, I kept my eyes on her to see if she was able to place and secure the bag. After several attempts, she finally got it onto a tray and, when I saw the CO close the door to the cart and lock it, my anxiety settled.

For all this, he better lick my shit, I thought.

CHAPTER TWENTY

U.S Department of Justice
Federal Bureau of Prisons

90056-066

FROST
MAKHI

Eye: GR   Ht: 6'03"

INMATE

Vending

MANIC

hen Keilani told me who the officer was that shook her cell down and wrote her the shot, I figured it was just him being on his best bullshit. But when she mentioned Grace was the serving lieutenant and what she told her, my mind started to wonder if Grace and Jones were in on shit together. With the kind of shit I experienced in life, I was always paranoid and thought the wildest shit, but most of the time, I turned out to be right.

"Yo, I just grabbed this from the kitchen for you," Touch walked in my cell and stated.

He handed me over a pill bag that was stuffed with something. I opened it and pulled out brown underwear and instantly smirked. Opening it up, I smelled it and inhaled her scent deeply.

"Mmm," I hummed.

"She really sent you her draws?" Touched asked with eyebrows raised.

"Yeah. I made her buss that pussy open and then send it up to me," I boasted with a devilish grin.

The way Keilani was submitting to me made a nigga want her even more. She was a whole fucking vibe that I wasn't used to. It was like I got everything in her. She was smart as fuck, sweet, a boss in her own nature, and a freak jawn. Not to mention, shorty was beautiful inside and out. Whoever was her nigga fumbled her badly, but I was grateful he did or else I wouldn't have had a chance to make her mine.

"Look at you, nigga, all in love," Touch voiced.

"Even if I was, fuck it."

When Touch made that statement, it got me thinking if I really did love her or was it just infatuation? I knew for a fact I loved her unconditionally and care for her deeply, but I also couldn't deny the fact I was falling in love with her too.

"Good you for, bro. Even a gangsta ass nigga needs real love."

I nodded my head in agreement. "Bae," I heard Kei yell through the bowl.

I looked at the time on my watch and saw it was the usual time she returned from work. "Yooo!" I hollered back.

Touch back-peddled out of the cell, giving us some space.

"Did you get that?"

"Yeah, I got it. You came through for real."

"Anything for you," she sang. "Oh yeah, I saw Ms. Walsh today."

"And what happened?"

"She took away my commissary for two weeks," she revealed.

"Damn, but honestly, that ain't too bad. Could've been worst. You need anything?"

"I wanted to get a few things, but I'll just buy it from the store."

Some inmates had stores where they sold items for the price and a half or double in return. I had a few stores in the building that I had ran by other niggas, including in my unit.

Then and there, I decided I was going to organize some shit and send it down to her through laundry. I was good with the CO that ran the department. I just needed my guy to pack up some shit, conceal it within the laundry clothes, and through the department to reach to Kei.

"Don't do that shit, baby. I'll make something happen. Hold tight, ard?"

"Okay, love. Let me go shower and settle in. I'll be back a little later."

"Ard. Give me them lips, girl."

"Muahhh." She made a smooching sound, and I sent a kiss back.

As soon as she was gone, I wanted to put shit in place for her. Touch was right outside the cell, talking to Zaine.

"Yo!" I called out to him.

He popped his head in the door. "Wassup?"

"I need Trouble to get her girl to catch this package coming their way," I told him.

Trouble dated someone who worked in laundry. Once we sent the bag down, she would grab it and put it in the designated cart to land at its rightful destination.

"Call Raf in here for me," I added, referring to one of the niggas that ran a store for me.

"Ard."

Not long after, Raf came through, and I gave him instructions on what to do. Without hesitation, he got right on it.

I laid back on my bunk and looked up at her pictures I had taped to the bottom of the top bunk. Shorty had me experiencing a foreign feeling. I always looked out for people I fucked with, but with her, shit was different. I was ready to give her the world and protect her at all costs. If I was her nigga, she wouldn't have had to do anything to land her behind the gray walls of FDC Philly.

With her heavy on my mind, I jumped up and headed to the computer to send her a message. Before I could compose a message to her, one came in from her.

Kei: My prayer for you tonight baby…

My prayer for you tonight baby...

Lord, I pray that Makhi will clearly hear the call you have on his life. Help him to realize who he is in Christ and give him certainty that he was created for a high purpose. May the eyes of his understanding be enlightened so that he will know what is the hope of Your calling (Ephesians 1:18).

Lord, when you call us, You also enable. Enable him to walk worthy of his calling and become the man of God You made him to be. Continue to remind him of You've called him to and don't let him get sidetracked with things that are unessential to Your purpose. Strike down discouragement so that it will not defeat him. Lift his eyes above the circumstances of the moment, so he can see the purpose for which you created him. Give him patience to wait for your perfect timing. I pray that the desires of his heart will not be in conflict with the desires of yours. May he seek You for direction and hear when You speak to his soul. In Jesus' name I pray. AMEN.

Sleep well baby, dream about me.

She never ceased to amaze me. Her messages and every-thing that came out her mouth were meaningful.

I got to typing and let out what was on my mind and heart.

Me: Your prayers and message really touched me. I just want you to know you have no worries and I mean that a hundred percent. I vow to you that I won't do you dirty or have you looking crazy, so don't worry. You're my future and you're in good hands. You changed a lot in my eyes, and I like that. You be having a nigga thinking about shit I never thought about before. I'm ready to change a lot of my ways for the sake of my family, my daughter, you, and especially myself. Also, I see a lot of my yelling and telling you things didn't go in vain. That's a quality I like; I hate a female that doesn't listen, but we don't got that problem. I'll continue to be your knight in shining armor. I love you, Kei. I really do.

I contemplated on whether to press the send button but remembered if I didn't really mean everything I said, I wouldn't have put it out in the universe and onto the computer.

Pressing send, I went and replied to my other emails and then stumbled back on our sex thread. The way she came after my part made my dick jump. I was ready to have her and was becoming impatient.

Later that night, right before lock down, we were wrapping up our conversation when she told me she'd be right back. She wanted to check the computer one last time before they shut down. While waiting, my nerves started to get the best of me. I rubbed my jaw thoughtfully, knowing the email I sent was possibly going to get through to her.

About ten minutes had passed before she returned.

"Babe?" she sang through the bowl.

I was sitting on my bunk in deep thought when she came back. "Yo."

"Sooo… you love me?" she asked in the cutest childlike tone.

I smiled, then cleared my throat. "I do, Kei."

There was silence on the line for a few moments.

"I love you, too," she expressed.

Letting out the deep breath I didn't realize I was holding in, I felt relieved that we were on the same page and shit wasn't one sided.

We spoke a little more before it was time to lock down. She was using someone's bowl who lived on my line. Usually, we'd go back and forth where I would use my boy shit that lived on her line and vice versa. I kept asking her to move on my shit so we could talk all night, but she was adamant about staying with one of her prison moms.

When it was time to go, we officially added a new line before parting ways: I love you.

I WAS WOKEN up from my cell door being unlocked. Grabbing my shank, I sat up in my bed. "Who that?" I asked.

"Wright. Come on," he stated.

I checked the time on my watch, which read two-thirty in the morning. There was only one reason I was being pulled out of my cell. Pushing my feet in my slides, I left out the cell and followed Wright to the library we had on the unit. Inside was LT Grace waiting for me. Wright closed the door, leaving us two alone.

"I miss you," she spoke softly.

"Mmm, I hear you," I responded nonchalantly.

She walked up to me and placed her hand inside my shorts, then proceeded to kiss on my neck. While I would've usually become aroused, I didn't. Grace was dead to me; I only wanted to conduct business with her.

"Makhi, wassup with you?" she asked, looking down at my shorts.

"Nothing, I'm just not in the mood. Matter of fact, I'm good off all this, ye mean?"

"What you mean?" she raised her voice a bit.

While I wanted to tell her to get the fuck on in the most disrespectful way, I decided to stay calm. I didn't know what type time Grace was on, but I knew she had been up to something and, when I found out what, I was going to handle her accordingly.

She took a step back and sized me up and down. "You acting like this because of that bitch, Milan, ain't you?" she questioned with malice in her voice.

"You drawn right now. Chill the fuck out."

"You always treating me some kind of way. After all I've done to prove to you I'm the one for you. I left my husband and all. This is the thanks I get?" she got emotional.

"Tiffany, I never told you to do that shit. I never told you we were going to be together. Stop with all that goofy ass shit, yo," I snapped.

This bitch is fucking delusional, I thought.

"Okay, Makhi. Mark my words when I tell you I will have the last laugh," she threatened.

Without uttering another word, I turned and left out of the library. There was nothing else to say to her crazy ass. I just prayed nothing backfired on me from fucking with her.

CHAPTER TWENTY-ONE

U.S Department of Justice
Federal Bureau of Prisons

75816-066

MILAN
KEILANI

Eye: BR   Ht: 5'03"

Vending

INMATE

KEI

I knew I told Manic I loved him, but I felt it
stronger when Monday mainline came around and
I received a hefty laundry bag with commissary. It wasn't

about the actual material things but the act instead. He showed me he was willing to go above and beyond to make sure I was good. He simply asked me to let him handle some shit, and he came through.

It had been a couple of months since we'd been dealing and I must admit, he made my bid so much easier than I expected it to be. I thought I was going to have constant sleepless nights and be in a bad depression, but that wasn't the case. That man came into my life and made me happy. I could only imagine what it would've been like once we became physically intimate.

Since I spent all of my time with him if I wasn't at work, I stayed out of any drama the ladies had on the unit. Some of the girls would say hi, but that's where I kept it at. I didn't have time to be around wishy washy people. Between running to the bowl, emails, and getting a quick workout in, I had no time to sit around with bitches anyway. Manic and I were continuously making plans for our future.

"Aye, this book is so good," Tamara blurted out of nowhere.

We had been locked down for about an hour. Her on her bottom bunk and me on the top. Our faces were buried in some urban fiction books.

"You have to let me read that afterwards," I told her.

"I got you because this shit here is a page turner."

"What's the name of it?"

"A Saint Luv'n a Savage."

"I think Manic told me about that series. He said he fucked with it hard."

"Mmmhmm, I can see why," she agreed.

"I want to write some books in this genre, ma. I have so many stories in my head from experiences; my jawns would be fire as hell."

"Then, what you waiting for?" she quizzed.

I asked myself that same question too. Procrastination was the devil himself.

"You right. I'ma get on it. I want to turn them into movies too one day," I added.

"Ayeee, that's my girl. I write scripts. When I get out, I'm going head first into the film industry." She sat up and went into her locker, pulling out a manila envelope. "Look, I started working on this one here." She showed me a movie script.

Tamara was so smart and ambitious. I had no doubt she was going to do everything she said she was.

We chopped it up some more about our plans and what we had to do to achieve our goals before returning to our books. I loved when we had positive and heart to heart conversations. It was a dope way to end the day after being in a fucked-up place we were in.

THE WARNING BELL SOUNDED, letting us know it was time for work. I just finished getting dressed, so I raced out of my cell and to the computer to check my emails. I clicked on Manic's first.

Manic: I love you, baby. You're my world and I can't wait to drop a load in you, so you can kick one of my youngn's out. I hope you have a good day at work. Hurry back, so you can jump on this dick.

I smiled wide as shit reading his message and instantly drifted off, daydreaming about us fucking.

"Milan!" I heard Williams scream, quickly snatching me out of my thoughts before I got too deep.

"Ughhh," I groaned out in aggravation. "I'm coming!" I yelled back, waving my hands so he saw me in the computer room.

I quickly wrote him back.

Me: I love the sound of that, baby. Thank you, King. I'll be home later to ride the shit out of you, but I'm sitting on your face too, so be hungry. I'm finna feed you.

I pressed send and logged off, then hustled out of the room to meet the rest of the workers walking out of the unit's door.

When we reached downstairs, as usual, everyone went into their designated areas and got to work. I placed my earbud in my ears and started to open the cans of vegetables that needed opening for the day's meal.

It wasn't even a half an hour in and one of the COs in the kitchen started to fuck with me. She was an older white woman who screamed racist. I ignored her on many occasions because Williams told us she had control issues. But the way shorty ran up on me, I wasn't feeling it.

"Milan, give me that MP3 right now," she demanded with her hand out.

We weren't allowed to take our players off the unit, let alone have it at work. It was the best way for most of us to get through the dreadful experience. But the administration didn't see that.

"Come on, Ms. Stewart. I'ma put it up," I pleaded.

Depending on their mood, they'd give it back at the end of the shift, or they'd hand it over to the lieutenant, resulting in a shot. I didn't know what she had in mind, so I tried to cop a plea with her.

"Give it here."

"Man, come on."

"If you don't hand it over, I'll just give you a shot."

"That's some bullshit," I gritted.

She moved closer and, as I was getting untangled with my headphones, I accidentally hit her in the face. *Oh fuck*, I thought.

Ms. Stewart pressed her panic button and pulled out her pepper spray in one swift motion. Spraying me in the face, I dropped to my knees instantly from the excruciating pain that hit me. My eyes burned so badly, I was sure I was about to lose my eyesight.

Without my vision, I wasn't able to see anything. I just

heard a ton of footsteps rushing my way. I was lifted off the ground by my hands and feet.

"That's crazy! Y'all ain't gotta do that girl like that!" I heard one inmate yell.

The kitchen went into an uproar with all kinds of slurs being thrown at the COs in my defense. I cried, hoping my tears would ease the burning.

"Please, my eyes," I pleaded.

"Shut up!" a CO yelled.

From the feeling, I knew we were in the elevator. But instead of going up a floor to where the unit was, we were on the machine for a while. Finally reaching the floor to wherever we were going, I was carried some ways before they placed me down on the ground on my stomach.

"Stewart hit the panic button on her. She claim she hit her," I heard one CO tell another.

I wanted so badly to say it was an accident, but it wouldn't have mattered in that moment. After lying on the ground for what felt like forever, the burning eased up from all the crying I did. A female guard took me to an eyewash station and helped me clean any spray residue that was left. I was then taken into a cell and told to strip out of my clothes. When I was completely naked, she pushed some clothes through the rectangle flap where they'd pass food trays through, but they were all orange.

"Where am I?" I asked through the door, already knowing but just needing confirmation.

"The SHU," the officer responded.

"What happens next?" I needed to know.

"They're writing up your shot now. You'll stay here pending investigation and, once concluded, you'll know your disciplinary action."

I can't believe this shit, I thought. It ran through my mind, my mother and brother were supposed to come visit me the following day. Manic also crossed my mind. I didn't want to be away from him.

About an hour passed when I saw two officers with two big green bags approach the desk outside the cell I was in. They turned and looked at me with such disgust.

"You just got into a whole other heap of shit, Milan," the same female officer exclaimed.

"What do you mean?" I was confused.

"They found drugs in your locker. You gon' be up here for a while." She shook her head.

"What? That shit ain't mine!"

"It was in your locker when we packed you out," one of the guys spoke, followed by a shrug.

"Ughhhrrr." I punched the metal cell door, hurting my right hand instantly.

A shock of fear and panic zipped through my heart. It felt as if it would explode or catch on fire. I slid down against the wall, holding onto my aching hand as tears flowed. The only person who could help me in my situation was God, so I talked to him.

Our Father, who art in heaven, hallowed be thy name; Thy kingdom come, thy will be done, on earth as it is in heaven. Give us this day our daily bread; and forgive us our trespasses, as we forgive those who trespass against us; and lead us not into temptation, but deliver us from evil. Amen.

"Please, help me," I whispered.

CHAPTER TWENTY-TWO

U.S Department of Justice
Federal Bureau of Prisons

90056-066

FROST
MAKHI
Eye: GR   Ht: 6'03"

Vending

INMATE

MANIC

"What the fuck!" I roared, tossing around shit in my cell.

It looked like a tornado had hit my spot. Anything that

wasn't bolted to the ground got slammed around the room. I was ready to kill someone.

"Aye, bro, chill the fuck out before they try to send yo ass up there too," Touch advised.

In that moment, I didn't give a fuck if they did do that, I would've been closer to Kei. When I got the news of what they did to her, I felt hurt and anger all at once.

"Nigga, I ain't tryna hear none of that shit," I spat, fuming at the mouth.

"Bro, maybe this is what you need. Some time away from her. I ain't gon' hold you, you been getting soft and haven't been focused on business."

I snapped my neck in his direction and burned a hole through his face with my eyes. "Nigga, you eating? Is money being made?" I took a step closer to him.

"I mean, yeah, but all you do is ride shorty ass. All I'm saying is, don't put these bitches before the bag and business."

"Says the same person who just married Noelle through the fuckin' toilet bowl. Nigga, don't talk to me about bitches. That's my fuckin' bitch. I can feel how I want to feel and do what the fuck I want to do."

Touch raised his hands in surrender and backed away towards the door. Nigga was testing me. Maybe what he said was somewhat of the truth and it was time I started acting like the savage I was. That wasn't going to change how I was about to go behind my bitch, though.

"Get your sister on my line now," I demanded. I needed to know what the fuck going on down there.

As he was popping the bowl open, Wright came by the door.

I waved him in. "What's the word?" I asked.

I knew he had to have some kind of information to be in our unit and he wasn't assigned to us.

"You don't even want to know what the fuck I found out." He shook his head in disbelief.

"What bul?" I barked.

"Grace was behind it all. Someone overheard her telling Stewart to fuck with shorty. And after the captain checked the cameras just now, he saw it was truly an honest accident of her hitting her. But when they were packing her locker, they found drugs, your drugs," he informed me.

I looked at Touch with a menacing glare. "Get your fuckin' sister on the line now."

I was the only nigga in FDC Philly that had product floating around. For it to be in Kei's locker, it had to be either Gia or Grace having someone planting some shit in it. Because those two were related and been set on making Kei's time tough, I knew they had something going on.

"Yo, she right here," Touch told me, stepping aside.

Wright was still standing in the doorway.

"Yo, Tee, what the fuck going on down there?" I inquired.

"A bunch of nut shit. I heard how they did Kei in the kitchen. But listen, word got around fast as shit about the drugs. It was Gia that went in there and slipped it in her shit. What you want me to do?"

I loved how on point Trouble was. She was lowkey than a muthafucker and out the way but knew everything that was going on.

"I would say kill that bitch, but get some bitches to beat her ass. I'm talking lock in the sock. Bust her fucking face open. I don't care how much the shit gon' cost. Get it done."

"Say less."

"What about Grace?" Wright questioned.

I started to pace the cell floor back and forth. "I'll deal with her. But it can't be right now," I concluded. "How she doing?" I asked Wright, referring to Keilani.

"She's good. They cleaned her up," he told me.

I nodded, then got angry all over again thinking about muthafuckers spraying and putting hands on her.

"Keep me in the loop. I'ma need a letter to go up."

"Ard, I'll come grab it from you by tomorrow and get it to her," he spoke and walked away.

At that point, Touch left out my cell too. I needed to be alone while I collected my thoughts. Before I flushed the toilet, I yelled for Lena. When she got on, I told her to make sure and reach out to Kei's mom and let her know what happened.

Once I was settled, I pulled out my pen and pad and poured my feelings out on paper.

Letter to Keilani:

Yo baby, I'm not even gone lie, you only been gone like a day and I'm missing you like crazy. I'm sick as fuck right now. You really my baby, I just hope you don't let this shit separate us because I really see us building something special.

I never in life vibed like this with a female that I didn't touch. You got a lot of good traits that I see making us go a long way. You make me proud to call you mine and I want you to keep it like that. I told you, me and you are bigger than all this in here. We really got something and I want to keep it that way.

All I can say is, don't let this shit break you and distract you from the goal. When I told you that you got me, I really meant that shit. I don't know how your big head ass did it, but you locked a nigga down. All I want you to do is use this time to refocus, work on things you want to do, and get some crunches in. Your time is moving and, before you know it, you'll be home with daddy.

I just had to lay this on your mind and let you know we're super straight, my love. You have absolutely not one worry while I'm in here. I'm going to stay out the way and make you proud to call me yours. When I touch those streets, you going to be a hundred percent good, that's on my life. I told you, loyalty is everything, and I meant that. I love you, my Queen.

-Your King.

CHAPTER TWENTY-THREE

KEI

*A*lmost a year later, I had been operating like a robot. My routine was the exact same every single day, except for Sundays when my mom and brothers visited. I would wake up every morning, pray and mediate, then eat whatever breakfast that was pushed through the door slot. After eating, I'd work on the book I started to write and write some verses to songs I wrote. Lunch would then come around; I may or may not eat it, depending on if it was nasty or not. On the days my prison moms, Lena and Tamara, worked, they made sure to send something decent up for me.

When lunch was over, the guards would take some of us out of our cells at times and let us get our one hour of rec. Rec was in a cage with just a little air from the top of the building entering. We were on the top floor of the massively tall building. When I went back in, I'd workout, stretch, then hop in the shower. I'd read a book until dinner came around. Once I finished eating, I'd return to writing, then back to reading until I fell asleep. I repeated that every single day for a year straight.

After the DHO, which stands for Discipline Hearing Officer, and SIS finished their investigation, they handed me all that time in the SHU. Out of all the time I sat in that boxed-in cell with a toilet, sink, and shower, I only had a cellmate once. At times, it sent me crazy and into a deep depression. I kept the bible close to me for whenever I felt like hurting myself.

Letters from Manic came at least three times a week, which was the only thing I looked forward to besides my visits from my family. He kept my spirit alive with his words of encouragement; he always spoke life into me. I missed hearing his voice so badly. I learned they once had the women located on the south side of the SHU, which would've given me access to speak to him, but they moved us, leaving me only with a letter to communicate with my love.

I remember the first time my mother visited me in the SHU. The moment we both laid eyes on one another, we cried. It was the hardest thing to be right near her and not be able to touch her, not be able to hug and be comforted by her. It was a thick glass separating us and only a phone to talk through. While regular visits we had from seven in the morning until two in the afternoon to spend time together, the SHU visits were limited to thirty minutes. If there was a cool officer on duty, we got a little longer.

Nevertheless, my mother was there to see me every single weekend right after she got off work from her job at the federal halfway house in Philly. Tired and all, she came to check on her daughter, not missing a beat.

Knock! Knock!

"Milan!" the CO called out to me.

"Yeah?" I sat up from my bed with a book in my hand.

"Pack up, you're dropping," he informed me.

"Yesss!" I shouted.

My heart thumped wildly as it doubled in beats. I was ecstatic and couldn't believe the day came that I was being released from the hole. It felt like I was being let out from prison rather than just another part of the building. It didn't matter to me; I knew I was under a year to the door and I was going to have back my wiggle room to do more shit. Most of all, I was going to be able to hug my family and talk to my man.

I packed up the little things I was allowed to have in the SHU and was ready for them to let me out. About twenty minutes later, he called me to the door and made me turn around so he could cuff me through the slot.

"Walk forward," he stated.

I knew the drill. In the SHU, you had to move a certain way and follow protocol. Anytime they took inmates out of their cells, they'd cuff us and make us walk away from the door with our backs still turned. Once the door was open, we'd walk backwards until they had our forearm.

"I know you are happy as hell to get out of here," he spoke.

"Hell yeah," I beamed.

"Lata Kei, be good girl!" one girl yelled, prompting the other ladies that were in the SHU to say their goodbyes to me.

"Y'all up next!" I yelled back before being taken off the wing.

The female guard on duty changed me out of the orange SHU clothes and gave me used threads like when I first came into FDC Philly. It wasn't the tan scrubs I wore, it was the green jumpsuit the men wore.

"You'll get your things from laundry when you get back downstairs," she told me as she noticed me being disgusted by what I had on.

"Okay."

Once I was dressed, she pointed at the two huge military looking bags that contained my belongings. I followed a male CO and dragged them through the door and onto the elevated. When we reach the third floor, he helped me off the elevator and to the unit door. He rang the bell and waited for the CO to open it.

The moment I touched the unit, I heard screams and hollers, which let me know someone had missed me. When I looked, it was Tamara and Sherrell. They hugged me so tight; I felt the love.

"Daughter," Tamara sang as she observed me. "You lost so much weight."

"Yeah, that's what the SHU would do to you. It's a whole diet in itself," I joked but was telling the truth.

Anyone knew if you went to the SHU and stayed for as little as a week, you would lose weight. You weren't allowed to have your commissary in there. The only thing a person could eat outside of the breakfast, lunch, and dinner provided by the institute was unsalted crackers and peanut butter.

"Well, tonight, we're going to cook you a ton of shit to get some meat back on those bones," Tamara stated.

"Now, that shit sounds great." I smiled. "Where's Lena?" I looked around the unit.

"Tamara and Sherell got quiet.

"Hello?"

"She got released last week; you just missed her, boo," Tamara revealed.

I felt a sting in my heart that I wasn't able to say goodbye, but I quickly remembered that we would link back up in the free world.

"Okay, good for her. I'm so happy one of us is gone and out of this hell hole."

"Right. Come on, let's get you settled. I know you want to talk to your man." Tamara smiled.

The CO gave me my cell assignment and, while I wasn't completely happy that my bed was no longer mine, I didn't allow nothing to bother me. I was out of the hole and able to move around.

The ladies helped me clean my bed, mattress, and locker. While they packed away my things, I went and took a long shower and washed my hair with Pantene shampoo and conditioner, instead of that cheap VO5 shit that was making my hair and scalp dry in the SHU.

When I walked back into the room from handling my hygiene, the bowl was popped with a mic in it. My new bunky was a younger girl and apparently lived in the bowl like how I did. In my mind, I knew it wasn't going to work out.

"Your man calling for you," she told me as she sat on her bed filing her nails.

"Thank you."

"Manic!" I hollered into the mic.

Moments later, I heard him yelling, "Ayooo Kei!"

"Hi, babyyy," I sang happily.

It was so fucking good to hear my man's voice. I was beyond elated.

"Wassup with your bald-headed ass?" He started his shit right away.

"Shit, I just got out of the shower and stuff. I missed you so much, King."

"I miss you more, baby girl. You good?"

"Yeah, as best as I could be. You straight?"

"Always. Aye, we coming into your unit tomorrow to paint the rec yard. They'll have y'all locked down, of course. See if you can switch rooms with the person who cell window faces the rec yard."

"That's Sherrell's cell," I told him.

"Even better. Holler at her and see wassup."

All I could think about was that I dropped back onto the unit at the perfect timing when he was going to be around. We continued to catch up a bit before it was time for four o'clock count.

The remainder of the day, I bounced back and forth from talking to him and chilling with some of the ladies. They had kept their word and cooked me a fire ass dinner with the things off commissary and the kitchen. The microwave worked wonders and always surprised me on how well it made certain meals.

I couldn't access my phone and email until the next day, but I made sure to tell Manic to reach out to my mom and let her know I was out of the SHU. During my time upstairs, he and my moms got close. They had phone calls and text message going. He even invited her to some of his court hearings.

My first day back in the unit was calm and welcoming. Even the mean girls said hi, speaking about Noelle and her crew. I wasn't worried about nothing; I had just endured the roughest year of my life and it wasn't anything else to trump that, or so I thought.

CHAPTER TWENTY-FOUR

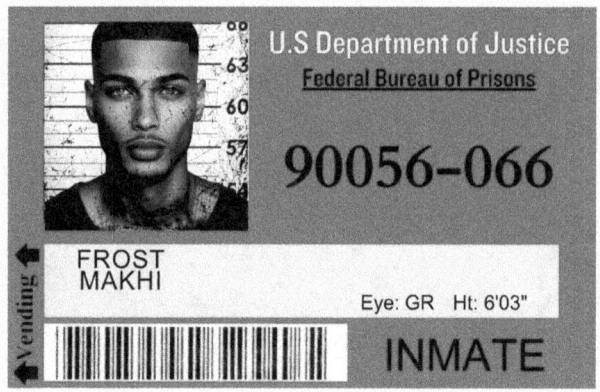

MANIC

 hen niggas came and delivered the news that my bitch was out of the SHU and back in her

unit, I felt my heart pause for a second. A nigga was too happy to even think straight. I had Touch find her and send her a message. With her recently touching down, I knew she was getting settled in. Once she was good and knew I was looking for her, she would come in the bowl.

She lived on some weird ass nigga's line who didn't play the bowl, so it made things much easier for me to get in his cell to speak to her. I sat there and waited for her to call since her new bunky told me she was in the shower.

Once I heard her sexy ass voice, I jumped off the chair like a stalker and ran to the bowl. We kept in contact through our letters, but actually hearing her voice and knowing she was okay made the moment even more memorable for me.

The following morning, I caught myself reading over one of the letters she sent me while she was in the SHU. It was a sex kite.

It read:

Picture this...

After a long hard day of hustling, you come home to a nice home cooked meal, clean house, and me in a silk robe with nothing under. I placed your food in front of you, giving you a massage while you ate. Once you're done, I sat on your lap facing you and started kissing you passionately. I stood up, smirked, looked at you in lust and walked away, leaving you sitting there with a hard dick.

Not too long after, you came following me into the bedroom. Grabbing me by the waist, you kissed on my neck while rubbing all over my body. Aggressively, you spun me around and snatched my robe off, leaving me wearing nothing but my birthday suit. I tugged at your pants, pulling your belt loose. Before you know it, I had the head of your dick in my mouth. As I slowly jerk it back and forth, I took it in my mouth inch by inch, then started to pick up the pace. Your dick ended up in the back of my throat. As I'm sucking the life out of you, you grabbed the back of my head, pushing your way in more while playing in my hair. I sucked and slurped until you came right down my throat.

You told me to get up and turn around; you bent me over and passed the palm of your hand on my pussy, sending chills up my body. I felt your warm tongue around my lips. You started slow and gentle, then started to devour my kitty. The feeling was unreal while you ate me out from behind. As I was about to come, you just stop, toss me to the bed, and turn me around. Taking off the rest of your clothes, you watched as I begged for you with my eyes while playing with my pussy. This gave you a sense of control, as you smirked.

Not wasting too much more time, you grabbed my legs up, gave my kitty a sweet kiss, then brought the head of your dick to my love box. You played around it, making me fuss and beg. You then started to enter inch by inch. It was painful but felt so damn good. You felt me tense up, so you kissed me gently and told me to relax, "Daddy got you", so I did what I was told.

Finally, you were all the way in me, giving me deep, slow strokes until I adjusted to your size. You picked up the pace and started to pound me forcefully. Right before I was about to come, you pulled out and turned me around, so now I was on all fours. You grabbed me by my hair and kissed me while ramming your dick inside of me, making me scream out your name. As you're hitting it from the back, I tried to run, but you weren't having it. You whispered, "Lil mama, take daddy dick." I started to throw that ass back and you went full force. I tensed up and you knew I was about to come, so you started to pound harder and deeper, as all my juices flowed out onto your dick.

I managed to get you out of me, then flipped you on your back. Now, I was on top. I planted both feet on the bed while I took my friend right into my love box. The pain was so intense but felt fucking good. I slowly grinded on you as you relaxed and closed your eyes. Hearing your moans made me want to go harder. I started to straddle you fast, started bouncing up and down on the dick. You couldn't take it no more. You grabbed me by the waist and started fucking me from the bottom, thrusting upward.

I felt you tense up. You flipped me on my back and started to dig in deeper as I plead. As I tensed up, you whispered in my ears, "Let it go baby girl." As you said that, I came and, right after you came, bumping all in me. You gave me a nice, long kiss. Grabbed me towards you, cuddled up, you kissed me on my forehead, and it all went blank. I was knocked out.

I can't wait until we can make this come true... I love you baby!!!! <3 xoxoxoxoxoxoxo.

"Frost, let's go!" I heard my work detail supervisor yell from the guard booth, snapping me out of my vision of Kei and me. The way she detailed her sex scenes, I just knew we were going to fuck like rabbits constantly.

Folding up the letter, I tucked it back in the folder where the rest of them were and made my way out of my cell. It was time to go down to the women's unit to paint their rec yard. I prayed Kei was able to get into her homegirl's cell without any issues.

When we reached downstairs, the unit was clear, as they had the girls locked in their cells. Once they saw we were on the unit, they started banging on the doors, making all kind of noise. We were about twenty deep. They wanted all hands on deck to get the job done in one day.

Walking into the rec yard, I moved near the cell window that was supposed to be Sherell's. At first glance, it looked like no one was in the room since the light was off. Moments later, I saw movement on the top bunk and a head appeared from under the covers.

There she goes, I thought.

Finally, I was able to lay my eyes on my girl. Kei looked like she lost a lot of weight but looked beautiful, nevertheless. She smiled and blushed as we locked eyes, just staring at each other.

"Alright, come and grab your supplies," our boss instructed. He was already hip to what I was trying to do. With some money his way, he told me to just be discreet for the camera.

As I took my time setting up my area, Kei kept peeking from under the blanket. My plan was to paint the same spot the entire shift, just to look at her ass. I didn't care if she just sat there staring at me. Being able to see her and be near her was enough for a nigga.

Time went on, and she just sat on the top bunk with her legs to her chest. Her eyes gazed with need and hunger, making me return the same look. Out of nowhere, she started to strip out of her clothes and put on her nightgown under the blanket. The lights were still off so, in order to see what she was doing, you had to be up close like I was. I didn't have any worries about anyone seeing her.

She positioned herself on the bed with her legs spread apart, showing her bare pussy. The whole act caught me off guard to a certain extent, but knowing her freak ass, I wasn't at all surprised.

Once she saw she had my undivided attention, she played

with her clit, rubbing it in a circular motion. Separating her pussy lips, she exposed the pretty pinkness of her love box. I drooled instantly, wanting to taste her.

Kei slipped a finger inside herself and started to move it in and out. She grinded against her hand as she used another finger to apply pressure to her button. Throwing her head back in bliss, her chest moved up and down as she enjoyed the pleasure she was bringing herself.

Watching her, I felt my dick rock up. I was ready to run into the unit, break down the door, and punish that pussy. I examined every inch of her body from where I stood, picturing my hands caressing her soft skin.

I quickly looked around the rec yard to make sure no one else was seeing the show that was only meant for my eyes. Everyone was hard at work, so I returned my attention back to my lady. That time, she was completely naked with nothing on, showing her full breasts that had the prettiest areolas I'd ever seen.

Massaging her breasts with one hand, she used the next to play in her pussy. In one swift motion, she turned around and was on all fours, bent over. The pink of her pussy kept peeking at me every time she leaned her chest onto the bed. She started to twerk and shake her ass in a circle, making her cheeks move in an enticing way.

She carried on the show for a while until she finally

reached her peak after finger fucking herself. I wished I was in the room to slurp her up dry. That's when my brain started working a thousand miles per hour. I had to get to her and as soon as possible.

CHAPTER TWENTY-FIVE

U.S Department of Justice
Federal Bureau of Prisons

75816-066

MILAN
KEILANI

Eye: BR   Ht: 5'03"

INMATE

KEI

oming down off my high of exploding, I ended up falling asleep. The cell door opening and letting in all the noise from the day room woke me out of my slumber. I looked outside the window and saw Manic was gone. It had me thinking, was I dreaming the whole time or was it real?

"Bitch, you were asleep in my shit?" Sherell joked.

"Girl, yes, I put myself to sleep," I stated, not getting into details.

I came down the ladder halfway and grabbed my blanket and sheet off her bed. My plan was to put on a show for my man from the moment he told me to be in that room to see him. Sherell was nice enough to let me stay in her cell while she was at work. The least I could've done was give respect to her sheets and shit.

Making my way back into my cell, I dropped my stuff on my bed, popped my bowl and called for Manic. Not long after, he came on.

"Aye, Kei!" he called out to me.

"Yes, baby."

"I'm gon' fuck the shit outta you," he spoke with so much bass in his voice.

Okay, it really wasn't a dream, I thought. "Oh yeah?" I cooed.

"On God. I sent you something, make sure and eat it."

Eat it? I raised a brow. "What is it?" I wondered.

"You'll see."

Manic was always up to something and full of surprises. I could have only imagined the type of shit he was going to do when we got home.

"Okay, baby."

We talked some more until I had to slide out for a minute to eat and make some calls. I had gotten access back to my phone and email. When I logged on, I saw a ton of messages from months back. It only showed until a certain time, so I knew a bunch of messages got lost in the sauce since I was up top.

I went and checked my balance and saw I had a hefty amount of money on my account. Blinking a couple of times to make sure I was seeing correctly, the figure never changed. Curious to know who put that kind of money on my books, I went and made a call to my moms.

"Hey, Lani, how you feeling?" my mom answered.

"I'm good, mommy. How you doing?"

"I'm hanging in there. I think I'm about to go and work inside the jail," she revealed.

"Huh, what? Why?"

"It's better pay and better opportunities. Besides, it's the same thing as the halfway house."

"Ummm, no, it isn't. But whatever you want to do, just make sure the decision is yours and yours only," I told her. "Aye, ma, who put all that money on my books?"

"We haven't put anything since you went to the SHU. Only enough for you to get the small amount of things you could've gotten. Why?"

"It's over five thousand dollars on my account, but the last name of the person it came from, I don't recognize."

The line got quiet, so I thought she hung up.

"Hello?"

"Yeah, Lani. It's from your boo," she exclaimed.

Manic?

"Seriously?"

"Yeah, I remember now. He had done that when you got your first shot."

"I see."

We talked for the remaining time on the phone. When I got off and was on my way back to the bowl, the girls that worked in the dish room came back to the unit from work. One of them approached me, so I motioned for her to follow me into my cell. She pulled out a letter taped to a honey bun.

"Thank you," I told her, and she left out.

I pulled the letter off the honey bun and unfold it.

It read:

After that shit you put down earlier, I had to race back to my cell and buss a nut to your pictures. The icing on the honey bun is from me, enjoy. I love you, baby girl. -M. A.

My eyes shifted to the honey bun in my hand. I opened it and sniffed it. Quickly remembering how fine that man was, how he made me feel, and all he'd done for me, I opened my mouth and bit into the pastry. I ate the entire thing and washed it down with a ginger ale.

Now, that's treatment for real niggas only.

A FEW DAYS had passed since I swallowed that man's nut for real. Events that happened that day made us closer and made us wanting each other more. If someone would have told me I would find my love, my soulmate, through a prison toilet bowl, I would've told them they were a lie.

"Milan!" I heard my name being called.

When I checked the call-out sheet the night before, I saw I was on there to see the doctor. I didn't put in a sick call request, so I figured it was just a normal follow-up or something.

"Yeah, I'm coming!" I poked my head out of my cell and yelled. I quickly threw on my tans since I had just got out the shower. Once dressed and ready to go, I made my way to the guard. I saw it was the same CO, Wright, who was the person to deliver all of Manic's letters to me and take mine to him.

"You ready?" he asked.

"Yeah."

I followed him out of the unit and onto the elevator. Before the door opened for us to get off, he turned to me.

"Just follow my lead."

I didn't ask questions, but I knew some shit was up. With so many thoughts in my head, I followed him off the elevator and through different doors until we reached medical. Instead of sitting in the waiting room or going into the doctor's office, he led me down a long hall that got darker by the second.

Opening a door to an office that had the window covered, he stepped aside for me to walk in, then closed the door. I heard the door being locked and started to panic. The lights were off, so I couldn't see anything at all.

I felt a presence in the room, so I reached my arms out to feel around. My hands landed on a firm chest, making me jump back and bump into an object. "Who's there?" I asked with my voice trembling.

"It's ard baby, it's me," I heard Manic's voice.

"Makhi?"

"Yeah." He touched my hands that were still extended in front of me.

"You scared the shit out of me." I hit him a few times on his chest.

He grabbed my hand and pushed me up against the wall. My breath got caught in my throat. Feeling his touch sent shivers down my spine. He aggressively palmed the back of my neck and brought our lips to one another. Kissing me deeply, I felt between my legs getting moist by the second.

"I want you," he whispered in between kisses.

"Then, take me."

He pulled down my pants and undid his jumpsuit. At this time, my eyes adjusted to the darkness as there was a little light illuminating from under the door. I was scared as hell that we would get caught, but it quickly went out of my head when he grabbed me. Lifting me up, I felt his hard dick at my opening. He rested me down on the head and inched his way in.

"Makhi," I whispered as I squeezed his neck. The pain from his size was more than I expected.

"Relax and let me in."

I nodded my head in the crook of his neck as I shut my eyes tightly. As he continued to push his way inside of me, I felt like I was tearing. But the way he held me with so much passion and love, I felt the pleasure within the pain.

"You love me?" he asked in a husky tone.

"I love you, Makhi," I whimpered.

He pushed the last bit of him that could fit, touching my g-spot.

"Oh, fuck," I cried.

Once he knew he was all the way in, he thrusted in and out of me, delivering long, deep strokes. After I adjusted to his size a bit, he sped up his pace.

"Damn, this pussy good as fuck."

I squeezed my walls around his dick as I felt my juices flowing. He pulled out and lifted my small body up in the air and around his neck. Burying his face in between my legs, I thought I was going to pass out when he latched onto my clit.

"Ma...khiii!" I cried out in complete bliss. My legs shook uncontrollably as I came again.

Dropping me back down on his dick, he started to punish my pussy like I disobeyed him. At this time, I opened my body up to him, so I felt nothing but waves of pleasure. I kissed his lips and inhaled his scent, which was so intoxicating. I felt myself coming, so I applied some pressure on my clit as he drilled in and out of me.

"Come for me," he demanded.

On his command, I reached my peak and creamed all over his dick.

"Good girl. Now, you gon' catch this load?" he asked.

"Yes, daddy."

He pulled out, and I descended to my knees. Swallowing his dick whole, I enjoyed the taste of myself mixed with him. I sucked the shit out of his dick because I didn't know when we were going to ever be able to touch one another again.

Feeling his dick pulsating, I toyed with his balls. Moments later, he exploded and shot his load down my throat. I made sure to catch every single drop.

"Shit," he huffed, stumbling backwards out of breath. He bumped into something, which made a loud bang sound.

"What the fuck was that?" I heard someone say out in the hallway.

Ah shit, I thought. My eyes grew wide like golf balls.

The door was unlocked and in walked LT Grace. Before neither of us could get a word out, she came straight for me with hate in her eyes. It was a reflex for me to defend myself, so I threw the first punch, connecting with her eye. She quickly snatched me by my hair, but I hit her a couple of times in her stomach, making her let go. Manic jumped in and broke us up.

"What the fuck is wrong with you?" he snapped at her.

"I told you shit wasn't going to end well if you chose her."

"Makhi, what the hell is going on?" I asked, confused.

He raised his hand up at me, signaling to give him a minute. Wright rushed into the room, looking lost as hell.

"Take her ass to the eighth floor," Grace told Wright.

"Aye, chill with all that," Manic tried to intervene.

"Fuck you, Makhi," she spat.

Wright solemnly led me out of the room. I looked back at Manic, who was fuming and red in the face. His eyes looked sad and defeated, as I gave him one last glance before we were no longer in each other's view.

BANG! Bang!

"Milan, let's go!" the CO ordered.

I got woken up out of my sleep and immediately looked outside the window and saw it was still dark. It had been about a month since Manic and I got caught having sex down in medical. While I sat there in the SHU, I didn't feel bad at all, nor was I mad. I was there for a good ass reason; it was all worth it, or so I thought.

A week later, I received a letter from Manic confessing everything he had going on with LT Grace, hence the reason she came at me the way she did. He went on to explain when he and I got serious, he cut her off and kept it strictly business.

Whether I believed him or not didn't matter. It was because of him that bitch sent me to the SHU. She wrote up a bullshit shot that I had a cell phone. DHO even showed me the picture of the phone. That's when I knew the hoe was crazy.

"Where am I going?" I asked.

"You're getting shipped."

"Shipped? Where?" I jumped up and ran to the door.

"I don't know. Get dressed, though. Taking you down to R&D in a few minutes."

What the fuck? I thought. I knew it was that ugly ass bitch's doing, and it wasn't anything I could do about it. Gathering the small items in my cell, I put the orange jumpsuit on properly and waited for him to come back around to get me.

Not long after, he reappeared at my door.

"You ready?"

I nodded.

Knowing the drill, I turned around and pushed my hand through the slot to let him cuff me. I walked forward and waited until he opened my cell door and took me out.

We made our way down to R&D, where I was switched out of the orange jumpsuit and into the normal tan uniform. I was then shown my property, as it was packed into boxes to be shipped. As I waited in a holding cell, trying my best to ignore the male inmates and their catcalls, two ladies joined me. One I knew of, while the other I never saw a day in my life.

"Kei, they're shipping you?" the white girl asked, all hyper.

"I guess," I simply answered. I hated nosy ass people.

Not long after, two white males that looked to be in their mid to late thirties entered into R&D from the tunnel entrance. Their shirts read U.S. Marshal. Paperwork was handed over to them as a CO came and unlocked our cell door. The ladies and I filed out of the room and stood in a line as instructed.

One by one, we were handcuffed and shackled. It was my first time being shackled, so my anxiety shot up almost immediately. The chain was connected from the handcuffs down to the foot cuffs and a belly chain wrapped around my midsection. I couldn't extend my arms or hand, and I couldn't walk normally; I had to shuffle my feet or take baby steps. It was inhumane to say the least.

They led us out of the tunnel door, which was the way I first came into the building on my self-surrender date. Walking down the long tunnel, we reached the underground parking garage and was placed in the backseat of a car. I made sure to get a window seat.

Within minutes, we were pulling out from the garage and onto the city streets of Philadelphia. Driving away from the building, I kept my eyes glued on it as there were so many memories of good and bad times inside, but most of all, my man was still there. The more we drove away, the more I felt sick to my stomach and saddened.

An hour into the ride, we stopped at a rest stop on the PA turnpike going towards Harrisburg. The Marshal parked at the side of the building away from the civilians. One stepped out while the other stayed put with us. He later returned with Burger King for everyone. I was shocked but grateful.

"Thank you," I told him.

He waved me off like it wasn't nothing. The two guys were cool for the most part. They talked to us like we were normal people and not what every person assumed prisoners were, murders. While we munched on our meals and continued to talk, we got back on the road to Harrisburg where the federal airlift was located.

Another hour passed, and we reached the airlift. Pulling up to a huge gate, the driver had to show his credentials to drive in. Surveying the place, I noticed there was a shit ton of men spread out with rifles and shotguns. As we approached the plane that read *Con Air* that was surrounded by busses, trucks, and cars, I felt like we were in a movie getting ready to do a business deal on the landing.

We sat in the car for a few minutes before the Marshal came and helped us out one by one. A huge buff dude with a rifle across his body approached us with a clipboard. He and the Marshal exchanged paperwork before he made his way in front of us.

"Keilani Milan?" he asked.

"Right here." I raised my hand as much as the restraints allowed me to.

He continued to call the other women I never saw before. When it came to the white girl that was on my unit back at FDC Philly, he looked confused.

"I don't have her on my list," he exclaimed.

They conversed back and forth until one of the Marshals we came with got on the phone. Moments later, he walked back to us.

"It's been a mix-up. She's going back to the detention center," he spoke.

No, take me, take me, I thought. I was jealous as fuck of her and wished like hell I could've been in her shoes.

"Where am I going?" I mustered up the courage to ask one of my transporters.

"I guess I can tell you since we're already out here," he stated and looked at his paperwork. "Waseca, it's in Minnesota."

Minnesota? What the fuck a girl like me know about the mid-west?

Fright started to settle in when I came to terms I was being sent across the country, away from my family. Those visits were going to end because of the distance and because I knew people had lives outside of me.

I watched on as a chain of male inmates came off the plane and went into different buses and vans. Once that fleet was off, the Marshal started to board the people who were outside waiting. When it was our turn, I shuffled as my long hair blew in the wind. I felt all eyes on me, especially from the male prisoners. *Don't trip girl, don't trip*, I told myself, watching my feet move.

When we reached the stairs to go up, it was even more

men with guns. That's when it really hit me to the core that I was a federal prisoner. I just couldn't describe the feelings nor make the shit up.

Taking my time up the stairs, I was helped to make sure I didn't fall. I peered over at the wing of the plane and saw the infamous tape many of the girls spoke about. They were always transport talks about the *Con Air* plane with the tape on the wing. People would make jokes about it being there for years and holding the plane together for dear life.

Once on the plane, I faced my reality of being amongst dangerous people, mostly men with different backgrounds and fates: murders, drug dealers, rapist, thief, and the list went on.

The plane was basically packed with only the ladies left to board. They sat us to the front where the Marshal sat. Before I took a seat, a woman officer asked me if I wanted to use the bathroom before liftoff. The only thing was the bathroom for the prisoners was through the male inmates at the back of the plane.

After drinking the Sprite from Burger King, I had to relieve myself and it was best I did it while the plane was still on the ground. Placing one foot in front of the other, I made my way through all the whistles and words from the men. My body tensed up, not knowing if anyone would've been bold enough to reach out and touch me. At the end of the day, we were all already locked up, what else they would've done to us if something like that was to happen?

As I reached the back, I saw in the last row they had two

prisoners in their own row with masks on their faces and mitten-like reinforcements on their hands. As I waited for the bathroom, curiosity got the best of me.

"What's the mask and hand thing for?" I asked the female officer in a hushed tone.

"Those are usually the most dangerous prisoners that need extra reinforcement. Ones that get out of their shackles and those who spit and bite," she explained with a faint smile.

It was my turn to use the bathroom. I looked at the officer to undo my cuffs, but she looked at me blankly.

"Oh, those don't come off. Take your time," she stated.

This can't be fucking life, I thought.

I went into the bathroom and took my time as I fought like hell to get my pants down. Once finished, I felt good that I got that out of the way so early on because it would've been hectic if I had to pass urine and couldn't hold it.

Shuffling back to my seat quickly, the woman strapped the seatbelt around my waist, making sure I was secured. I sat in the window seat, so I looked outside until the plane revved its engine.

Looking across the landing, I saw the Marshal that brought us to the airlift get in his car after watching the plane for some time. Once the door to the plane was closed, they proceeded off the premises, leaving with the wrong inmate in the back of their vehicle.

The wheels started to turn, and we moved slowly down the runway. Eventually picking up the speed, the plane lifted into the air, and that's when I knew it was truly no turning back. I was heading to Minnesota.

I blinked away tears that threatened to fall and closed my eyes to picture myself on the day of my release. It was something I always did to escape my reality and, in that moment, I needed to go to another place mentally.

CHAPTER TWENTY-SIX

MANIC

f I hadn't been behind the walls and Tiffany Grace wasn't a lieutenant, her head would've been smashed into the brick wall. I literally wanted to tear her apart limb from limb. It was one thing to send Kei back to the SHU, but to plant a cellphone that time around to make sure she was shipped to another facility was on a whole other level.

Ever since Grace caught Kei and me in the office, she'd been ducking me. I literally didn't see or speak to her for a month or more. I saw her in passing, but once Keilani was out of the building and it got around she was, Grace got low. The only thing that held me back from ruining that bitch's life was my integrity as a man.

Snitching was off the table, so I couldn't see myself speaking on what she and I had going on. That would've been a real weak nigga move. Plus, it could've potentially opened up a can of worms about my operation that I fought so hard to keep under wraps. She might've thought she won, but she had another thing coming. I was just playing shit cool and smart. Revenging my bitch was top priority, especially since she was mad at a nigga.

While Keilani was still in the SHU, I came clean and told her everything. I had no other choice but to let her know since she caught the wrath of it all. She didn't deserve any of it, and it was fucking with me mentally everything she had gone through because of me.

"Yo, call Ms. Ellis and tell her I need to speak with her," I told the unit officer.

He got on the line and made the call right away. When he hung up, the bell to the unit rung, and the door opened.

Walking over to her, I peeped how she sized me up and down, but I wasn't on that type of timing.

"Hey, what you need?" she asked in a sweet tone.

"I need to get on the phone with my lawyer, like now," I told her.

She took a deep breath in and out, then waved me over to follow her out of the unit and into her office. As soon as I sat down, she gave me the phone to use. Dialing up Hash's number, it rang a few times before he picked up.

"Hello, good afternoon," he answered.

"Hash, it's Manic," I told him.

"I was scheduled to call you today. Your sentencing date has been pushed up and it's in another week," he informed me.

After going back and forth to court for the past year, my lawyer and I settled on just pleading out. The U.S. attorney gave a good deal for the bullshit charge, or else they would've kept putting off my court dates like they were for no reason.

"Shit, that's good. I didn't expect that when I called, but fuck it. Aye, I need you to do something for me though."

"What's up?"

"I need you to look into someone for me. She just got shipped from here. I need you to find out where she is and have them to ship her back."

"I'd have to enter as her lawyer."

"Then, do that. I'm retaining you for her."

"Okay, what's her information?"

In under a minute, I gave Hash all of her information, plus

her mother's number, which I knew by heart since I called her often.

"I'm on it. I'll come and see you before we go to court."

"Ard, bet."

While I held my phone conversation, Ms. Ellis stood outside of her office door. Once she saw I was off, she came in and sat across from me at her desk. When I stood to my feet, she had a dumbfounded look on her face.

"Why have you been so distant this past year?"

"Because I'm good, shorty. No hard feelings," I simply told her.

She hung her head in defeat and embarrassment.

As I was walking out of her office, Grace walked through the door that separated the units and the elevators.

This bitch here, I thought.

"You haven't learned your lesson, huh?" she asked with a scowl on her face.

"I ain't see yo ass in forever and, as soon as you peep me on the camera in her office, you want to show your face?" I quizzed. "I wasn't even on that type timing anyway. I had a legal call, so get the fuck on." I waved her off.

"Makhi—"

"Manic!" I turned and roared with my voice traveling through the hall, making her jump. "I told yo ass to get the fuck, you outta pocket. I thought you was a solid one that knew how to keep your emotions in check."

She looked at Ms. Ellis through the window to see if she was listening, then back at me with sorrowful eyes.

"I—"

I raised my hand to stop her from talking. Turning to signal Ms. Ellis to open the door for me, she quickly came out her office and let me back into the unit.

With court right around the corner, I was looking to most likely have time served. And even if I still had to do a little more time, they were going to ship me out from the building. I would no longer have any dealings with Grace's sheisty ass.

Returning back to my cell, I laid on my bunk and just looked at Keilani's picture. Watching her face just brought so much calmness and peace to me. I missed her something crazy and needed to speak to her before a nigga went mad.

TWO DAYS PASSED, and I received a legal visit from Hash. We went over things for court and, then, he jumped into giving me information on Keilani's whereabouts.

"So, she just got to FCI Waseca, that's in Minnesota," he revealed.

"Minnesota? Nah, they drawn sending her all the way out there." I got agitated.

"I'm in the process of getting in touch with Grand Prairie."

Grand Prairie was where the Federal Bureau of Prisons

decided on which facility inmates would go to and also calculate their sentences.

"Get on it fast. She don't need to be that far. She used to get visits from her family every weekend. I know it's gon' fuck with her mentally," I pleaded.

"I got it. Who's this person to you?" he pried.

There was nothing to hide, so I told him. "My future wife," I simply stated.

Hash's eyes bucked as he nodded and curled down the corners of his mouth. "Well, let me go and get your future wife back to Philly." He stood and left out of the visiting room.

Yeah, you do that.

As soon as I went back to the unit, I called Keilani's mom, Ms. Milan, and spoke to her. I gave her a message to give to Kei and hoped her emails would be up and active so we could talk. Shorty was literally the only thing on my mind despite me having my sentencing coming up.

CHAPTER TWENTY-SEVEN

KEI

$\mathcal{A}$fter a few days of being in transit, I finally arrived to Federal Correctional Institution Waseca. While I thought the plane was going to drop me there on that same that, I was sadly mistaken. Every inmate in the federal system had to go through the Oklahoma transfer center when in transit. Although when I got there, it was over capacity, so I was sent to a nearby county jail.

At this jail, I felt the most disgusted, worse than being in a SHU. It was literally an open warehouse with a ton of bunk beds and a section for a table to eat and watch a TV. The showers were open, so I had to bathe while other women gawked at me. The food was distasteful, and the mattress was uncomfortable. When they called my name around two o'clock in the morning to get ready, I was more than happy that I was going to Waseca.

The plane finally landed and, as we descended the stairs, I saw Marshal agents spread around the premises like they were in Harrisburg. There was a bus waiting right at the bottom with a prison officer in the FBOP uniform posted outside with a rifle. We climbed onto the bus one by one and took our seats.

While on my first flight, I only rode with a small amount of females. There were more than forty women getting off the plane and on the bus to go to Waseca with me. They carried on conversations since some of them knew each other prior. I just stayed quiet and to myself as I observed everyone around me.

About a half an hour later, we finally reach our destination. From the outside looking in, the grounds looked huge. We all got off the bus, bypassing several armed officers, and made our way inside the building. Once through the front building, we walked outside and onto the path to another building. Down the stairs we went and ended up at the facility's R&D.

My time spent in R&D was lengthy due to the massive influx of inmates at one time. I went through the same process I did at FDC Philly, the only difference was we were placed in our tans right away and not a jumpsuit. I sighed out loud as I waited my turn to take my picture for my ID.

"You good over there?" a stud asked me.

There were a handful of studs on the bus coming in. It wasn't new to me being around them since I played basketball with them all my life. But that one in particular looked cute and clean. She was light-skinned and had dreads with an average build. Her lips were full and shaped beautifully, like ones I'd suck on.

"I am, I'm just ready to shower and rest. And I'm starving."

As soon as I finished my sentence, in walked a guard pushing a cart with drinks on top. I assumed inside were food trays.

"I guess God heard your cries," she cracked.

"I guess so." I smiled.

They handed out the food trays to us, which was surprisingly good. It was mashed potatoes and beef with gravy. We even got a huge chocolate chip cookie as a dessert.

"Damn, they do it like that here?" I quizzed.

"Where you coming from?" she asked.

"FDC Philly. You?"

"I was in state holding out Chicago. What's your name?"

"Kei, and yours?"

"Don."

We continued to talk and get to know one another while we waited to be seen. She explained to me that she referred to be called him, that by law she was considered a man. While I found it strange, I respected his wished. I looked around and figured the other studs felt the same way.

When we got our roll of blanket, sheets, and toiletries like I did at FDC Philly, we were escorted to our housing unit. Don and I ended up in the same place, B-Unit. The officer told us our bed and room number, prompting us to go and find it. A lady showed me where I was, which was in the basement of the three-level building. When I reached the bottom, I looked and saw it was a bunch of bunk beds out in the open in cubicles. I cringed at the sight, especially when I saw my bed was directly in front of the restroom, which was open with no doors.

"I know, everyone hates that bed," a Spanish girl spoke.

She must've read my body language and facial expression to know I wasn't pleased with my living arrangement.

"Do I have to stay here?" I asked.

"When Mr. Bennette comes in tomorrow, go see him. He'll change you."

"Who's that?"

"Our unit counselor."

"Okay, thanks."

I went and made my bed to the best of my ability. Nine o'clock count was near, so I just stayed put until then. And once that was over and the light were turned off, I curled up on my bunk and relaxed. I didn't get much sleep that night. Being exposed in the open with complete strangers, criminals at that, was unsettling.

"CAN I MOVE NOW?" I begged Mr. Bennette. "You said a week. It's been that."

It had been exactly eight days since I approached him about moving my bed. I barely slept with the constant flushing, foul smell, and noise of running showers. Not to mention, the girls used the bathroom as their meetup spot to chill and talk, especially at night time.

"Ughhh. Milan, it looks like you'll be a pain in my ass," the middle-aged white man stated.

"Give me what I want and I won't be." I raised my eyebrow.

He stared at me with squinted eyes and leaned back in his chair. "Alright. Go look for an empty bed. Ask the folks if they're alright with you moving in and come back and tell me," he stated.

Sounds familiar, I told myself.

"I'll be right back." I rushed out of his office and made my rounds about the unit. I already spotted a few open beds. I just needed to double check and talk to the people in the rooms. On the top floor, I narrowed down a few rooms and gave in to ask this room that had three people in it, with only two bunks. That was the least number of people I was going to get to be around. Other rooms held a larger number.

"Hi, I just got here last week. I wanted to know if I could move in. I'm currently in the basement and it's driving me crazy," I proposed.

The two ladies looked over at the stud that occupied the room. It was over him I would've been living with. He went on to ask me a few questions about what I did daily, how clean was I, amongst other things. In the end, he said it was cool for me to move in. I raced back to Bennette's office and told him. He made the switch, and I moved into my new space right after count that day.

"Oh, you damn near right across from me," Don stated.

We bumped into each other in the hall while I was going to the bathroom.

"Yeah, it seems so."

"What you finna get into?"

"Nothing, read."

"Come out to the rec center with me."

I thought about it for a while and gave in. Within that week I was there, I barely left out the unit unless it was to go to a callout or chow in the cafeteria.

"Aight, come on."

I used the bathroom, then went into my room to grab my

ID. They made it clear we needed to always have it around our necks once outside of the unit. We waited another few minutes for the compound control to announce the move.

A controlled move was when we only had ten minutes to move from one part of the compound to the next. It happened at the beginning of every hour. If you were caught still moving around after it was closed, it was considered being out of bounds, which resulted in receiving a shot and then a sanction.

Don and I made it down to rec where it had a library, basketball court, gym with all kinds of cardio and workout equipment and outside it was a huge track surrounded by tables scattered throughout the yard. It was definitely a big difference from FDC Philly. I was able to stretch my legs and breathe.

I spent time with Don and his friends he knew prior. Some looked like actual men with facial hair and deep voices. They explained to me that there were on the shots, hence the reason for the extra testosterone. I found it interesting and didn't judge. Shit, some of them were looking good. I felt a lot of them checking me out but didn't say much because I was always walking around with Don.

After I got some fresh air, I returned back to the unit once they called recall. We had nine o'clock count; then, I ran to the computer to check my emails. Kayla had reactivated my text service, so I was being to speak to more people. When I browsed through my messages, I saw multiple ones from Manic.

I rolled my eyes and got irritated at the thought of him. Everything happened because he couldn't keep his dick in his pants and because he couldn't control his hoes. I was seconds away from clicking on his message, but I decided not to. Manic had a way with his words, and I wasn't ready to forgive him or fallback in. He needed to understand that he fucked up, and in a major way.

Later that night, I relaxed on my bunk as everyone in the room read a book. Lights were out and, for the most part, ninety-five percent of the unit was either already asleep or just kicked back.

I reached a sex scene in the book I was reading and instantly got horny. I clinched my legs together tightly as I had thoughts of Manic and my escapade. It was like I felt him inside of me touching my spot with every stroke. I was upset with him, but there was no denying how much my body yarned for him.

Not being able to take it any longer, I jumped off my bunk, grabbed my shower things, and went to take a cold shower. There was no one in the showers since it was past the time. I was taking a chance, but it was going to be a quick one.

I got undressed and stepped in under the cold water. My body jumped at the temperature as good bumps formed all over my body. I washed and rinse and repeated three times before the water cut off on me with soap still on my skin. The showers were programmed to only stay on for seven minutes and took a little while before turning back on.

So much for a quick shower, I thought.

I knew I had to shower-hop like I saw the other girls do before. Pulling the curtain back and stepping out with my naked body exposed, I ran head first into Don.

"Oh, shit. Sorry."

"Nah, you…" his voice trailed off as he looked at my bare skin.

The way his eyes roamed unapologetically turned me one for some reason. I was still feeling aroused, which didn't make things better.

"Late shower, huh?" I asked, running into the shower across from the one I was just in.

"Yeah, but I'm tryna get in with you." His eyes continued to dance around my body.

As I was about to protest, I remembered what Noelle once told me about adjusting for the time being. Use what's around to escape my reality.

"What you waiting for then?" I smirked.

Don dropped his things and got undressed in seconds. Stepping into the shower, he pulled the curtain back and immediately attacked my lips. His hands found its way to my other set of lips, which were soaked and not with water.

Slipping a finger inside of me, I gasped as waves of pleasure shot throughout my body. Our chests, which his still had breasts, touched together as I raised my leg, giving him more room to play in my pussy.

"Ohhh," I cooed, resulting in him placing his hand over

my mouth quickly. For a moment, I forgot I was in a prison shower.

The water fell on our bodies, as he had me pinned against the wall. It was a way he finger fucked me and pressed on my knob, sending me into a complete frenzy. Out of nowhere, he pulled her finger out and placed it in my mouth to taste, which I always enjoyed tasting myself. He placed his finger in her mouth while staring deep into my eyes.

I wanted to say I felt bad that I was enjoying a woman, technically, but I didn't. At that moment, I had a need, and it was being satisfied. Don made me come again two more times, but when we heard someone come into the shower, we ended our heated moment.

CHAPTER TWENTY-EIGHT

MANIC

I know she's getting my messages. Why the fuck she not answering me though? I asked myself as I stared at the computer screen. There weren't any emailed from Kei, and I found it wild since I knew her service was back up and running. I shot her moms a text to tell her I was missing her and that I was sorry. It wasn't like Kei to just not respond or to ghost a nigga, so I knew she was really in her feelings.

Knock! Knock!

I turned and saw Wright at the window. Looking at the time on the computer, I saw it was time for me to go to my medical call out to see Dr. Gannon. I logged off and followed Wright out of the unit.

There were barely any words spoken between him and me because my mind was far gone. Keilani had me fucked up and, if she knew better, she would've gotten her shit together.

We entered the medical wing and bypassed other people who were waiting. Once inside the office, Dr. Gannon took my vitals and checked my weight.

"How have you been feeling, Frost?" he asked.

"Empty," I simply answered.

"Well, I'm not a psychologist, but I hope you have someone to talk to."

"I'm good, doc. What's the word?"

He went into the usual spot and pulled out a medical duffle bag. Resting the bag beside me on the examination bed, I observed the contents inside.

"Yeah, this it," I confirmed.

He secured it back and took a seat at his desk.

"What's going to happen when you're gone?"

It was like everyone in my circle was asking me that same exact question. While I had a gut feeling I was going to walk when I went to court the following day, I also wanted to leave room for disappointment and the unexpected.

"We'll cross that bridge when we get there. We'll be in touch."

I hopped off the table and opened the door to leave. Wright took me straight back upstairs to the unit, where I went into my cell and brainstormed my next few moves.

"FROST," I heard on the speaker.

I was dressed and ready to go to court. The night before, I didn't get much sleep because my mind had been all over the place. My anxiety of possibly going home had my adrenaline pumping. But the thought of them doing some bullshit and keeping me in also had me on edge.

Walking out of my cell, I met the CO at the door with two other niggas who had court as well. We were escorted down to R&D to be processed out, then through the tunnel, and up to the Marshal holding cells. I sat in there for about three hours until my case was finally on the docket to be called.

"You ready?" Hash asked me.

I looked over at the fat ass U. S. District Attorney who had a bothered look on his face. "Yeah, I'm ready."

Moments later, the court officer announced the judge.

"All rise for the honorable..."

Everyone started to fade while my mind drifted off when I turned around and saw Ms. Milan walk in the courtroom. It was like I saw Keilani. They looked so much alike. I always got that feeling when I saw her mother. I not only saw her on the visits, but she would come to my court hearings to show support.

Automatically, my mind went to her and how much I wanted shit to work for us. I couldn't wait until she was released and I could give her the world and more.

"May the defendant rise." I felt Hash nudged me back to reality.

I stood to my feet and looked at the judge as I was about to be sentenced for the assault charges. My stomach was turning every which way, making me feeling nauseous. My nerves were bad and my throat felt blocked while I tried to swallowed.

"The defendant is sentenced to forty-eight-months, which twenty-eight months is to be served in prison and the rest on probation. The defendant is to pay a fine of fifty thousand dollars. Furthermore, the defendant will receive credit for the time served during his incarceration."

I'm a free fucking man, I thought.

A nigga wanted to scream out so badly. I felt like I was on top of the world in that moment. That's how fucking happy I was. Hash gripped the top of my shoulder firmly and smiled. I turned around to see everyone in tears and smiles. Makaela wasn't sure what was going on, but I mouthed that daddy is coming home, and she beamed.

It's go time.

CHAPTER TWENTY-NINE

KEI

$\mathcal{S}$omehow, word got around about what Don and I did in the showers. The other studs were looking at me like they were hungry, while the other girls gave me death stares. It wasn't a large number of guys(studs) on the compound, so the ratio was totally off, especially when there were a lot of horny fems. This one stud had three girlfriends, and they were all cool with it, like sister wives.

When a lot of drama started to come my way, I fell back from Don. Granted, we never made anything exclusive or even did anything outside of our first encounter, but being cool with him brought too much shit. Girls would approach me about him and do or say all kinds of slick shit. It started to be over-bearing, and it wasn't worth it when that shit wasn't even my life.

The prison compound was a different world by itself. There were people in their serving life sentences, so they did what any other person would've done, adapt. For me, I didn't have much time to go; I was already near the door. It would've been foolish of me to sink into their claws and get mixed up in their prison bullshit and set myself back.

While the compound was constantly in an uproar with arguments, fights, and so on, I saw a group of Muslim sisters all the time together. The way they just moved carefree and stayed to themselves intrigued me. One day, I approached them and started to learn more about the religion because I was completely ignorant of the matter.

Day by day, I grew a perfect understanding, which then turned into a passion and love for it. I decided to take my Shahadah and revert back to Islam.

They said when all humans were born, they were Muslims

because they know of only one God, but when they grew, they learn about different religions. So, the proper way to say someone was a Muslim was to say they reverted back to Islam.

I refocused my energy on my studies of Islam, writing my novel and movie script. When I completed my book and word got back to my boss, which I got a job in education as a tutor, I was asked to do a class on how to write a novel.

While all these changes were occurring over a month's time, I still hadn't written Manic back. Whenever I spoke to my mom, she would try to tell me something about him, and I told her not to mention him until I was ready.

Once I received my property and went through it, my heart strings were tugged on when I saw his pictures.

"Ohhh, who's that?" my bunky asked.

I paused to think about the answer I should. Last he was my man, but then, I had no clue where we were at that point. "He's my love," I answered, keeping it short and simple.

I came across his letters I had tucked away very well since I wasn't supposed to be in possession of them nor his pictures. It was forbidden for inmates to have any kind of communication unless they were co-defendants and had approval.

Rereading his words sent me to a place I hadn't been in a while. I missed him. I missed his voice, his laugh, his rough- ness, his love and admiration for me and, of course, the nasty side to him.

"Kei, come on, let's pray," one of my Muslim sisters came and told me.

I rested everything on my bed, grabbed my prayer rug and went to meet the girls. We tried to do as many prayers of the day together as possible. We had five obligatory prayers to offer.

After we completed it, I felt a whole new feeling after giving it all to Allah. I prayed for guidance and patience when it came to love. I'd been hurt so many times, I was almost numb to it, but what I had with Manic was different than anything I ever had. That's when I decided I needed to go and make things right with my man.

I raced to the computer and logged on. Finally wanting to, I clicked on all his messages he sent one by one.

Manic: Bae, I didn't know I was going to be missing you this much. Like my whole little bid is fucked up because my day used to be centered on you. I'd sleep while you at work, wake up, and talk to you for the rest of the day. Now I'm super dried out and missing you like crazy. I'm not gon' front, I can't wait to suck on that pussy when you come home. I love you, gorgeous.

Manic: I heard you're good at your new spot. Remember to stay low and out the way. You're right by the door and your nigga will be there when you touch down. I love you.

Manic: Damn, Kei. So you really not fucking with a nigga? I'm sorry baby, I didn't mean for any of that shit to

happen to you. On God, I promise you I wasn't fucking with no one else when I got with you. That's all news. You don't have to worry about no more heartache or turmoil coming from something I did, even though I really ain't do shit. Bitches just be trying to feel relevant when it's obvious I chose my place. We super straight, Queen. I love the shit outta you.

Manic: I vow to never leave you, Keilani. I love you.

Guilt started to take over me as I read all of his messages with tears in my eyes. From the moment I laid eyes on Makhi, I felt something. As we started to talk, he applied nothing but pressure, straight gas, and no brakes when it came to me. He showed time and time again that he loved me and would do anything for me. As a woman, I saw my fault in not hearing him out completely. I only thought about myself. I'd been fucked over so many times, I thought that's what I had to do.

I finally wrote him back, hoping he wasn't mad and over me. Manic wasn't exactly the type to chase bitches, so I knew it would've been an only matter of time that he threw the towel in on me.

"To ACCEPT THIS CALL, PRESS FIVE," the operated stated.

I had dialed up my mother the following day when I saw I didn't get a response from Manic.

"Hey, baby. Sorry I was so busy doing overtime in the jail,

and you know I can't have my phone in there," she quickly spoke.

"It's okay, ma. I miss you. Are we still on for our video visit later?"

At that facility, they offered thirty-minute video visits. It was the best thing for me since I was far across the country.

"Yes, we are."

"Okay, good. Ahhh, did you speak to Manic?" I finally mustered up the courage to ask.

She tried to speak to me about him on so many occasions, and I felt bad about how I dismissed her and him.

"I'm happy you asked. Keilani, Makhi, went to court and got time served," she revealed.

"What? Oh, my God. He's home?" I squealed in excitement.

He kept saying that the same scenario was going to happen when his sentencing came around. I was just beyond happy it came through.

"Not exactly. When he was being released, the state came and picked him up from FDC Philly. He had to go do a few months there because he violated his probation by catching a federal case," she explained.

"No wonder he didn't respond to my email," I spoke somberly.

"Yeah, I haven't spoken to him either. But don't worry, both of y'all will soon be home. Keep your head up."

"I got you, ma. I'll see you later for the visit. I love you."

"Love you more, Princess."

After I got off the phone with my moms, I headed upstairs to my room. On the way there, I bumped into a stud I befriended after meeting him through Don. We bonded and became like brother and sister in the short period of time.

"You good, sis?" Cash asked.

"Yeah, just processing some shit. You know how that go."

"I feel you. You ever finished that book? I'm tryna read it." he asked, referring to one of the urban fiction novels I had just read.

"Yeah, come and get it," I told him.

He followed me to my room, where I climbed up on my bed for it. Quickly coming off the ladder, I went to the room's entrance and handed it over to him.

"Good lookin'." He took off, eager to read.

Those urban fiction novels had everyone in a chokehold in prison. From men to woman, even the COs indulged at times.

"Yo don't have that nigga at my door no more," my bunky, Chris, who lived beneath me, ordered.

I snapped my neck at him like he lost his rabbit ass mind. "Excuse me?"

"You heard what the fuck I said." He stood up.

Chris was a whole of a person, standing at about five feet, ten inches compared to my five-three petite frame. He was also on the heavier side, weighing four times my weight.

"You ain't my daddy, and you ain't my nigga. Go check your bitch."

"Like I said, don't have that nigga come to my shit no more." He pushed past me, bumping my shoulder on his way out of the room.

Why do I always get these weird ass controlling cellmates? I asked myself.

My other two roommates just sat quietly and gave me a sympathetic face. It was like they knew something was about to go down. And, indeed, it did.

About ten minutes later, Chris came walking down the hall yelling all kinds of shit.

"Somebody better tell this little bitch I ain't the one to fucking play with!" he ranted.

I looked out the room and down the hall to see him posted up on the wall talking to his girlfriend.

"If she knows what's good for her, she will get her mutha-fuckin bed changed, asap," he added.

His girlfriend got him to go downstairs and away from the room. Few people came and checked on me, one being this girl that I got cool with when I'd just arrived; her name was Tally.

"What the fuck is going on?" she asked, walking up to my room.

"He started trippin' over Cash coming by the room. I told him he ain't my daddy or my nigga, and the muthafucker went off."

She slapped her hand on her face and shook her head. "Bitch, I suggest you put a lock in a sock and keep it on you as all times."

"I ain't scared of his ass."

"It ain't about being scared, it's about being smart. Baby, you finna go home soon. That big muthafucker has life in prison. He can catch another body and it won't matter."

"Wait, what? He in here for murder?"

"Yes."

My heart dropped to the pit of my stomach. I ain't no pussy bitch, but I also didn't want to lose my life over something so stupid. People like Chris, I needed to stay clear of. They had nothing to lose, making them the most dangerous people to walk the earth.

Out the corner of my eye, I saw Chris speed walking coming down the hall.

"You getting out or what?" he stopped in front of me and asked.

"No."

"Okay, we'll, I'ma put you out."

He went into the room and start grabbing my things, so I went and snatched them out his hand. We tussled for my laundry bag until he got the best of me and snatched the bag real hard, causing me to crash into the locker.

"What's going on in here?" Two COs ran in our room.

Chris start to run his mouth like the true woman he was. The CO didn't want to hear nothing else; they cuffed us both and took us to the SHU for a threat assessment.

"Milan, a legal call request came from your attorney. Let's go," a CO said.

"Legal call?" I quizzed. I hadn't spoken to my lawyer since I was sentenced.

"Yes. Turn around, hands behind your back."

I did what I was told and got cuffed. It had been two weeks in the SHU, and I was over it. It seemed like I spent most of my time in the hole. So, whenever I was able to leave out the small cell to stretch my legs, I was grateful for it.

He took me into an office that had the phone off the hook. Before leaving out, he motioned for me to pick it up.

"Hello?" I answered.

"Ms. Milan, my name is Joel Hash. I was retained as your attorney through your fiancé, Makhi Frost," he introduced himself.

Fiancé?

"Hi, what's this about?" I was confused.

"I've been working on getting you transferred back to Philly. And since learning of your current SHU status, things just got a bit easier for us."

"How so, sir?" I needed him to enlighten me.

"I need you to refuse housing when they try to send you back into the general population. If they ask why, just continued to say you refuse. I will work things on my end. Okay?"

"Okay," I answered, slowly trying to figure out his angle.

"I spoke with SIS already on your matter; they'll be trying to release you in the next day or two. But don't go. Before you know it, you'll be back on your way to Philly."

"Sounds good, but I don't need you to be selling me no dreams."

"You sound just like Makhi." He chuckled.

Whatever that meant.

"Hang tight and be good. We'll talk soon."

When the call ended, I was taken back to my cell, where Manic was the only thing that plagued my mind. He always had something up his sleeve. The lawyer sounded like he knew what he was doing. And the fact he was one of Manic's folks, I knew he couldn't have been no weak attorney. I placed my trust in him and prayed he came through.

ONE MONTH LATER...

"Milan, let's go." A CO banged on the door.

I woke up from my slumber, confused. "Go where?" I stretched.

"You're shipping out."

I didn't even respond. I just sat on my top bunk and smiled so hard. Hash really came through. Everything he said was going to happen, happened.

The following day after we first spoke, they were ready to

release me from the SHU. I refused that time and every other time they came and tried to let me out. After several attempts, they apparently got tired of it and stopped coming. That morning, I understood why; I was on my way off their compound.

Climbing down off the top bunk, I sprang into action to handle my hygiene. Packing up the little things I had, I patiently waited for them to get me out of the cell. I knew the routine all too well.

They took me down to R&D to get dressed out in the appropriate clothes for the trip. I went through my property and watched them box it up to be shipped out. Not long after, I, with five other girls, was loaded onto the bus and taken to the airlift to get on the plane.

Since I experience everything already, it was a little easier that time around. I wasn't as emotional nor was I bothered by the men and their catcalls. The only thing I had in mind was seeing my family again.

When we reached Oklahoma, I was ready to stay there for a few days, but I was out the very next day. I just knew Allah was on my side because the process was so smooth; I had no complaints. Before I knew it, I was back at FDC Philly.

While being processed through R&D, lieutenant Grace waltzed her ass in. I hadn't felt so angry in a while to where I was about to risk it all just to beat her ass. Good days didn't mean shit to me because I didn't have any. Due to her over-jealous ass, I lost all my good time from all the incidents that led me to the SHU. They all had her prints all over them.

"Oh, you back, huh." She stood in front of me and smirked.

"She came from the SHU. Apparently, she kept refusing housing. Send her to three-south or all the way up?" the CO that was handling my intake asked Grace.

I didn't move my eyes from off her. It was no fear in my heart, and I needed her to know that.

"Send her up," she told the officer without taking her eyes off me.

I shot her a smirk and kept it cute. People in her position thought they had all the power when, in reality, they were weak as shit. Remove the clothes and the title, she would've been a regular ass bitch on the street. And that's the thing she forgot. She lived beyond the walls of FDC Philly, and I didn't have life outside.

After the officers were finished with me in R&D, I was taken to the SHU, where I settled in and got ready to walk down my days.

Release Day...

THE NIGHT BEFORE, I couldn't close my eyes. The excitement I felt was out of this world. I was raring to get from behind the cell door and walls of FDC Philly altogether.

Weeks prior, I mentally prepared myself to re-enter back

into society. My family came to visit me, even though I was in the SHU and was getting out soon. They stood ten toes down the entire ride from the moment I caught the case up until my last days.

Because I didn't have access to the computer or phones, they made sure to send me in letters to keep me occupied. The last time I had a long stay in the hole, Manic was the person to keep me going with his kites.

I hadn't spoken to him, and my mother never mentioned anything else about his situation to me. While I missed him and was dying to see him, I had to focus on getting home and settling down. Once I was good, I'd see what was up with him. That's when I'd know if everything was real or just for the time being.

"Milannn," a female CO sang.

"Yesss," I sang back happily.

"You know what today is?" She stood by my cell door, peering in the window.

"It's time for me to get evicted." I smiled.

"Damn right. You ready?"

It felt good that not all the officers were dickheads. Some were cool as shit and wanted to see us do well.

"Turn around and cuff up," she instructed.

I cheerfully turned around and pushed my hands through the slot. Feeling the cold handcuffs touch my wrist was a sweet feeling because it was going to be the last time I felt it.

She took me out of my cell and escorted me down to R&D

where my outfit my mom sent in for me to wear home was waiting for me.

"That shit cost a nice little change," the R&D officer pointed out.

I looked at the fit, which was a Fendi dress and a pair of Balenciaga high-top sneakers, and nodded my head in agreement.

"My moms know what I like." I smirked.

"Lucky you. Better keep your ass out of here," she added. "Go and change."

I took my clothes and went into the changing room. I stripped out of the orange jumpsuit while an officer looked on and tossed it on the ground. With every piece of prison clothes making its way off my body, I felt a load lifted.

Bare in my birthday suit, I stood there feeling free and proud, instead of the shy, embarrassed, and timid woman. I made it through all trials and tribulations that were thrown at me. I stood ten toes and didn't fold. I was the true definition of *you may bend but never break.*

Putting on my new threads, I felt a new journey starting. It signified a fresh start, as I threw away the past with the prison uniform. Walking out the changing room, all eyes were on me from COs to inmates, and I took it all in.

"Are you taking your belongings with you or you want us to mail it?" the officer asked.

"Mail it. I want my arms free to hug my family," I told her.

She smiled at me and nodded her head. "You ready to go?"

"Hell yeah."

She handed me my discharge papers with instructions regarding my probation and other resources.

Following behind her, we exited out of R&D but through the facility instead of the tunnel. We made our way through the halls, onto the elevator, and to the ground floor.

"Make sure you check her paperwork," I heard someone say.

When I turned, it was none other than the bitter Lieutenant Grace. I shot her a wink and turned around, as the officers at the main gate checked over my paperwork.

"Be great," the guy told me.

"See you girl," the R&D officer told me.

I smiled at them and walked over the threshold of confinement. Standing in the lobby of the building, I anxiously walked towards the exit doors and, when I opened it, my heart thumped widely as I laid eyes on a sidewalk full of people.

"Welcome home!" everyone shouted in a unison.

I stopped in my tracks, bent over and broke down crying. It was all too overwhelming. I couldn't believe I made it out and in a sane state.

Everyone came and took turns hugging me. I saw far distant relatives, people I knew who lived out of the state, also present. It meant a lot; I was truly loved.

"My Princess free." My mom held my face and kissed my cheek. "I have a surprise for you."

"What is it? A car?" I joked.

"Something better."

I turned around for a split second and saw LT Grace standing at the entrance of the building looking on. When I turned back to face my mother, she moved out of the way and there stood Makhi Manic Frost.

My body got so weak; I felt like I wanted to faint. But before I could react, he was hovering over me with his tall frame. His cologne tickled my nostrils, making the hairs on the back of my neck stand up.

"You thought a nigga was playing about you?" he asked.

My mouth was open, but no words came out. He was fucking fine as ever. His green eyes penetrated my soul by the way he stared into mine intensely.

"Makhi," I finally spoke, swallowing the whole lump in my throat.

"All I want to know is, are you mine or not?" he asked.

I quickly nodded my head and smiled.

He pulled a box out of his pocket and dropped down on one knee. Opening the box, he exposed a huge diamond ring that looked like it cost a grip. My eyes watered instantly while everyone started to yell and make noise.

"Keilani Milan, will you marry me?"

"Yesssssssss!" I screamed.

Manic slipped the rock on my finger and picked me up. Wrapping my legs and arms around him, I kissed his lips deeply.

"You sure you're ready to be Bound to a Savage?" He pulled back and asked.

I nodded with tears in my eyes.

"I love you, King."

"I love you, Queen."

The End

ABOUT THE AUTHOR

P. Wise (Pretti Wise) is a National and International Best Selling author of fiction literature, whose experiences and imagination have shaped her to write about her ideas. She is originally from Trinidad and Tobago but grew up in Bed-Stuy, Brooklyn; also spent a great deal of time in Philadelphia and Chester.

Having experienced and witnessed different events in her life, she has a variety of perspectives that almost any and everyone can understand. The love to write stemmed from a young age, as she enjoyed essay writing and penning her journal.

Coming from a lower-class family, she's a first-generation college graduate, but also, the first to enter and survive a federal prison sentence. With ambition, intelligence, and absurdly high tenacity, she'll have her place in the fiction game.

P. Wise has a 3 year old daughter, who's her world and reason for her grind.

This is P.Wise's 24th book since starting her career in January 2022.

Photos from my time inside.

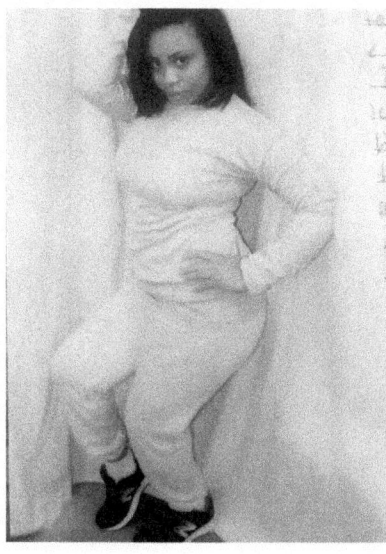

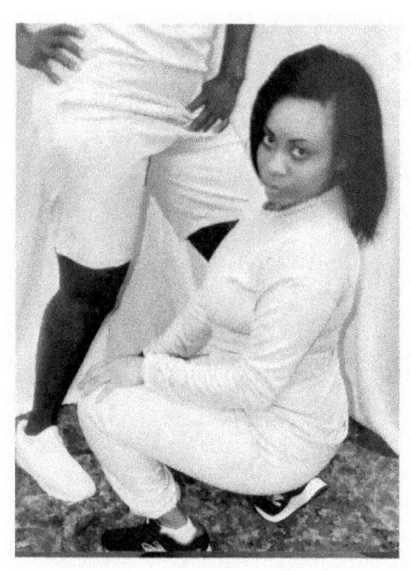

STAY CONNECTED!

Website/Mailing List: PrettiWise.com
Instagram: @CEO.Pwise
Facebook: Author P. Wise
Facebook Business: Authoress P. Wise

Facebook Group: <u>Words of the Wise (P. Wise Book Group</u>)

P.O Box 923
Brookhaven, PA 19015

COMING SOON

ALSO BY P. WISE

Melted the Heart of a Menace

My Curves Captivated a Hood Millionaire: A BBW Love Story

My Curves Captivated a Hood Millionaire: A BBW Love Story 2

Come Play In It: An Urban Erotica

Heir to the Plug's Throne

Heir to the Plug's Throne 2

Gorgeous Gangstas

Gorgeous Gangstas 2

Gorgeous Gangstas 3

Luchiano Mob Ties: Snatched Up by a Don Spin-Off

Snatched Up by a Don: A BBW Love Story

Snatched Up by a Don: A BBW Love Story 2

Snatched Up by a Don: A BBW Love Story 3

A Saint Luv'n A Savage: A Philly Love Story

Luv'n a Philly Boss: A Saint Luv'n a Savage Spin-off

Kwon: Clone of a Savage

Kwon: Clone of a Savage 2

Welcome to Cherrieville: Bitter & Sweet

Summer Luvin' with a NY Baller

Tamia & Tytus: A Toxic Love Affair

Diary of a Brooklyn Girl

Sex, Scams, & Brisks

Sex, Scams, & Brisks 2

www.ingramcontent.com/pod-product-compliance
Lightning Source LLC
Chambersburg PA
CBHW051059030726
47504CB00006B/1693